Building  Bridges

Tales from Grace Chapel Inn®

Building Bridges

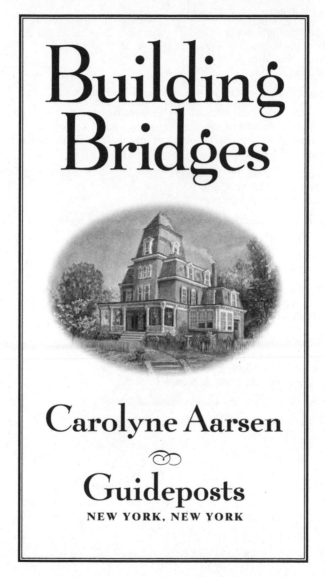

Carolyne Aarsen

Guideposts
NEW YORK, NEW YORK

Building Bridges

ISBN-13: 978-0-8249-4757-6

Published by Guideposts
16 East 34th Street
New York, New York 10016
www.guideposts.com

Distributed by Ideals Publications
2636 Elm Hill Pike, Suite 120
Nashville, Tennessee 37214

Guideposts, *Ideals* and *Tales from Grace Chapel Inn* are registered trademarks of Guideposts.

The characters and events in this book are fictional, and any resemblance to actual persons or events is coincidental.

All Scripture quotations are taken from *The Holy Bible, New International Version*. Copyright © 1973, 1978, 1984 International Bible Society. Used by permission of Zondervan Bible Publishers.

Library of Congress Cataloging-in-Publication Data has been applied for.

Cover by Lookout Design Group
Interior design by Cindy LaBreacht
Typeset by Planet Patti Inc. & Nancy Tardi

Printed and bound in the United States of America

10 9 8 7 6 5 4 3 2 1

Acknowledgments

To my many lovable nephews and nieces. You made it easy for me to write this book.

—Carolyne Aarsen

Chapter One

I don't usually beg, but I am begging you now. Please help me out."

Jane Howard anchored the phone between her ear and her shoulder. One part of her mind was listening to the slightly breathless woman on the other end, while another part was occupied with a list of groceries she was scribbling on the back of an envelope she had found lying on the butcher-block counter.

Upstairs, the vacuum cleaner wheezed and whined as Alice, one of her older sisters, did the final cleaning of the guest rooms. Nearby the washing machine swished through its last cycle of linen.

Multitasking was alive and well at Grace Chapel Inn.

"I am absolutely at my wit's end," Stacy Reddington continued, her voice rising as she grew more upset. "My caterer canceled on me two days ago, and there is no caterer to be had in Potterston, and the hall I booked had a fire in the kitchen, so it's out of commission. I'm expecting ladies from Canada, the Netherlands and all the way from New Zealand and Japan . . ." Stacy stopped, exhaling heavily, and Jane felt a moment of sympathy for this obviously overwrought woman.

"What organization are you with?" Jane asked.

"It's not an organization per se," Stacy replied. "I belong to the Potterston Chamber of Commerce and these women belong to the Chambers of Commerce from towns we've twinned with in different countries. They've been touring, and I'm in charge of this dinner, their last one in our area. I want it to be the highlight of the tour, but I think it's going to be a disaster." Stacy continued after she had composed herself, "Could you please, please help me out?"

Jane hesitated, torn between her obligations to running the bed-and-breakfast that she and her sisters owned and her genuine desire to help this woman. Catering was a small sideline for Jane, and she took on jobs when she could for the extra income to purchase items for the inn.

And high on the list of extra things is a new vacuum cleaner, Jane thought, as the grating sound upstairs was finally silenced.

"What day would you need me and for how many people?" Jane asked, scribbling "ear plugs" at the bottom of the grocery list. If she and her sisters, Louise and Alice, had to use that vacuum cleaner much longer, all three of them would go deaf.

"Twelve women this coming Saturday, and I have no place to go . . ."

As Stacy revisited her problems, Jane pulled off the apron covering her pale-blue shirt and walked to the front desk tucked under the stairs. A quick check of the appointment book showed Jane the other reality of their situation. The inn would be full to bursting from tonight, Tuesday, until Sunday morning. A group of seven young people were in town for a football reunion, which would keep them busy Friday night, all day Saturday and Saturday evening. Catering the event on Saturday would be tight, but with organization she could make it work, especially because the inn's guests were gone all day and a large part of the evening.

"Do you need an answer today?" Jane asked, trying to

buy some thinking space, though she had to admit the idea appealed to her. International guests meant she might experiment with a varied cuisine.

"I'd like to know as soon as possible. I know I'm groveling, but, Ms. Howard, I'm desperate. These women are coming Saturday. I promised I would take care of this. I would make it worth your while," and she named her figure, which gave Jane pause.

Jane tapped her pencil on the desk, contemplating. She loved cooking and baking, and the challenge of doing this for a group of unknown people gave her a delicious tingle.

And, she had to admit, the figure Stacy quoted would add nicely to the inn's quickly depleting maintenance fund.

She had to run it past her sisters before she made a firm commitment, however. Money or not, the busier she was with a catering project, the less she was available for any extra work their inn guests might require.

"I'll see what I can do," Jane said. "I'll call you tomorrow with my answer."

"Thank you. Thank you so much. I really appreciate that you would even consider this, but could you let me know as soon as possible?"

"I'll do my best," Jane assured her. Jane listened to a few more breathless *thank you*s, and then Stacy said good-bye.

Jane closed the appointment book and leaned her elbows on the desk, staring toward the front windows of the inn. Raindrops slithered down the windows, obscuring the dreary day outside. The rain, which had started the day before, had put a damper on her plans to clean out the garden and ready the flowerbeds for fall. Though it was only late August, some of the plants had come to the end of their lifespan and needed to be cleaned out to make room for the still-producing plants.

If the rain continued today, she would have to wait another day just to let the ground dry out.

Jane had time on her hands, and her thoughts returned to Stacy's phone call and panicked request. Should she do this meal? If the rain continued, she would have time.

If she did cater this meal, what should she serve? Jane could draw on her work as a gourmet chef in San Francisco as well as on her experience from cooking at the inn.

The more she entertained the thought of catering for Stacy Reddington, the more the idea appealed to her. A challenge—just what Jane needed to energize herself.

The thumping of the vacuum cleaner getting moved down the stairs pulled her back to the present. She hurried around the desk to help her sister.

Alice Howard stood on the landing, her usually pleasant face puckered with frustration. She slipped her hands over her auburn hair, then checked her hands as if looking for something. "Are you quite sure you changed the bag on this machine, Jane? It still seems to have minimal suction. In fact, I'm fairly sure it's spitting out dust instead of sucking it up." She brushed down the front of her oxford shirt, checking it and her twill pants for more dust. "At any rate, there is something wrong with it."

"Okey dokey," Jane said, hastening to her sister's side. "Let me help you bring that downstairs and I'll have a look at it."

They manhandled the machine the rest of the way down the stairs. At the bottom, Jane opened it up and was immediately enveloped in a dusty cloud. She coughed and tried ineffectually to wave the dust away from her face.

"Oh dear," Alice lamented.

Jane waited for the dust to settle, then took another look inside. "Here's part of the problem." Jane pointed to the place where the hose entered the bag. "This connection is broken."

"Part of the problem? Is there more?"

"Besides causing migraines every time we use it?" Jane asked, brushing off her blue jeans. "This machine is going to make us deaf if we don't replace it."

"We can't do that now," Alice said. "When Fred Humbert came over to do the annual inspection, he said we should replace the gutters and make repairs on the north roof. That will use up most of our maintenance fund."

Jane stared down at the semiuseless piece of equipment, thought of the dollar figure Stacy had quoted and made a sudden decision.

"Don't worry about it. We'll have enough to buy a new vacuum cleaner in a few days."

"I suppose you'll just head out to the money tree we have growing out back?" Alice teased as Jane closed the cover.

"I believe I'll cater a dinner. I just got a phone call from a woman who is desperate." Jane paused, pursing her lips in a thoughtful gesture. "That could either be a compliment or an insult, couldn't it?"

"Take it as a compliment." Alice flicked some lint off her pants. "And what do we use to clean the inn in the meantime?"

"I'm sure Aunt Ethel has a vacuum cleaner we can borrow." Jane poked their moribund vacuum cleaner with the toe of her running shoe. "As for this . . . thing . . . we should banish it immediately."

"We can put it on the back porch for now." Alice closed up the vacuum cleaner. "When did this request to cater a dinner come up? Are you going to have enough time?"

"Of course. I'm a super supper caterer," Jane said flapping her hand at Alice's concern. She opened the door, letting in a gust of cold, damp air, and together they dragged the now-defunct appliance onto the porch. "I'll phone Fred to see if he can send José down to pick this up and take it to the landfill."

Alice stood a moment, looking down at the machine. "It seems a shame to get rid of this vacuum cleaner. Are you sure we can't get it fixed?"

Jane put her arm over her sister's shoulder, giving it a squeeze. "I'm sorry, Alice." She pretended to sniff, her voice taking on a melodramatic tone. "We did all we could. We didn't give up. Even Fred said this faithful cleaner was on its last legs . . . er . . . wheels. But its time has come. We must accept this and move on. It was a good vacuum cleaner in its day. It worked hard, but you have to admit, the last few years it was a bit of a whiner."

Alice started to chuckle. "I suppose even appliances must die."

Jane nodded solemnly.

"Are we done here?" Alice said, shivering. "I'm getting chilly."

"Shame on you, Alice," Jane said with mock severity. "Have some respect."

"I'd sooner have some tea, thank you very much."

"All right then." Jane saluted the appliance, pulled open the door, tucked her arm in her sister's and walked with her to the kitchen. "I'll clean up the dust later."

As Alice filled the kettle, Jane called Stacy to tell her what she had decided.

"Jane, you are a lifesaver," Stacy gushed. "An absolute lifesaver. I can't thank you enough."

"Not a problem. Now, did you have any preferences as to a menu?"

"I discussed that with the other caterer. I still can't believe he just up and quit on me. I had something memorable in mind but not too out there. You know how you can go to these gourmet restaurants, and you get a concoction that looks like it took hours to put together, and you hardly know where to start eating it? I don't want that. Good food, yes, and of course not too plain. Yet I want them to get the idea that care was taken. I want them to think we've put ourselves out a bit, but, as I said, not too out there. Does that help?"

Jane scribbled a few words on a pad. "So, elegant yet simple?"

"Not too elegant. But tasty. Whenever I think of elegant I think of tiny portions that don't fill a person up."

"How about an international flavor? Would that appeal to you?"

"Oh yes. I like that idea."

"Okay, we could go with a mixture of some ethnic foods—"

"Not too ethnic. I'd like every dish to be something anyone would enjoy eating."

"Okay. I think I have an idea of what I can do," Jane said, taking a few more notes. This dinner sounded like a challenge, but Jane was confident in her abilities to pull it off.

"Could you let me know fairly soon what you plan?"

"As soon as possible," Jane said.

They chatted a bit more, and then Jane hung up the phone.

She went to the cupboard holding her library of cookbooks and started pulling some out.

"Planning already?" Alice asked, setting cups out on a tray.

"There's no time like the present," Jane said, laying them out in a fan on the butcher-block counter. "So many recipes, so little time," she said, though with a smile of delight rather than regret.

Quiet reigned once again, broken only by the sound of pages flipping—Jane thumbing through her cookbooks and Alice immersed in a mystery book she had picked up at the library.

Wendell, the inn's resident feline, strolled into the room, looked about as if trying to decide where to sit, then hopped up on a chair, settled in and promptly began purring.

Jane looked up and smiled. For a while all was peaceful, restful.

Then the kettle started whistling, the back door flew open and excited voices spilled into the room. Louise, the oldest of the Howard sisters, and their Aunt Ethel bustled into the kitchen. Ethel looked flustered, Louise slightly annoyed.

"Are you sure you're all right, Louise? That didn't look very good to me," Ethel was saying, holding Louise's arm. "You ran right into that young boy and his truck. My goodness, he wasn't happy with you about the accident."

"What did you say?"

"You had an accident?"

Jane and Alice spoke at the same time.

"Nothing happened more than a very minor smack of bumpers and one flat tire," Louise said, holding up her free hand to keep her sisters at bay. She shrugged out of Ethel's grip, set a stack of papers and envelopes on the table, then removed her raincoat. She took off her glasses, letting them swing from the chain to which they were attached. In spite of her assertion that nothing had happened, Jane saw in her older sister's bright blue eyes that all was not right in Louise's world.

Jane pulled a chair out from the table. "Sit down, Louise, and tell us what happened. Is your car drivable?"

"Nothing happened, and I'm fine, thank you very much," Louise said. "My car is at the mechanic's getting checked over."

"But she won't let herself get checked over," Ethel harrumphed. "Seems a bit odd. Besides, that accident didn't look good from where I was standing."

"You were standing inside Time for Tea and I bumped into a truck at the other end of the block," Louise said dryly, giving Alice and Jane a quick smile.

"You never mind. I saw it all happen. And I'm a little worried about you," Ethel said, all concern and frowns. "You might want to see Dr. Bentley and have your head examined."

Jane wasn't going to look at Alice or Louise because she was sure if she did, they would burst out laughing.

"I'm sure that is a given regardless of my circumstances," Louise replied. "Alice, could you please make that kettle stop its infernal whistling?"

Jane was closer so she hurried over and turned off the flame underneath the now strident-sounding kettle.

"Some tea, Louise?" she asked, as she lifted the lid off the teapot.

"Tea would be lovely."

When Jane brought back the tray that Alice had prepared, Ethel was still insisting that Louise see a doctor.

"Truly, Aunt Ethel," Louise said, her voice firm, "My car is worse off than I am, and my car has a mere scratch. The boy's truck had rubber bumpers, so not much chance of damage there."

"But these days you never know. You can get whiplash like that," Ethel snapped her fingers to emphasize her statement. Only nothing happened. Ethel frowned. "Like that," she repeated, trying to snap her fingers again. "Well now, isn't that something. Whatever is wrong with my fingers? I used to snap them all the time. I hope it's not arthritis."

"I'm sure you would have noticed some pain if it was," said Alice.

Ethel flexed her fingers, frowning. "I think I'm starting to feel a few twinges. Feels like, well, almost like . . ."

"Needles?" suggested Alice helpfully.

Ethel's frown deepened. "Possibly. Yes."

"Sometimes the weather can affect how your hands feel."

Ethel sat up as if something had just occurred to her. "Why just this morning I was having a discussion with Florence about this very thing. I told her the other day my hips were sore and I was sure it was because of the changing weather. She told me that was nonsense, that I was just imagining it. Then I told her that every time the weather changes, I can feel it, and then she said weather has nothing to do with how I'm feeling. I'm afraid we had a bit of a falling out over that. She can be quite opinionated, you know." Ethel looked around at each of her nieces as if seeking confirmation of that very fact.

"Imagine that," Jane said with a wry note in her voice.

Ethel glanced down at her hands. "So I'm sure my problem is arthritis." She looked around the table with a lugubrious expression.

"So tell us about this accident," Jane said, settling down to a cup of tea.

Louise simply shook her head, the overhead light glinting off her silver hair. "It was nothing. My tire went flat and as a result the car veered to one side and I bumped into a young man's truck. Thank goodness his truck is fine. I must confess, however, I felt rather foolish. I've never been in a car accident before. And I was clearly at fault."

"That young man wasn't a happy camper either," Ethel put in, patting her lips with a napkin. "He came storming out of his truck, took one look at the car and the truck and got upset with Louise."

"Oh dear. How unfortunate," said Alice.

"Nerve-racking," Jane agreed.

"Did you have to call the police?" Alice asked.

"We called them for insurance purposes and to be on the safe side," Louise said. "I'm glad to say the young man's truck didn't sustain any damage."

"I wanted to call an ambulance . . ." Ethel put in.

"But I found that unnecessary. As for that young man's attitude, as I said before, he was simply concerned about his truck."

"He still didn't need to be so angry with you," Ethel added, her pale blue eyes darting over the rest of the available brownie squares, trying to decide which one to have next. "I'm sure if you had been hurt, he still would have been more concerned about his precious truck."

"I hope that would not have been the case," Louise said, unbuttoning her peach-colored cardigan.

"Well, he was impolite. I hope I don't have to see him again soon."

The front doorbell rang, and in unison all three sisters pushed their chairs back, put their hands flat on the table and got up in one smooth motion.

Alice laughed. "You could say we've been living together too long."

"The Synchronized Innkeepers," Jane joked. "We could take our show on the road."

"We could become famous."

"We could answer the door," Louise commented, already walking briskly toward the front of the inn.

Jane winked at Alice and followed Louise. They, in turn, were followed by Ethel who was always vitally interested in the comings and goings of the guests at Grace Chapel Inn.

Though Louise had pooh-poohed Ethel's concern over the accident, Jane knew Louise well enough to understand that she would be disappointed with herself, no matter how slight the accident may have been.

Yet in spite of that, Louise was the consummate hostess. Smile in place, ready to greet and welcome prospective guests, she was the embodiment of Grace Chapel Inn's motto: "A place where one can be refreshed and encouraged, a place of hope and healing, a place where God is at home."

Louise opened the door to the sounds of lively chatter. A group of young people were gathered on the porch.

Behind them Jane heard Ethel's gasp.

"That's him," she said in a stage whisper, plucking at Jane's shirt. "That's the boy Louise hit with her car."

Chapter ⌐ Two

The young man staring back at her appeared as surprised as Louise felt. With his dark brown eyes and thick brown hair, he looked like a young movie star. But a deep frown marred his handsome features.

It was the same frown he directed at her after their collision. Of course, he had done more than frown then. As Ethel said, he seemed quite upset over a minor incident.

And now, here he was on her porch. Had he come to make amends? Or worse, had he come to charge her with something?

But he looked back over his shoulder at a young woman whose short black hair was spangled with rain, as was the bright red windbreaker she wore. She ran up the steps, joining the group of chattering and laughing young people.

Was this the party of seven Jane had booked two months ago? Jane's scribbled note had merely said, "Cobalt High School alumni-reunion," and Louise had drawn her own conclusions about their age. Cobalt was a town near Potterston. *Well, I overestimated,* she thought, taking note of the group's youthfulness.

"Hey, Carita, you sure this is the right place?" the dark-haired young man said.

"Yes, Lynden, it is," Carita replied. "You know, the sign? Grace Chapel Inn? That was the first clue."

The young woman, Carita, shook rain from her hair and favored Louise with a smile. "I am giving the right information, aren't I?"

Louise nodded.

"See. Right place, Lynden." She glanced up at him as if challenging him to question her authority.

Lynden looked back at Louise, then shrugged. His dark leather jacket glistening with moisture, the torn T-shirt, the faded blue jeans, the frown still creasing his forehead, all combined to give him the same edgy look that had made Louise feel uncomfortable in his presence after their accident.

But it appeared that he was now their guest, so Louise stepped aside, pulling the door farther open. "Please, come in out of the rain. And welcome to Grace Chapel Inn."

As the other young people tumbled past Lynden into the front hall, laughing and joking, Louise glanced back at Jane, who seemed as surprised as she was at just how young this group of guests was. Why, most of them barely looked old enough to vote.

Obviously, Jane had not verified their ages either.

"My name is Louise Smith, and these are my sisters, Jane Howard and Alice Howard. We're the owners of the inn. And this is our Aunt Ethel. She lives in the carriage house behind us."

"I'm Carita. This is Lynden, Rick, Matthew, Herbie, Isabel and Pete."

Carita reached out and shook Louise's hand, then Jane's, Alice's and Ethel's. The rest of the group nodded their heads in greeting.

Carita smiled. "Okay. That's settled. What's next?" she asked, fingering her damp hair.

"Jane took your reservation, so she will sign you in. Then I'll show you to your rooms upstairs."

"This is a great place," Carita said, glancing around the foyer. "Love the wallpaper. Whaddya think, guys? Did I do good or what?"

"Yeah."

"Great."

"Nice place."

Louise thought that, despite their responses, Carita's friends seemed less than enthusiastic about the accommodations. She wondered what they had expected.

"Rick and Matthew, can you please help me get our luggage from the van?" Carita asked, smiling sweetly at two of the young men.

They spun around, ready to assist the young woman.

Lynden hung back, one hand in the pocket of his blue jeans while he stood looking at the floor, the reception desk, the nails of his fingers, anywhere but at Louise, Jane, Alice or Ethel.

Isabel whispered to one of the other boys and, it seemed to Louise, sent furtive glances her way.

Was there a problem?

Once Jane had them signed in, Louise led the way up the stairs to the guest rooms.

"We have four rooms, and I notice there are seven in the group," Louise said, stopping in the main hall, "so six of you will double up. We do have extra cots if you are uncomfortable with sharing a bed.

"Each room has a name," Louise continued, opening the door of the Garden Room, a room at the front that was decorated in shades of green with a floral border along the wainscoting. She moved across the hall. "This one is called the Sunset Room," she said, then opened the door to a room with terra-cotta ragged paint. "The Sunset and Garden rooms each have a private bath, so I thought either of these might be suitable for the girls."

"The Garden Room looks okay," Isabel said. "Carita told me to pick it. Besides, I kinda doubt the boys will appreciate flowers and stuff."

"Unfortunately, one of the other rooms for the boys is called the Symphony Room and it does have flowers," Louise said. "And stuff."

"Yay for us," one of the boys said. Louise clearly heard the irony in his voice.

Undaunted, she showed them the other rooms, letting them decide. Lynden just hung back, not responding to anything the other boys said.

Louise glanced at him from time to time, but he appeared not to notice her.

She waited while the boys made their choices, growing increasingly uncomfortable with their obvious lack of enthusiasm. It appeared the inn wasn't what they had expected either.

Carita rejoined the group. "So? Everyone got his or her rooms picked out? You pick the Garden Room, Isabel?"

"Just like you told me to," Isabel replied.

"Awesome. My cousin told me about this place. Said it was awesome and you ladies were super-duper hostesses." Carita flashed a smile that Louise was pleased to return. At least Carita seemed enthusiastic about the inn. "Hey, Lynden, whaddya think?"

"Yeah. Good," was all he mumbled.

Louise chose to ignore his reticence as she glanced around the hall at the gathering of young people. She knew she shouldn't care, but for a moment she felt very . . . old. To have so much youth and vitality all gathered in one place seemed to underscore the age difference between her and her guests.

Still undaunted, however, Louise went over the basic house rules, telling them when breakfast was served and how their linen was handled. "We have a number of brochures downstairs by the desk in case you are interested in touring Acorn Hill. I understand you are going to be visiting Cobalt for something called Spirit Night on Friday and a school reunion on Saturday?"

"Go, Cobalt Cougars," one of the young men called out, pumping his fist in the air.

"Herbie and Rick are our reps in the flag-football game on Friday night," Carita said.

"And there are going to be bonfires," another boy said with obvious relish.

"I'm sure you will all have a wonderful time, but if there's anything we can do to make your stay here more comfortable, please don't hesitate to let us know." Louise glanced around the gathered young people. "Does anyone have any questions?"

"Can I check my e-mail here?" a short, slightly overweight young man asked. Louise tried to recall who he was, but the introductions had been such a flurry of names, she could attach only a few names to faces.

Lynden she had already identified. Matthew's hair was cut close to his head and Pete wore a baseball cap. She'd have to work on the others.

"You can use the library downtown."

"You need to limit your surfing, Herbie." Carita wagged her finger in a mock reprimand. "You spend way too much time on MySpace."

"MySpace being . . . ?" Louise asked with genuine interest. She had only recently mastered the rudiments of searching the Web and had discovered the joys of "googling" various topics. She hadn't heard about MySpace yet.

"A huge sprawling mess of interconnected personal Web pages." Carita's dismayed look telegraphed her opinion of said sprawling mess. "If you're really interested, Mrs. Smith, I can show you some time. You have to be a member to log in though."

"I could help you set up a page. For the inn," Herbie offered.

"Would that be helpful?" Louise asked.

"Well, yeah. You could set up a really cool friends' list and then you can post bulletins." Herbie slung the bag he carried over his shoulder onto the floor.

"Give Mrs. Smith a break," Matthew said.

Louise held up her hand. "Please. Feel free to call me Louise. Mrs. Smith makes me feel old."

Herbie frowned, then glanced at Lynden still slouched against the wall. "But she is old," he whispered.

"What do you mean?" Louise asked, delicately placing her hand on her chest. "I'm a mere sixty-five."

"And not deaf either," Matthew shot a warning glance at Herbie who simply shrugged.

"So, if everything is satisfactory, then I shall leave you to your unpacking." Louise's glance touched each one of them and then she turned to leave.

"She seems okay," she heard Herbie whisper. "For an old lady."

"Hey. Remember. Not deaf," she heard Matthew warn.

Louise smiled as she walked down the stairs. So perhaps it was just an age gap that made some of the young guests seem unimpressed with the inn. She resisted the urge to jump a step, just to show them. *One is only as old as one feels*, she reminded herself as she came to the bottom.

"Got our new guests settled in?" Alice asked, looking up from the dishwasher she was filling.

"I hope so. Where is Aunt Ethel?"

"She went to get her vacuum cleaner."

"Why is she doing that?"

"I forgot to tell you. Our vacuum cleaner has expired. It

bit the dust, once literally, but now metaphorically," Jane offered, glancing up from the cookbooks she was paging through.

"But that machine is quite new."

"I bought it eighteen years ago, Louise," Alice said.

Louise frowned. "Are you sure? I had exactly the same type when Eliot and I lived in Philadelphia. I'm sure I bought it when Cynthia was . . ." She stopped there and shook her head, then sighed. "I guess it is old, and I guess I am older than I think."

"Where is this coming from?" Jane said, folding her arms over her chest.

"Our guests. They seemed somewhat dismayed."

"At what?" Alice asked. "They seem much like many of our other guests. Tired, excited to be doing something different."

"I am quite sure they were expecting much younger hostesses," Louise replied. "As I was expecting much older guests." She sent a questioning look Jane's way.

Jane lifted her hands in a gesture of surrender. "Mea culpa. When Carita said they were alumni, I pictured older men in scarves and jackets looking all very Harvardish and reserved."

"Wrong picture," Louise said.

"Well, I'm not going to start asking guests' ages when they phone for reservations," Jane said.

"Of course not, but they are so young and energetic . . ."

"Now Louise, you know we want to model our Lord here. Everyone is welcome."

"Of course they are. It's just . . ."

Alice wiped her hands and walked over to her sister. "Louise, what is the problem? You seem upset. Could you have hurt yourself in the accident?"

"No, I didn't. Truly, I'm fine." Then Louise sighed and shook her head. "However, I still feel foolish for running into

Lynden's truck, and though nothing serious happened, I'm uncomfortable with how I felt afterward. And then, just a few moments ago one of our guests made a comment about being surprised at how old I was. I usually don't feel old, and I maintain that one is only as old as one feels. But today, I have to confess, I do feel old."

"Now, Louise, we're always going to be older than someone, but the upside is we're always going to be younger than someone too," Jane said, adding an infectious grin.

Alice, however, truly understood Louise's concern. Though she still felt quite fit, there were times, especially when the young, bright and seemingly tireless student nurses would come into the hospital to work under her supervision, that she had "elderly" moments. But that soon subsided when she realized all the experience and wisdom she had to offer these young girls. Often, by the time the students moved on to another ward or graduated, she and the young women had achieved understanding and mutual respect. They ceased to be young students and an older woman; they were simply nurses, united in a common cause to alleviate suffering.

Other than the half-hour sessions with her piano students, Louise did not have as frequent an opportunity as Alice to interact with young people over longer periods of time.

"You put things quite well, Louise, when you said that you're only as young as you feel. I don't think you're old at all."

"You realize you have a vested interest in consoling me, Alice," Louise said with an ironic tone. "You're only a few years younger than I am."

"And I feel as young as I ever did," Alice said with a decisive nod.

"That may be, but sometimes reality intrudes and today it has." Louise straightened her shoulders. "I must be realistic.

I remember reading an advertisement in the *Acorn Nutshell* about a refresher course for seniors who still drive. I think I should register."

"You don't need that," Jane protested. "There have been no major breakthroughs in the transportation department. We're not strapping on jet packs yet, as I once thought we would be by now." She sighed, looking almost wistful.

But Alice, being just three years younger than Louise, understood her sister. "I think that might be a good idea," Alice said, by way of encouraging Louise. "I have a number of days off coming up. I might take it with you."

"I'll have to look into this course," Louise said, pressing the palm of her hand on the table like a judge considering a sentence. "It would be the prudent thing to do."

"Could someone help me with this?" Ethel's call was followed by some thumping noises punctuated with some unladylike grunts.

Alice scooted across the kitchen to the door, and a few moments later Ethel's ancient vacuum cleaner took up one corner of the kitchen and Ethel sat on a chair, fanning herself. Her hair was plastered to her head and the vacuum was spotted with rain.

"Mercy me, that old thing is heavier than I thought. I had to stop three times between here and my house."

"You should have asked us to help you," Alice chided gently as she maneuvered the machine into a corner.

"Why? I can certainly manage to get a vacuum cleaner from point A to point B. I'm not some helpless little old lady," Ethel protested.

Jane snorted and then covered it up with a cough.

"Are you all right, Jane?" Ethel asked, her bright eyes flicking to her youngest niece.

"I'm fine, really," Jane responded, adding another cough.

"Sounds a bit croupy to me. I would get that checked

out." Ethel turned back to Alice. "Now the vacuum should be running like a top. I won't need it for a couple of days, so feel free to use it all you want. The carriage house doesn't get very dusty in this weather."

"You didn't need to bring it over in the rain," Alice said.

Ethel patted her hair and sniffed. She cocked her head, listening. "Those kids still here?"

"They are settling in." Alice made a trip to the laundry room, and when she returned, Ethel was quizzing Louise on their new guests.

"Seems odd a bunch of kids like that wouldn't want to stay in a motel so they can whoop it up till all hours of the night. I remember when Bob and I were traveling. We ended up in a town during a big hockey tournament. We couldn't find a room anywhere. We wound up in a little motel with walls no thicker than my pinky and stayed in a room beside a group of young kids who were louder than a marching band at Macy's Thanksgiving Day Parade. Except without the instruments. They didn't need instruments, the way they were trumpeting on and on and playing music loud enough to wake the dead." She shook her head as if still amazed at the memory. Ethel frowned at Alice. "These kids won't be loud, will they? I mean, the carriage house is a ways away, but still, noise does travel at night."

"I don't think so," Alice said reassuringly. "I'm sure if they wanted to whoop it up, as you say, they would have chosen a motel."

"One of the girls, Carita, said her cousin recommended the inn," Louise said. "I think it's always wonderful when previous guests are so satisfied with their stay that they pass that information on."

"Word of mouth. Best advertising in the business," Jane said from her perch, making a note on a piece of paper.

"What are you doing, Jane?" Ethel asked.

"Looking for new and exotic recipes." Jane tucked the pencil behind her ear and paged through another cookbook. "Though I'm coming up empty-handed."

"I'm sure our young guests don't need exotic breakfasts," Louise said.

"That's not the only thing I'm looking up recipes for," Jane said.

"Jane might be catering a dinner Saturday night," Alice put in.

"Won't the extra work leave you in a bind?" Louise frowned, adjusting her glasses. "We will still have all these guests."

Jane shrugged. "They'll be gone most of Saturday and I see this as a challenge."

"Who is the dinner for?"

"A Stacy Reddington from Potterston. She sounded desperate and 'really, really, really' wanted me to do this dinner." Jane held up her hand as if to forestall Louise's correction. "Her words, not mine."

"Where would this dinner take place?"

"She hadn't settled on a venue. I'm sure she's checking that out as I speak."

"Are you certain you won't be too tired?

"Stop fretting, Louise. I've got loads of energy."

Louise pushed herself to her feet. "Very well. I see I can't dissuade you. However, I have my own work to do. I'll be in the office." She gathered up the papers she had brought in and left the kitchen.

"How did this lady find you?" Ethel asked, folding her arms on the kitchen table.

Alice could tell that her aunt was settling in for a session of chatting, but she could also see Jane was buried in her cookbooks and preferred not to be distracted.

Seven guests and an upcoming dinner meant hours of

planning on Jane's part, and Alice was sure Jane would prefer peace and quiet while she planned.

"I heard June Carter at the Coffee Shop made some raisin pie today," Alice said, getting up from the table. "Why don't I treat you to some, Aunt Ethel?"

Ethel got the hint, and together they left Louise to her bills, Jane to her planning and the group upstairs to their unpacking.

Chapter ⌐ Three

"Hi, ladies. What do you want to order?" Hope Collins asked, stopping at Alice and Ethel's booth with a full coffeepot. An array of bobby pins held up her hair in an intricate style.

Ethel had selected a booth by the window to keep her eye on the comings and goings in the town. Light rain fell steadily, obscuring the buildings across the street, drizzling down the glass.

The walk to the Coffee Shop had been damp and cool, and Alice was glad to be inside again.

"I'll have a piece of raisin pie," Ethel said. "With some ice cream on the side, but not too much. I should be watching my weight."

"And you, Alice?"

"I'll also have the raisin pie, but without the ice cream, thank you." Alice too was watching her weight, and in spite of her regular walks with her friend Vera, the struggle was an ongoing one.

"Will do," Hope said as she poured coffee for Ethel and brought the usual tea for Alice. "And how is Louise? I heard about her fender bender."

"More like an embrace of bumpers," Alice said.

Hope frowned, setting the coffeepot on the table. "I heard the police were at Wilhelm's?"

"Just a formality. Neither Louise nor the young man she hit was hurt, nor were the vehicles damaged."

"Road must have been slippery," Hope said. "I can't imagine Louise being even the teeniest bit careless. She is a lot like your dear father. Rev. Howard was methodical and careful."

"She said something was wrong with her tire. That's what caused the accident."

"I saw the whole thing," Ethel piped up, only too eager to share any bit of news with Hope. "Seeing that car slide into that truck put my heart smack dab in my throat. Very scary, though Louise won't admit it. She's going to take a seniors' refresher course now."

"I can't think of her as a senior," Hope said with a chuckle.

"Tell Louise that," Alice said. "She's been feeling a bit elderly today."

"If she's feeling that way, I hope June isn't counting on her."

"Counting on her for what?" Ethel asked.

"I'll let her tell you. I should get back to work."

"Do you have any idea, Alice? I can't imagine June would plan something and not tell me. I was talking to her just the other day and she said nary a word about any plans."

Aunt Ethel looked peeved, and Alice tried not to smile. Her dear aunt liked to be in the forefront of any new gossip in town. Of course she would never call it gossip. "Generous sharing of information" was her preferred phrase.

Alice saw June Carter, the shop's owner, walking toward them, wiping her hands on her apron. Flushed cheeks and a smudge of flour decorating her forehead indicated that she had just taken a break from cooking and baking chores.

"Maybe June is coming over to tell us now," Alice assured her aunt.

Ethel twisted around. "*Yoo-hoo*, June, come join us." Ethel slid closer to the window to give June room.

"Hope told us you have something going on," Ethel said as June settled next to her. "Is it a big secret or are you allowed to share?"

"No secret, Ethel, though I don't know if you'd be interested. I'm going to be involved in helping with Habitat for Humanity. They're building a house for a young couple."

Alice was taken aback. She couldn't imagine June swinging a hammer.

"You look surprised, Alice," June said with a laugh. "I'm surprised myself. But if first ladies can do it—"

"Who?" Ethel asked.

"A number of first ladies and female governors set up an affiliate to build houses. They've been doing it for many years now. In fact, sometimes Habitat for Humanity sets up building crews made up entirely of women—they call it the Women Build program. Helps give women a safe place to learn how to use a hammer and operate a skill saw."

Aunt Ethel's eyes lit up. "A skill saw," she said in a reverential tone.

Alice tried not to imagine her dear aunt in possession of such a tool and the potential havoc she could wreak. As a nurse who had seen many accident victims in her time, she knew all too well how much damage a saw, wrongly handled, could do.

"I imagine they leave the operation of dangerous tools to experienced people," Alice commented.

"Absolutely. They believe in safety first," June said.

"So this project is a women-only project?"

June shook her head. "We were hoping, but we can't seem to get enough women. For now, we're just content to get enough volunteers."

"Can anyone volunteer? Do they have an age limit?" Ethel put in.

"You have to be over eighteen and, I guess, reasonably fit. I imagine they don't want people having heart failure once they start hammering," June said. Hope set down cups and plates of pie, then bustled away.

Ethel glanced down at her hands, and Alice guessed she was pondering her arthritis. Then Ethel flexed her fingers and straightened her back as if a small thing like twinges and aches wasn't going to keep her away from doing her duty by her fellow man.

"I'd like to volunteer," she said.

"Are you sure you should?" Alice asked, envisioning her usually spry but slightly plump aunt trying to climb a ladder or straddle a roof.

"I could probably do something. Maybe bring water or clean up behind the workers."

"Good afternoon, ladies."

Florence Simpson stood at the end of their booth, her brown hair teased and sprayed to glazed perfection, her deep red earrings and necklace sparkling in the overhead light. Her gaze merely flicked over Ethel, but Alice and June got a full-fledged smile.

"I overheard you talking about this building project, June," Florence said. "I heard about it previously and I am very interested. Could I get some more information?"

"I can only give you what I received from the project co-coordinator," June said.

"I might be interested," Florence's eyes skipped over Ethel and rested on June, "if there's a place for me on the crew."

"Don't worry," June assured her with a laugh. "From what I understand there will be many different jobs to do once they get started building. You might find the perfect place to help."

Though Ethel and Florence were taking great pains to avoid speaking, Alice saw her aunt squirming with curiosity.

"Did you put this information in other places, June?" Ethel asked, pointedly ignoring Florence. "I'm just wondering how people would hear about this." Ethel dug into her pie.

"Martha Bevins told me while I was getting my hair done at the Clip 'n' Curl," Florence said, aiming her comment at June and only June. Florence could ignore a person as well as Alice's aunt could.

June gave Alice a puzzled glance as if trying to figure out why Florence and Ethel were channeling their conversation through her. The two women's relationship could be stormy, but sooner or later Ethel would have something she simply had to tell someone, and Florence, always a willing recipient of any news, big or small, would forgive her.

In the meantime, however, Alice felt uncomfortable and a bit sad for these two friends.

Florence tapped June on the shoulder. "I don't have arthritis, so I could probably help out. What could I do?"

"Lots of things," June said, stifling a smile at the gymnastics she was going through to maintain a conversation with these women. "I'm sure you could handle some of the heavier work. It's always a cooperative effort, so it's not like you have to build the house on your own," June explained, warming to her subject. "In fact, the future owners of the house are required to help, which I think is very interesting."

"Do you need training?" Alice asked, growing curious herself about the project. "I don't believe any of us here has used a hammer for anything more than putting nails in walls or doing minor repairs."

"There is usually a supervisor on the project, and she or he will tell you what you need to do and help you. I'm sure after a few days, you'll get better at it."

"And how do they get the money if they need assistance?" Florence asked.

"The cost of building the house itself is pretty low.

Apparently much of the material and the time to build the house is donated, or provided for Habitat at a deep discount. In addition, as I mentioned, the people who will receive the home have to commit to working at least five hundred hours on the project, either building or collecting funds or whatever else might need to be done to help raise money or raise the house."

"How interesting and how motivating." Florence looked impressed.

"It is. I visited my sister a few years back when she was involved in a similar project. I went to help her for a day and have been wanting to do this ever since. The day I was there, the family had to decide on paint colors. One of the volunteers was helping the woman, a single mother, and the dear girl was so excited and so happy that she was crying while she was picking out the colors."

"I'm in," declared Ethel, slapping her hand—somewhat cautiously—on the table for emphasis. "I think this is a wonderful example of faith in action. I want to be a part of this."

Alice saw an answering spark in Florence's eye. "Well. If some people can forget their disabilities, I am sure I can be of help. I will also volunteer," Florence declared in a loud voice, as if making sure June and Ethel—as well as others in the shop—would not doubt her meaning. Alice glanced from Ethel to Florence, who were still studiously avoiding each other. If Ethel and Florence were helping, it would be prudent if Alice volunteered some time to keep an eye on the two of them.

"I'm interested as well," Alice said.

"This is wonderful," June said, beaming at the assembled group. "I'll let my contact person know and she can give you all the details."

"When do we start?" Ethel said. "I need to prepare myself."

"You can go to the building site tomorrow if you like," June said. "I may not go until Thursday."

Ethel turned to Alice. "If you're coming, I can ride with you."

"I'll ride with you, June," Florence said.

Alice exchanged a smile with June. "I guess that's decided," she said.

"Good, and I better get back to my kitchen. I'm excited about this and so glad Acorn Hill will be well represented."

"I don't know how well Acorn Hill will be represented, but we will be represented," Alice said with a smile.

After June and Florence left the table, Ethel leaned closer to Alice, her blue eyes fairly snapping. "Can you believe that Florence? I think she's deliberately setting out to goad me."

"What makes you say so, Auntie?"

Ethel sniffed. "That comment she made about not having arthritis. Then that one about ignoring disabilities. She's just trying to get me riled up."

"Why would she do that?"

Ethel sat back, crossing her arms over her bosom and glancing out the window, her dyed red hair bouncing with suppressed indignation. "She can be that way, you know," was all Ethel would say.

"I see," Alice said, even though she wasn't sure that she did. Ethel and Florence had fallings-out before, but not over something this trivial. She suspected there was more to the story, but for now Ethel wasn't telling her.

She also suspected she would receive even less information from Florence herself.

However, Alice had hopes for her aunt and for Florence. Working together on this project could be a good opportunity to bring them back together again.

Ethel sighed, glanced over at her niece and was suddenly all smiles. "Are you done with your tea?" Ethel said, leaning closer to peer into Alice's cup.

"Not quite." Alice couldn't help but smile herself. Her aunt could be easily provoked, but she bounced back quickly to her usual sunny nature.

"Okay." Ethel leaned back, drumming her fingers on the tabletop, glancing out the window, then around the Coffee Shop, then back at Alice's teacup.

"Are you in a hurry to leave, Auntie?" Alice asked.

"If we are going to be working on this house tomorrow, we'll need some tools."

"I'm sure they will be provided."

"Are you positive?"

"Well, not positive. I've never done anything like this before."

"Then we should be prepared, shouldn't we?" Ethel's face fairly beamed. "I'd like to stop at Fred's Hardware. The more we provide ourselves, the less they have to, right? And we should probably stop at the Nine Lives Bookstore to see if Viola has any books on carpentry in stock. We might find some information to help us be better prepared when we get there."

Alice finally caught the gist of where her aunt was headed—shopping.

"I'll be done in a few sips," she said, smiling at her aunt's enthusiasm. One thing about Aunt Ethel, she never stayed down long.

❧

"And when would this course begin?" Louise asked, writing down a figure on the message pad on the reception desk. "And it is every day, starting tomorrow? Then I'm glad I contacted you as soon as I did. I shall see you tomorrow."

Louise hung up the phone and ripped the paper off the pad. She paused a moment, wondering if she was doing the right thing.

Well, of course she was. She had been fortunate nothing worse had happened this morning when she ran into that truck. For what seemed like the twentieth time, she replayed the scene in her head. But what else could she have done?

According to Harlan Green, her tire had been wearing down for a while. Simple maintenance and regular observation would have prevented the tire's going flat, he had said. That was something she should have been aware of.

Louise was always of the opinion that preparation for potential problems limited the potential for future problems.

As a result, she decided to be proactive and find a way to be prepared. And, thankfully, she remembered reading that piece in the *Acorn Nutshell* about this refresher course. Now that she was registered, she felt better.

A blast of music from upstairs gave her an unexpected jolt. Had there been other people staying at the inn, Louise would have asked their current guests to turn down the music. As it was, no one was complaining, and as long as they didn't keep the music playing into the night, she and her sisters would simply have to put up with the noise.

Louise was surprised these young people chose to stay at the inn when there were many other places in Potterston that would seem to have been better suited for their purposes.

Louise tucked the paper into the pocket of her narrow gray skirt and wandered back to the kitchen, where Jane was hunched over her recipe books, talking to someone on the phone.

"I understand. I could make some traditional American recipes," Jane made a note on a pad of paper lying beside the books, nodded, then scratched it out. "We don't *have* to do traditional American. I could try to find something more cosmopolitan . . . no, I don't mean fancy, I just mean . . . more . . . European? I see." She nodded, spoke some more, said good-bye and then hung up the phone.

"Haven't settled on the menu?" Louise asked as the door to the dining room swung back and forth behind her.

Jane pushed her long hair back from her face and sighed. "Stacy specifically said she didn't want exotic ingredients—she's concerned about possible allergies—nor did she want something too 'out there,' wherever 'there' is, or too plain, or something that's been done before. That narrows the list. So I thought of an international menu, but she didn't like the idea, and, well, you heard the rest of the story." Jane gestured at the telephone.

Louise caught a note of frustration. "Are you already regretting taking this on?"

Jane's forehead puckered a moment as she flipped through her recipe books. Then she shook her head. "If anything, I'm becoming more determined."

The timer for the dryer buzzed, and Louise moved toward the utility room to remove a load of clothes.

"I'll get it," Jane said, holding up her hand. "You just sit down."

"And why should I do that?" Louise asked.

"Well, I'm just, you know, a little concerned . . . I mean, you did just have an accident."

"Nothing happened, Jane," Louise said. "I'm fine and I'm not going senile and there is nothing wrong with my coordination." She frowned, glancing upward as a particularly loud blast of music boomed above them. "I didn't realize the ceilings and walls were so thin."

"What do you mean?"

Is she deaf? Louise wondered exasperatedly "That thumping music carries with remarkable effectiveness throughout the inn."

Jane frowned, cocking her head as if to listen. "I hadn't really paid much attention."

"How could you not? That bass chord is practically shaking the floor."

Jane's smile showed Louise once again the differences in their ages, and in their musical tastes as well. "Maybe I should get them to play their radios in the parlor."

"They would completely fill up that room. Why would you want to do that?"

"Soundproof walls."

The music stopped, and Louise breathed a sigh of relief. Too soon, it seemed, because only a few moments later, country music wailed through the halls of the inn.

"I'm going to go out for a while," Louise said. "Unless you need any help here?"

Jane smiled at her sister, obviously recognizing the source of her discomfort. "There's not much to do, so go ahead. Maybe by the time you come back, they might have switched to classical."

"I don't think I can be gone that long," Louise said with a wry smile. "I'll be at Viola's bookstore."

"Would you like a ride?"

Louise stared at her sister. "No. Nine Lives is not far. I'm walking."

Jane held up her hands in a gesture of surrender. "Fine. Good. Walking is healthy and invigorating. Make sure you take your umbrella."

Chapter ⊤ Four

A few moments later Louise was striding down the wet sidewalks, inhaling the fresh, albeit damp, air. Dark clouds still hung low over the area, dropping a light drizzle on the town—enough to spangle the trees with moisture and to keep Jane out of her beloved garden, yet not enough to inhibit a good, brisk walk.

She waved at a neighbor and slowed to admire the flowers filling a corner flowerbed near Grace Chapel. *I should appreciate them while I can,* she thought, bending over to touch the bright chrysanthemums. Soon the killing frost would come, the plants would die, and the trees of Acorn Hill would display their glorious colors as a muted song of praise to God for His creation.

But not yet, Louise thought, tucking her hands deeper in the pockets of her raincoat. For now the grass was still green, plants were still alive and the leaves still clung to the trees.

She paused at the street crossing, looked both ways, then looked again as if to make sure she didn't have a second accident this morning. Then she crossed over.

Though she had waved off her sister's concern, her confidence in her own driving ability had been shaken. She realized that drivers made mistakes all the time, but hitting that truck was a reminder of how much power and weight a vehicle had.

Louise paused at the entrance of the bookstore, removed her rain bonnet, shook out the moisture, then pulled open the door of Nine Lives. The faint jangling of the bell created a welcoming, homey sound.

All was quiet inside the store. Louise looked around the crowded shelves and felt a familiar pull of anticipation. The sight of all the new, still unopened books, the potential adventures, and the information stored inside the shiny new covers never ceased to create a gentle thrill. *All this just waiting to be plucked from a shelf and read.*

"Hello," she called, wondering where her good friend was. Usually when the bell rang, either Viola or one of her many cats were there to greet her.

But no one came, and the only cat Louise saw was resting on Viola's desk in the back of the store.

Where could she be?

She finally heard a faint murmuring of voices and followed the sound to a far corner of the store where the how-to books were shelved, a section Louise seldom visited.

"I need to know if there's a right or wrong way to hold a hammer."

Is that Aunt Ethel's voice?

Louise peered around a bookshelf and there was her aunt squinting at a book as Viola was pointing out something on one of the pages.

"From what it says here you want to hold the hammer near the very end. I would imagine you get better leverage that way."

"This doesn't give a person much information."

"If you want more detailed books, you could check with Nia Komonos at the library," Viola said.

Aunt Ethel snapped the book shut. "Maybe I'll just figure it out on my own. Alice, I'm ready to go to Fred's now."

Alice is here as well?

Louise coughed lightly to make her presence known. "Hello, Viola, Aunt Ethel," Louise said.

Viola spun around, her expression slipping from humor to worry. "Louise. How are you?"

"I am the picture of health and vitality." Louise held up a hand to forestall any concern on Viola's part. She should have known something as minor as two vehicles bumping each other would have already spread across the width and breadth of Acorn Hill. And she should have known that her friend would have already found out. Louise was certain that Ethel had seen to that.

Louise turned to her aunt. "I thought you and Alice were having pie at the Coffee Shop."

Ethel shrugged Louise's comment aside. "Well, we were." She put the book back on the shelf. "But now we're here."

Alice appeared around the end of the bookshelf holding a couple of books in her hand. Mysteries, Louise saw from their covers.

"These just came out, didn't they?" Alice asked.

Viola fiddled with the floral silk scarf draping her shoulders. "Yes. I just finished shelving them." Sharing Louise's less-than-enthusiastic regard for mysteries, she gave her friend a "what can I do" look, which merely made Louise smile.

One would think that after all these years of running a bookstore in Acorn Hill, Viola Reed had resigned herself to the varied and, at times, ordinary tastes of her patrons.

"Wonderful. I wondered when this author's new book would come out. I love reading her stories. They may not be great literature, but they are great fun."

"I set a new anthology of Walt Whitman's poetry on the display table," Viola suggested in an encouraging tone.

Louise gave Viola high marks for maintaining her campaign to raise the literary bar for the residents of Acorn Hill.

Over time some had succumbed and slowly purchased a number of Viola's more challenging suggestions. But by and large, her biggest selling item was popular contemporary fiction.

Alice wrinkled her nose, giving Viola a sly smile. "Thank you, but I prefer a good rollicking read."

Viola shrugged. "Well, then rollick away," she said, leading Alice to the front of the store.

"May I ask why you are looking at books about construction?" Louise asked Ethel, her curiosity piqued.

"Alice and June Carter and I are going to help build a Habitat for Humanity home. It's a wonderful opportunity and it's going to be so much fun."

Louise considered remarking on her aunt's developing arthritis but thought better of it. "So where is this house being built?" she asked.

"Just outside of Potterston. It's going to be a fulfilling experience. June filled us in on all the particulars. She said the people for whom we are building the house are going to be helping. This is a good chance to use the gifts God has given me to help someone else. That's a good thing, isn't it?" Ethel asked.

"I think it's a wonderful opportunity," Louise agreed, though she was secretly relieved Alice would be working with her aunt. Ethel's exuberance could, at times, get in the way of good sense. Even though she was not exactly reckless, the picture of Ethel wielding a hammer was somewhat disconcerting. "I hope you will be careful."

"Of course I will." Ethel patted Louise on the arm, reassuring her niece that all would be well. "Now if you'll excuse me it looks like Alice has paid for her books. We've got to get moving. Lots to do before tomorrow. We want to be up at the crack of dawn." Ethel paused a moment, tilting her head to one side. "Your Uncle Bob always said that, but you know I never really knew what it meant. Dawn doesn't exactly crack, does it? I mean the sun, it usually kind of slips up over the horizon. *Hmm.* I wonder where that saying came from. I'll have to check that out when I do some more research on this Habitat program." Ethel's face brightened. "I'm so excited about this. You should come too."

"I have other fish to fry," Louise said with a smile. "But if I have time, I might stop by at the site to see you and Alice at work."

"You do that. Now I need to get going." And Ethel was off.

As the bell above the door provided Alice and Ethel a tinkling send-off, Louise glanced over the how-to books, wondering if she could find something on driving. Not that she needed to start from the beginning, but some helpful tips might come in handy.

"Are you trying to find out how to build a house too?" Viola asked, adjusting her glasses as she looked at Louise.

"I don't think you'll find me scampering about on a building site anytime soon," Louise replied with a smile. "No, I've just come to visit. And to see if you carry any books on driving."

"Because of your accident this morning? Louise, you hardly need to worry about your competence in that department. Accidents are called accidents because they are, by their very nature, unintentional."

Louise felt comforted by her friend's enthusiastic defense of her abilities.

"Nonetheless, I have decided to enroll in a seniors' refresher course at the library that I read about in the *Acorn Nutshell*. I was able to get in on short notice."

"What can they teach you that you don't already know?"

"I believe I could use some brushing up. The longer a person drives the less attentive she gets. I really do not want a repeat of what happened today."

Viola looked thoughtful. "Refresher course? I wonder if I

wouldn't benefit from that as well?" She fingered the fringe of her silk scarf.

"Could you get me the information? Then I can enroll as well." Viola turned, tapping her chin with her fingers as she studied a nearby shelf. "As for books on the subject, I'm afraid you'll have to go to the library. I don't have much demand for material of that sort."

"That's fine. The books were mostly an excuse to come here. The inn is filled with young people, and they were listening to music when I left. Quite loud and noisy music."

"Can't you ask them to turn it down?"

"They are guests, which means we invite them to make themselves at home." Louise simply smiled.

"How old are they?"

"Not that many years out of high school. They seem like an exuberant and friendly group of kids."

"You are using your 'I have my doubts' voice," Viola teased.

"They vastly outnumber Alice, Jane and me."

"You're not expecting a guest insurrection, are you?"

Louise laughed. "No. Usually our guests come to the inn to enjoy the peace and quiet. These guests seem to have other plans."

"Sounds like you need a cup of tea and some conversation," Viola said. "Wilhelm just brought in a new brand of Indian chai, which can be most welcome on a dreary day. I'll be glad to fix some."

Though she had already had a cup of tea at the inn, Louise welcomed the opportunity to visit with her friend. "That sounds lovely. You can tell me which books will be coming out this fall."

Viola's expression brightened. "I just got some new catalogs from two of my favorite publishers. I'll show them to you."

A few moments later a cat lay curled up on Louise's lap,

a cup of tea stood steaming at her elbow, and she and Viola were leaning over brightly colored brochures discussing the merits of various authors and publishers.

The bell over the door tinkled, and Viola leaned sideways to look out of the office. Louise also glanced back.

Florence Simpson entered the shop. She caught sight of them and came striding over.

"Hi, ladies. Ah, Viola," Florence said. "I was wondering if you have any books on carpentry."

∽

A cough caught Jane's attention. She looked up from the towel she was folding to see Carita standing in the kitchen doorway, her hands tucked in the pockets of her blue jeans. Herbie stood behind her, peering over her shoulder.

"What can I do for you, Carita?"

"We were wondering if you could recommend a good place to eat." She poked her thumb over her shoulder at Herbie. "He's starving."

"The Coffee Shop has a fine reputation, and it's not expensive."

"Burgers?" Herbie stretched his head to peer more closely into the kitchen.

"Some of the best you'll ever have."

"Score!" Herbie slapped Carita on the shoulder. "I'll go tell the others."

Carita, however, didn't follow him. She stayed in the doorway watching Jane work as if waiting for something.

Jane felt obligated to make some conversation. "How long has this group known each other?" Jane asked.

"We all hung out in high school, and most of us now go to college together."

"Most of us . . ." Jane prompted.

"Lynden ducked below everyone's radar the past year.

Didn't phone, e-mail, nothing. Of course he doesn't really need to learn a trade or get a degree. His grandma has oodles of money. Lynden could just hang out the rest of his life and not do anything if he wanted." Carita stopped, pressing her fingers against her lips. "Sorry. I shouldn't be yapping about him. He doesn't like it."

"I won't breathe a word."

Carita stepped farther into the kitchen, fluttering her hand in the direction of the hallway. "I noticed the name on the library door. Was that your dad?"

Jane set the still-warm towel on the pile on the table. "Yes, he was an avid reader." Jane picked up another towel, her mind slipping back to memories of her father sitting at his desk, a book open in front of him, a pad of paper beside him, fountain pen in his hand as he made notes on what he was reading. "The library also holds many valuable concordances of the Bible and reference books he would use to make his sermons."

"So you were a preacher's kid too," Carita said with a grin.

"Too?" Jane asked.

"Yeah. Lynden's dad was a preacher at the church my father and mother went to, until he died and Lynden went to go live with his grandma." Carita leaned against the doorframe, looking like she was settling in for a chat.

Though Jane and her sisters tried to maintain boundaries between their guests and themselves by keeping the kitchen a separate place, occasionally they bent the rules. Talking to Carita across the expanse of the kitchen seemed awkward.

"Come on in," Jane said, lifting her chin in the direction of a chair by the kitchen counter.

"You sure? I don't want to intrude." But even as she put forward her mild protest, Carita pushed herself away from the doorway.

"Please, I'm not doing anything too demanding."

Carita bounded into the room and sat down. "You want a hand with that?" Carita asked, pointing to the still full laundry basket.

"I'm not about to make a guest work." Jane glanced at the oven timer, and her heart gave a quick jump. She'd almost forgotten about the cookies baking in the oven. She dropped the towel she'd been folding, snatched the oven mitts off the counter and yanked the oven door open.

Thank goodness the cookies were a comforting, golden brown.

She drew the cookie sheet out of the oven, and, one by one, scooped the cookies off and set them to rest on a cooling rack.

"Wow! Those look good," Carita said.

"I smell something outrageously wonderful."

Pete stood, licking his lips, his blond hair anchored by a black cap this time. Herbie stood behind him, peering over Pete's shoulder.

Their eyes widened when they saw the cookies. "You just made those?" Pete asked.

"Well, she didn't just pick them up from the store and heat them up in the oven," Carita said, shaking her head at Pete's question.

"I don't think my mom ever baked anything," Herbie said, casting a longing look at the cookies.

"Would you like some?" Jane asked.

Herbie didn't need urging.

Jane piled some cookies on a plate. She had planned on setting the plate on the table and putting out some napkins, but by the time she rounded the end of the counter, Herbie and Pete were there. They each whisked a cookie off the plate faster than she could say "Help yourself."

"You can take two," Jane said.

The words had barely left her mouth when the two boys acted on her offer.

"Things are looking up at Carita's inn," Pete said.

"These are fantastic." Herbie licked his lips and ate the second cookie in three bites. "Butterscotch cookies are my number-one favorite, and yours are the best."

"I appreciate the compliment. These are a favorite of mine too." Jane beamed.

"You two guys don't believe in savoring your food, do you," Carita teased.

"Savor?" Pete asked, his frown indicating his opinion of that particular exercise, his own cookie disappearing in record time.

"You know. Take your time and enjoy it? Like this?" Carita lifted a proffered cookie, took a bite and closed her eyes, chewing slowly.

Jane laughed at the dumbfounded looks on the boys' faces. They looked at each other, then at Carita, shrugged and each took another cookie.

"Thanks, Ms. Howard."

"See ya later, Carita," Pete mumbled around a mouthful of cookie.

"Yeah, thanks. These were the best," added Herbie.

Carita sighed as she watched them leave. "Barbarians," she grumbled.

The sound of feet thumping down the porch stairs drew her and Jane's attention.

"You sure you don't want to go with them?" Jane asked, surprised that this young woman would choose to stay behind.

"I'm tired. I drove the rented minivan most of the way here."

"And Lynden took his own vehicle?"

"He arranged to meet us here." Carita pressed her index finger against a few scattered crumbs lying on the counter and popped them in her mouth.

"Which of you likes to listen to the music?"

"Was it too loud? I told Matthew to turn down the volume.

We thought your sister might be annoyed, but he said she told them to make themselves at home. The guys thought that was cool of her."

"If we had other guests, we would probably ask you to tone it down, but if none of your fellow travelers objects, you go ahead and listen to what you want."

"Maybe Matthew should put on earphones." Carita smiled.

"So when do the festivities start?"

"Friday. We're talking about having a tailgate party earlier."

"And what will you be keeping busy with while you are here?"

"I've got some plans. I hope everyone goes along with them. And I really hope Lynden wants to play along."

"He strikes me as a taciturn young man."

"He can be." Carita fiddled with the knife block, shifting it back and forth. "But he's one of those 'still-waters-run-deep' kinds of people. He was pretty smart in school."

"Sounds like you know him well."

Carita ducked her head, popping another cookie crumb in her mouth, the faint blush in her cheeks telling Jane what Carita's silence didn't.

"How long have you and your sisters run this inn?"

Her sudden change of subject made Jane wonder about Carita's relationship with Lynden, but she wasn't going to pry. "We've done this awhile now."

"You don't mind sharing your home with people?"

Jane shook her head as she scooped out more cookie dough. "I enjoy meeting new people and finding out where they come from. But I have to confess I find it interesting that a group of such young people would come to a bed-and-breakfast."

"Totally my idea," Carita said. "I wanted to come to a quiet place and a place that felt more like a home for this reunion. I heard about this inn and this town, and figured this would be a good place to stay." Carita shrugged. "It's fun to be together again."

"Well, I'm glad you came. It's been a while since we've had such a young group." Jane slipped the cookies into the oven and leaned on the counter.

"Trouble is, I didn't think they'd all want to come this soon, and this group needs someone to get them moving, so now I have to come up with something to do on the days there isn't anything planned. I'm trying to make up an itinerary," Carita pulled a small notebook and a pen from her shirt pocket and set it on the counter in front of her. "Do you have any ideas?"

"Acorn Hill doesn't have a lot of things to do, so you will probably have to spend most of your time in Potterston."

"I already have a movie night planned, and we're hoping to check out some of the local tourist stuff in some of the surrounding areas. Matthew was talking about a car show. I was trying to think of something I could do around here. None of us has a lot of dollars except for Lynden, it seems."

Jane scratched her chin. "Paintballing?"

"Possibility," Carita said.

"The only other thing on my list of activities would either be an Easter egg hunt, which is rather out of season, or a town scavenger hunt, which is pretty lame," Jane said with a laugh.

"How does a town scavenger hunt work?"

"That was a joke."

"I'm not joking. That might be something fun. How would you do it?"

"It would require prep work."

"So what would you do?"

As she told Carita, she had thrown the idea out as a joke. Now, it seemed, she actually had to come up with something for the young woman. "I guess you could divide the group into teams, then make a list of things to find in the town.

Maybe pick up a business card from Time for Tea, that's Wilhelm Wood's teashop, a muffin from the Good Apple Bakery, a matchbook from the Dairyland convenience store, describe an item in Humbert's Hardware. That kind of thing." Jane shook her head, and laughed. "Just a silly suggestion. I think Alice did something similar with the girls group she works with, the ANGELs. They're younger than your group, so a scavenger hunt might seem a bit immature for you. Forget I mentioned it."

Carita pursed her lips as she considered the suggestion. Then she smiled. "Trust me, this is exactly what these guys would enjoy. When guys turn nineteen or twenty, it's like they regress. The only trouble is that a scavenger hunt would take some planning."

"If you're serious about this, I could help you. I know the town, and I think Alice still has something lying around from when she and her girls' group did the hunt."

"That'd be great." Carita made a quick note in her book, then tapped her pen on the counter. "As long as it's not too much work for you."

"I need to run a bunch of errands tomorrow anyway. If you're not busy with your friends, we could compile a list. Add Alice's stuff and I think we could keep them busy."

The timer started beeping for the second batch of cookies and Jane pushed herself away from the counter to answer the insistent summons.

"You sure it's not too much to ask?"

Jane glanced out the window. The weather was still damp and chilly. She doubted she'd be getting much done in the garden for the next few days. She still had Stacy's dinner to plan, but she was fairly certain that she had that taken care of with a sure-fire menu item. "I have time," Jane assured the engaging young woman.

"Great. I'll see you about it tomorrow." Carita glanced at her notebook, pausing a moment.

"Anything else I can help you with?" Jane asked, setting the cookie sheet on the cooling rack.

Carita looked pensive, and then shook her head. "No. Not really. But I am feeling tired. I think I'll grab a nap. I'm beat from our drive."

Jane watched Carita leave, then turned her attention back to her cookies. But as she took more cookies off the sheet to cool, she sensed Carita wanted to talk about something other than her friends' entertainment.

Before she could ponder more about the young woman's situation, the telephone rang. Jane answered it.

"Jane, have you figured out a menu yet?"

Jane stifled a groan. Stacy Reddington. "I've got a basic concept in place."

"I hope you're not going to do anything with noodles . . ."

Jane sighed as she walked over to her sure-fire menu and scratched her entrée off the list. "Why don't you tell me what you would like," Jane said, settling in for what would be a long chat, as all chats with Stacy were turning out to be. She would never admit this to Louise or Alice, but her second thoughts about taking on this dinner had become third and fourth thoughts two phone calls ago.

Chapter ⊤ Five

"T his one should do," Ethel said, tilting the hammer back and forth, as if testing its weight. "What do you think, Alice?"

"It seems okay now, Aunt Ethel, but I'm sure if you had to wield it all day, you might be sorry you took such a heavy one."

"But Fred said these Estwings are the best."

"For a carpenter, maybe, but I think we might want to stick to something with less heft." Alice held the hammer a moment, then put it back. "We don't need to get the nails in with one blow."

"But I want to be a help, not a hindrance." Ethel grabbed a smaller hammer from the pegboard and pretended to hammer a few nails. "This one seems a bit light. And according to that handyman book in the library, you want a head with cross-hatching." She turned it over to check the head, then put it back with a grimace. "Smooth as glass. No hitting the nail on the head with this hammer. It will be bouncing around all over the place and then there'll be hammer dents in the wood. Won't look professional is all I can say. I want to do the best job I can."

"That's important," Alice agreed, "but if you get too tired using your hammer, you might have the same problem."

"This is true," Ethel said and considered the display in front of her. "So I suggest a compromise. Not too much weight, but not too light." She pulled another hammer off the display. "This one will do quite nicely." She dropped it in the pull-along cart. "Now we need pouches."

"I'm fairly sure those will be provided," Alice said, glancing over the list she and Ethel had compiled.

"Cotton things," Ethel said with a dismissive wave of her hand. "We need the real McCoy. The leather ones with the metal hammer handle. After all, that hammer will wear out those cotton aprons in a New York minute. Now mind you, I always thought minutes were minutes. You can't change time in spite of what the daylight saving time people tell us."

Alice looked decidedly puzzled. "Auntie, I—"

"But I figure if I'm going to spend my time wisely, I don't want to bother those Habitat folks every time my hammer falls off my pouch because the hammer sling broke." Her emphatic nod told Alice precisely what Ethel thought of that idea and how far Alice was going to get trying to dissuade her.

Not very far.

Alice decided to humor her aunt. Despite having urged her to consider that Habitat would probably provide tools, she knew that Ethel had enough money to supply her own tools, and her aunt was insistent she do her part on this project to the best of her ability.

"Besides, the more I provide of my own supplies," Ethel continued, striding down the aisle toward the section carrying leather pouches, "the less they have to, and the more money they'll have for the people they're helping."

They made an abrupt halt at the end of the aisle. "Only two to choose from?" Ethel frowned. "That makes it difficult."

Alice actually thought that made deciding much easier and was secretly relieved. She and Ethel had spent a good part of their afternoon at the library, checking Habitat Web sites, reading up on tools usually provided and tools that volunteers might bring along. Even though they weren't told exactly what they were expected to supply, Ethel had a take-no-prisoners attitude and was marching full force into the fray.

Alice was willing to help her aunt and had even purchased a few items herself. She understood that having one's own hammer was beneficial, and even though they had a finishing hammer at the inn, she got a heavier one for herself here. She also decided that a few extra pencils probably wouldn't hurt, but she had put her own spending on hold when it came to pouches, chalk lines, box cutters, hand planes, metal rulers or calculators.

Ethel finally decided on a pouch and dropped it into the basket.

"Can you think of anything else we might need?" she asked, casting a critical eye over her current choices, then glancing down the carpentry aisle again. She shook her head. "All this time, and I never knew half of these things existed. It's like a whole new world of shopping has opened up for me."

"I'm sure you have everything you need and then some," Alice said, glancing surreptitiously at her watch. She didn't want to leave Jane alone to prepare and serve dinner.

Though the inn didn't offer dinner to its guests, they did, on occasion, offer an evening snack. Alice had a feeling the alumni at the inn were a snacking crowd.

"You want to go?" Ethel said.

"You don't miss a thing, do you?"

"That's the third time you've looked at your watch in the past minute. I've been trying to hurry, truly, but we can go now." Ethel marched down the aisle, pulling her well-stocked little cart behind her.

"Looks like you've got some big plans. I've been wondering about your new interest in tools," Fred said as he rang up their purchases. "Doing some renovating at the inn?"

"Alice and I are going to work on the Habitat for Humanity house they're putting up outside of Potterston," Ethel said.

"Now that sounds fascinating," Fred replied. "Does Vera know?"

Alice shook her head. "This just came up. And I mean, just."

"June told us about it at the Coffee Shop," Ethel put in, bending over to take the other items out of her cart.

"I thought I should volunteer," Alice said, and then poked her index finger down at her aunt, who couldn't see what she was doing. "Keep an eye on her," she mouthed to Fred, who grinned and then nodded.

"I'll be glad to be one up on Vera," Fred said, bagging their purchases. "You'd think running a store would give me the upper hand on news, but somehow Vera always comes home from school with one anecdote or piece of information that is new to me."

"Little pitchers. Big ears," Ethel said, lifting the last of the items. "People say all kinds of things around children and don't think they hear. When my three were young, they were pretty good at cobbling bits and pieces of information together when Bill and I were talking about things we didn't think they should know."

Fred gave Ethel the final tally, and as she paid, Alice saw her aunt glancing around, as if afraid she had missed something.

"I suppose we'll need a visor," Ethel mused.

"I think they'll provide us with hard hats," Alice replied.

Ethel nodded, but Alice was fairly sure Ethel would be back here again, only too happy to be searching through some aisle of the hardware store she had never explored carefully before.

They packed the crinkly plastic bags back in the cart, and slipped their rain bonnets on, getting ready to venture out into the wet.

As they stepped outside, they almost collided with a young man walking at a brisk clip. His jacket was pulled up around his ears, his hands shoved deep in his pockets.

Lynden, Alice thought, recognizing his dark hair and handsome features.

He skidded to a halt, his blue eyes glancing from Alice to Ethel.

He gave them a curt nod, then stepped around them and kept walking.

Ethel glanced over her shoulder, looking peeved. "He seems like a rather rude young man, don't you think?"

"Maybe he didn't recognize us," Alice said.

"Oh, I'm sure he did. I saw the minute he clapped eyes on us he knew exactly who we were."

Alice had inclined toward the same conclusion as Ethel, though she preferred to give Lynden the benefit of the doubt.

As they walked back to the inn, avoiding puddles and chatting about the project coming up, Alice wondered what was on that young man's mind.

∞

"Wonderful dinner, Jane," Louise said, gently patting her mouth with her napkin. "I especially liked the way you prepared the prawns. An unusual flavor."

"Too unusual or just interesting unusual?" Jane pushed an uneaten prawn around on her plate, suddenly unsure.

"Is this one of the dishes you want to serve at Stacy's dinner?"

"I thought I did, but somehow I think it might be a little too 'out there,' which Stacy specifically warned me to avoid." Jane sat back and crossed her arms over her chest. "She called me several times today, and each time she had another suggestion and another idea. It's like she's trying too hard."

"Which in turn puts pressure on you," Alice offered.

Jane nodded, tapping her fingers on her arm. "This afternoon I was thinking in terms of a simple but elegant dinner à la Jane Austen. This evening I'm leaning more toward a meal worthy of Lucretia Borgia."

"Without the complication of poisoning, one would hope," Louise added.

"Well, I can't say that hasn't crossed my mind." Jane held up a hand to forestall her older sister's reprimand. "Joking, dear Louie, just joking."

"Could you call it off?"

Jane rocked back and forth in her chair, shaking her head. "I'm a gourmet chef, for goodness sake. I help run an inn. I've fed mothers, daughters, fussy businessmen, easy-going guests and persnickety guests. Surely this dinner shouldn't confound me."

"And it won't because I think you have a winner with this meal," Louise said.

"It's superb," Alice added.

"I quite like it myself."

"Then isn't it nice to have that out of the way," Alice said. "Now all you need to do is decide what to make for dessert."

"I already decided on dessert, lemon ginger cheesecake, which should complement the flavors of the main course." Jane released a light sigh of contentment. She had spent quite a few hours hunting down all the ingredients for this recipe. Now that she had them in the house and she had already done a trial run of the meal, her preparation time would go down considerably. So far so good.

Louise pushed herself back from the table and retrieved the Bible from its drawer in the buffet and handed it to Alice. "I believe we agreed upon devotions for this evening."

Alice opened the Bible at the last place they had read, cleared her throat and was just about to begin when the doorbell rang.

The sisters glanced at one another, and Jane got up and walked to the door. A woman wearing a light-green raincoat stood outside, her brown hair falling in soft waves back from her pale face. She started when she heard footsteps, then recovered when Jane opened the door.

"Hello. I'm Stacy Reddington." Stacy held out her hand to Jane, her smile bright. "I thought I would stop by and see you face to face. Go over a few things for the dinner."

This was completely unexpected, and for a moment Jane was taken aback. But good manners overruled telling Stacy that it would have been wise to make an appointment. "Please come in. May I take your coat?" Jane held out her hand to do so, but Stacy waved her off.

"No. No. I'm not staying long. I'm running around the area, checking out halls for the dinner." She glanced around the foyer of the inn. "This is a lovely place."

"It's our family home and has worked quite well for our business," Jane said as she led the way down the hall. She kept a smile on her face, trying to keep her voice pleasant. Talking to Stacy every hour on the hour had been bad enough; now she was stopping in unexpectedly?

Stacy paused at the entrance to the dining room. "How many people can stay at the inn?"

"We have four bedrooms, and this weekend they are all taken. Seven guests."

"That's a lot."

"My sisters and I are just finished eating," Jane said, leading Stacy toward the kitchen. "In fact, the meal was one I was thinking we could make for your dinner."

"Wonderful." Stacy's eyes brightened. "I'm excited to see what you've come up with. I've heard some enthusiastic reports about your cooking. That was one of the reasons I called you."

"Well, I'm flattered."

Jane introduced Stacy to her sisters and then pulled out

a chair for her. "If you want to sample dinner, I still have some left."

"I would love to try it out."

While Louise and Alice kept their newest guest occupied, Jane quickly put a plate of food together, and heated it up, added the salad she was going to serve and then set it on the table.

"I have to say it myself—this dish is quite tasty," Alice said as Stacy glanced at the plate.

Stacy only nodded, picked up a fork and isolated a prawn. She frowned as she found another one. "Seafood?" was all she said.

Jane nodded, trying not to feel upset. This was ridiculous. As she said to her sisters, she was a gourmet chef. She shouldn't be so uneasy around this woman.

But the truth was, she was.

"I'm so sorry. I forgot to tell you one of the ladies is allergic to shellfish," Stacy said, giving Jane an apologetic look.

Of course, Jane thought, mentally scratching a black line through much of the work she had done this evening.

"I hope this isn't a problem."

"No. I'll work around it," Jane said, her "pleasant" voice getting a real workout.

"I realize I should have told you when I called earlier. I know you did ask me about allergies, but I've been so busy trying to find a venue. Unsuccessfully, as it turns out." She sighed as she looked around the kitchen of the inn. "My, this really is a lovely place—so welcoming and friendly."

Stacy paused and Jane was fairly sure she knew what was coming next. "I don't suppose you could recommend a place in Acorn Hill?" Stacy's voice held a plaintive note.

Jane felt a tickle of a premonition. She had seen the look on Stacy's face when she saw the size of the dining room and was fairly sure Stacy could count as well.

Twelve chairs around the table and she was going to

entertain twelve guests. "I'll see if we can find something for you," Jane said.

She scurried to the reception area, tucked a pen behind her ear, slipped a pad of paper into the pocket of her blue jeans and grabbed the phone book, flipping through it as she walked. By the time she got back, she had found the section of the yellow pages that she wanted.

She laid the open book on the table in front of Stacy, set the pen and paper beside it. "There. This should help."

Stacy nodded slowly, but Jane saw from the set of her mouth and the downward tilt of her eyebrows that she was less than impressed with Jane's solution to her dilemma.

Out of the corner of her eye Jane saw Alice lean forward and she intuitively sensed that her dear, generous sister was going to offer the inn. Jane zeroed in on Alice and gave a quick, tight shake of her head.

Alice sat back and Jane breathed a sigh of relief.

"I can see I have limited options," Stacy mumbled, glancing through the book.

As do I, thought Jane. She was tempted to call off the entire thing, but she couldn't do that to Stacy, knowing that she was a last-minute hire.

And there's still the vacuum cleaner, Jane thought.

This wasn't a major stressor, but the reality of a full inn meant that having a vacuum cleaner was even more pressing than usual. Borrowing Aunt Ethel's machine was strictly a short-term solution. Very short term.

"Obviously I have a number of phone calls to make," Stacy said, scribbling down some numbers. "I'll get back to you when I know more."

"As for the guests, any other food allergies or problems I should know about?" Jane asked, glancing over at her cheese-cake, thinking *lactose intolerance.*

"Not that I know of," Stacy said, a distinctly defensive note creeping into her voice.

"I'm sorry, but time is working against us here," Jane replied diplomatically. "And the more information I have, the better I can plan."

"I'm sorry for all the difficulties." Stacy heaved another sigh, looking at Alice and Louise as if trying to garner sympathy. "I had so hoped to make a good impression on these women, to give them an experience they've never had before, and every time I turn around, I'm faced with another obstacle."

"And I'm sure your dinner will turn out fine," Alice assured her. "And with Jane's cooking, I'm sure it will be a resounding success."

"Thank you," Stacy said, and Jane saw the tension around the woman's mouth ease.

Alice has that ability, Jane thought. A few words in her mellifluous nurse's voice and you felt as if all your problems had shrunk.

"You simply need a location," Louise put in, adding her own brand of assurance. "For a small group like yours, that shouldn't pose an insurmountable difficulty."

"Thank you so much, ladies." Stacy got up and turned to Jane. "I'll call you as soon as I find something."

Jane kept her smile intact, trying not to glance at the calendar. *Tick tock,* she thought. "That'd be great. In the meantime, I'll continue trying to find a dish everyone will enjoy."

Stacy put her hand on Jane's arm. "Don't get me wrong. What you made was wonderful. Just . . ." she shrugged, ". . . the prawns. Not such a good idea. You need to be aware there are people who are allergic to seafood."

"I'll take that under advisement," Jane said, trying not to be irked by Stacy's unwanted advice.

She walked Stacy to the door, bid her a pleasant farewell, then closed it carefully, looked upward, and offered a prayer for patience and wisdom.

By the time she got back to the kitchen, Alice was clearing the table and Louise was putting out cups for tea and coffee.

"So did you get the problems ironed out?" Alice asked, placing the dinner dishes on the counter.

"If you'll allow me to extend the housekeeping metaphor," Jane said, "there are still a few wrinkles." She gave her sister a quick smile to alleviate the faint concern she had heard in Alice's voice. "I made dessert that was supposed to go with the meal we just had."

"Was?" Louise asked, pouring tea.

Jane pulled the cheesecake out of the refrigerator. The only decorations she had put on the top were curls of lemon, creating a simple yet elegant touch. "Now that prawns are off the menu, I'm thinking I might be better off going with a simpler dessert. This dessert perfectly complemented that meal. So I don't know. The cheesecake is a bit heavy and wouldn't fit with every meal. However, cheesecake freezes well."

"Why don't you offer two desserts," Louise suggested. "Freeze this one for Saturday and offer it along with a lighter option."

Jane weighed the idea and offered a noncommittal "That could work."

"And for tonight's dessert, we can have some of those cookies you made earlier," Alice suggested.

The tension gripping Jane's neck slowly released. Her sisters were right. She could nicely check off one item for Saturday.

"*Yoo-hoo*," Ethel's voice called out from the back door. "I'm here."

Louise pulled out another cup and plate for their aunt, and Jane did a double take as Ethel strode into the kitchen.

A bespattered painter's cap held down her red hair, she wore an old pair of denim coveralls over a twill shirt, and circling her waist was a leather carpenter's apron, its pockets bulging with nails and pencils. A tape measure was clipped to one side of the carpenter's pouch, and a hammer swung from the other.

"What do you think?" Ethel asked, doffing her cap and doing a slow twirl so that her nieces could more fully appreciate her transformation.

"I think you look like you mean business," Jane said, scratching her head with one finger. "Are you moonlighting as the town's handyman?"

Ethel wagged a warning finger at her. "Silly girl. This is what I'm going to wear tomorrow for the Habitat job." Ethel shot Alice a frown. "Do you know what you're going to wear?"

"I thought I could get away with blue jeans and a plain shirt," Alice said.

"What happened to your pants?" Jane asked, glancing at the dirt circling the bottoms of Ethel's coveralls.

Ethel glanced down, then took a quick step back toward the porch. "I'm so sorry. I didn't think I would get muddy."

"What were you doing?"

Ethel bent over and brushed off what dirt she could onto the rug just inside the entrance, then bent down and rolled up the cuffs of the coveralls. "I was practicing my nailing. There were some boards loose on your tool shed."

"And you fixed them."

Ethel raised one hand in a vague gesture that could have meant anything. "I'm sure I'll get better with practice." Ethel double-checked her pants, then walked to the kitchen sink to wash her hands, wincing as the water hit her fingers.

"And what happened to your thumb?" Jane asked, noticing a deep purple mark on her aunt's thumbnail.

Ethel turned pink, and curled her thumb into her palm. "Nothing. Well, just a little tap. I hit the wrong nail on the head."

"Let me see that." Alice reached for Ethel's hand.

"It's just a bruise. It doesn't hurt...much." Ethel winced again as Alice gently manipulated the thumb, checking for more injuries.

"You shouldn't be swinging a hammer with such force," Alice said.

"I need the practice . . . as you can tell," Ethel said, holding up her thumb. "It's better now, anyway."

"When did you do this?"

"When we got back from Fred's. I was so excited to try my new hammer, and it works well. Lovely heft, and swings nicely. I'm sure that in time I won't have to hit the nail so many times to get it in." Ethel glanced over the counter. "Well, doesn't that look lovely," Ethel said, her eyes falling on the cheesecake. "Is that for tea?"

"I think Jane wants to freeze the cheesecake," Alice said, sparing Jane from having to douse the expectant light in her aunt's eyes.

"I'll try to save some for you," Jane said.

Just then the front door burst open, slamming against the stopper, and boisterous voices filled the inn with noisy laughter.

Alice was still busy with the dishwasher and Louise with pouring coffee, so Jane volunteered to greet their guests.

The boys stood in the foyer, shaking water off their coats, laughing at a joke one of them had just told. Only Lynden and the girls were missing. Jane wondered about the elusive Lynden.

"Hey, Ms. Howard," Herbie said, his round cheeks shining with moisture from the rain falling outside. "Sorry about the wet."

"That's fine. How was your evening?"

"Great. Hey, you got any of those cookies left? I was telling the guys about them."

Before she could reply, Herbie turned to the rest of the

group. "I'm telling you guys, you have got to try these cookies. Best Pete and I ever had. Homemade."

"Can we take some to eat in our rooms?"

Jane imagined crumbs all over the rooms and thought of Ethel's wheezing vacuum cleaner. She made a snap decision. "Why don't you join us? We were just going to enjoy some coffee and dessert."

As she walked to the kitchen she sensed the boys hot on her heels, as if afraid she would change her mind.

Louise glanced up as the group swept into the room. "Hello, everyone. How was your evening?"

"We went to the Coffee Shop. Great food."

"This is some kind of town, though," Matthew said, rubbing his hand over his buzzed hair. "Saw some woman pushing a baby buggy. When she went past I thought, whoa, that's the ugliest baby I've ever seen. Then I saw it was a pig. Freaked me out."

"Clara Horn and Daisy," Ethel put in. "She loves that pig like a baby. It's a miniature pot-bellied pig."

Matthew pulled back his head as if assimilating this information. Then he grinned. "Cool," was his succinct summation.

"Would any of you like a cup of tea or coffee?" Alice asked.

"Could I have some water instead?" Pete asked, pushing his cap back from his forehead.

Jane gathered what chairs she could, then angled her chin toward the refrigerator. "There's a jug of water in the fridge, just help yourself. The cups are in the cupboard over there," she pointed in another direction.

"Anyone else want some?" Pete asked, pulling open the door and glancing over the contents of the fridge. "Wow! Look at all this good food."

Jane had already prepared a fruit platter for breakfast to go with the French toast she was going to make in the morning. She had decided to forgo gourmet breakfasts for this group, assuming that the heartier food would probably be more welcome. She assumed Pete was interested in the plate of cinnamon rolls and muffins she had prepared and covered in plastic wrap.

"Look at this Rick," he said. The tall, lanky fellow disengaged himself from the wall and sauntered over, his long, dark hair bobbing as he walked.

"Oh . . . my . . . goodness . . . this is better than television." Rick leaned closer to the fridge, the dragon tattoo on the back of his hand looking oddly out of place against the appliance. Jane didn't know how long he would have stayed there, but he had to move when Pete pulled out the water pitcher. He poured a cup for himself and one for his friend.

Matthew joined them, his eyes growing wide at the sight of the food. "Hey, look at that. I haven't seen a fridge so full of good stuff since I lived at home."

"Do you and your sisters eat all this food?" Pete asked.

"Most of that is for breakfast tomorrow morning." Anticipating time to be spent with Carita to work on the scavenger hunt, Jane had done as much prep work for the following day as possible. Unfortunately, this seemed to be creating an irresistible temptation for the boys, and she knew she would be unable to turn them down if they asked for some of it.

"For us? Tomorrow? Whoa, I don't know if I can wait that long." Matthew rubbed his stomach as if underlining his statement.

Jane saw all her hard work disappearing in one fell swoop and made another quick decision.

"I have some cheesecake . . ."

Ethel's eyes lit up. "Yes. Cheesecake. Just the thing."

And so, after a few quick strokes of a knife and a few flips of a serving spoon, the cheesecake began disappearing almost as quickly as Jane could pass it around.

"This is awesome," Pete exclaimed, his hazel eyes beneath the brim of his cap sparkling with pleasure.

"Jane is the best cook in town," Ethel advised, tucking into her own piece of the dessert.

"Why did we go to that Coffee Shop then?" Matthew asked, swiping his finger over the plate, gathering the last of the crumbs and cream.

"I dunno," Herbie said, licking his lips as he settled his bulky figure into a more comfortable position.

"I thought Ms. J doesn't cook dinner for us," Pete said, casting a longing eye at the remaining half of the cheesecake.

"We generally don't serve dinner," Jane agreed, catching the hint and getting up to cut the rest of the cheesecake.

"That's too bad," Herbie said, following her, holding his plate like an oversized Oliver Twist, wanting to ask for "more."

"It would simply make us too busy," Louise said. She followed Jane's lead and, opening up the cookie tin, made up a plate of homemade cookies.

"Fair enough. There are a few good places in Potterston from the looks of it, and Lynden has got something planned for game night on Friday anyway. Tailgate party," Pete said in an aside to Jane. "We should get you to come and cook for us."

"I feel honored to be asked, but I don't think a tailgate party at a football game is somewhere I want to be Friday night," Jane said with a smile.

"Hey, who should we start in the first quarter?" Rick asked, settling with his plate. He was eating a little slower this time, as if savoring the treat.

"Probably Harris. He's a real winner. Quick off the snap." Herbie leaned against the counter, emphasizing his point with a wave of his fork. "We'd be crazy not to."

Jane served the last of the cheesecake, bemused at the quick change in conversation.

Comments ping-ponged as the young men pontificated on the various strengths of their team and the opposition teams they would be playing. Louise, Jane, Ethel and Alice settled in at the table, listening, while the boys devoured the cheesecake.

Jane enjoyed the energy the young men brought to the kitchen, but as Matthew got up and walked to the fridge to help himself to a glass of orange juice, she wondered if she had too easily erased the carefully guarded boundary she and her sisters had always maintained between the kitchen and the rest of the house.

"Did you boys have some cookies?" Ethel asked, getting up and passing around the plate Louise had arranged.

"Herbie told us about these," Matthew took one quickly. "Gotta be pretty good for him to say they're the best he ever had."

"Jane's baking skills are also quite renowned," Ethel said, seeming only too glad to brag about her niece. "In fact, she's going to be catering a dinner for international guests on Saturday night."

"Wow! Impressive," Rick said, nodding his head as he took another cookie from the plate Ethel was passing around.

"Hey, what happened to your thumb?" Herbie asked when Ethel came by him for the third time.

"I was doing some repair work on the inn's shed," Ethel said, pride sounding in her voice.

"That explains the getup," Pete said. "Nice hammer. Estwing?"

"They are supposed to be the best." Ethel put down the cookies and pulled the hammer out of its metal sling.

"Nice. Well balanced. Perfect hammer for a lady," Pete assured her.

"I'm going to be working on a Habitat for Humanity home."

"Cool!"

"Is that where you get together with a bunch of people and put a house up in one day?" asked Matthew.

"You can't put a house up in one day." Pete punched Matthew on the shoulder, as if reprimanding him for his ignorance.

"Hey. I've seen it on TV." Matthew protested, punching Pete back. "The Amish do it all the time."

"Yeah, well, they can put up a barn really fast."

"How fast?"

"I dunno." Matthew leaned past him to address one of the other boys. "Hey, Rick, you worked construction last year. How fast do you think the Amish could put up a barn?"

From this the conversation switched to construction and jobs and trying to find a job and what jobs they had been doing over the summer to help pay their college tuition.

Jane sipped her coffee, content to listen to the scattershot discussion. She glanced sidelong at Louise, wondering how she felt about this male domination of the kitchen.

Louise was leaning back in her chair, smiling and feeling more comfortable with their guests than she had at their arrival. Ethel was standing beside Herbie, her arms crossed over her chest, looking for all the world like she belonged with this circle of young men.

Alice was laughing at some of the jokes being bandied about.

"Hey, what's with the invasion?"

Carita and Isabel stood in the doorway, their eyes going over the group in the kitchen.

"Come on in," Matthew said, waving his hand. "The ladies are serving us cookies and cheesecake, and you should see the awesome food they're going to feed us tomorrow."

Carita gave Matthew an indulgent smile. "Where's Lynden?"

Matthew glanced at Pete, then shrugged. "Dunno. Herbie, you know?"

"Yeah. He's up in his room. Reading."

"Is he feeling okay?" Carita sounded concerned.

"Yeah. He's hibernating," Herbie said.

"And missing out on awesome cheesecake." Rick licked his fork, then glanced over at the counter. "I think there's a piece left if you girls want some."

"No thanks." Isabel wrinkled her nose.

Jane motioned for Carita and Isabel to join them. "Come on in."

Isabel shook her head as she took a step away from the doorway. "I think I'll just go to bed, okay?"

"I'll be right up." Carita glanced at Isabel's retreating figure, then at the kitchen, and Jane saw she would have preferred to join the party in the kitchen. "I should go too. We'll see you tomorrow." She walked away, then turned and came back. "Almost forgot. What time is breakfast?"

"I usually start serving breakfast about seven thirty. You can come down anytime after that until about ten," Jane explained.

"Whoa, that's early." Matthew sounded incredulous.

"No, it isn't, you lazybones. Besides, I thought you and the boys were going to check out that car show in Potterston," Carita said. "You'd have to leave early for that."

Matthew snapped his fingers. "Yup. Totally forgot about that." He shot Jane a grin. "Guess I'll be up early tomorrow anyway."

Carita laughed. "See you bright and early, boys."

As she left, Pete pushed himself to his feet. "Probably should hit the shower and then bed anyway." He put his plate on the counter and paused, eyeing the last piece of cheese-cake, adjusted his ball cap as if making a decision and grabbed a cookie instead. "Thanks for dessert," he said, waving his other hand at Jane. "Goodnight, ladies. You be careful with that hammer tomorrow, Aunt Ethel."

The rest of the boys soon followed, each of them thanking the sisters and a couple of them taking a last cookie upstairs with them as they left.

Jane shook her head as their conversation faded away up the stairs. So much for her ingenious plan to avoid having them eating in the bedrooms.

"Wasn't that fun," Ethel said, stacking up the plates and bringing them to the dishwasher. "Reminds me of when Bob would get crews in to help on the farm. Always young boys with big appetites and full of stories. My, what fun we used to have when they were around. And, oh, the food they could inhale."

As Jane walked past her refrigerator, she had a sudden flash of misgiving. She certainly didn't think she would see an entire cheesecake, supposed to serve twelve, disappear in minutes.

What if she hadn't planned for enough food for tomorrow's breakfast?

Chapter ⊤ Six

Wednesday morning dawned sunny and cheerful and found Louise sitting in the parlor, her Bible on her lap. The quiet of the morning surrounded her, creating a sense of sanctuary.

Her only company was the antique doll collection in one corner of the room and Wendell, draped over the tapestry-covered stool pulled out from Louise's grand piano.

The piano had been a gift from her beloved husband Eliot, and Louise treasured it as much as she did the ivory velvet piano shawl, a gift from her sister Alice.

In fifteen minutes she, Jane and Alice would be getting breakfast ready for their guests and then she and Viola were scheduled for the first lesson of their senior drivers' course.

Besides being a chance to spend time with her friend, the course offered Louise an opportunity to learn something new and useful.

Louise reread her Bible passage for the day from Romans 5:1–2: "Therefore, since we have been justified through faith, we have peace with God through our Lord Jesus Christ, through whom we have gained access by faith into this grace in which we now stand. And we rejoice in the hope of the glory of God."

Louise let the words enter her heart, relishing the peace they gave her. As her gaze rested on the piano, she thought of the moments of sorrow she had felt after her dear husband's death. She had felt as though she could never smile again, as though all the light had been taken out of her life.

Yet, coming back to Acorn Hill and starting up the inn with her sisters had combined to give her a purpose she had thought she would never find again. Together they encouraged each other in their faith and helped each other express that faith to their community and to the guests who stayed at the inn.

She bowed her head, once again thanking the Lord for the love He showered upon her every day and for the blessing of her work. As she prayed, her thoughts and prayers touched on each member of her family, the greater community and each of the guests at the inn. Her prayers included the multitudes in the world who had so much less, reminding her of her blessings and her obligations.

And, as she always did, she asked for a blessing on the day.

She kept her head bowed as she finished, allowing God's peace, the peace offered her in the passage from Romans that she had just read, to settle over her.

She drew a long, deep breath, closed the Bible and looked out the window. The sunshine made little prisms of the droplets of water still clinging to the leaves of the trees, sending out bright showers of light, like little promises.

Today was going to be a good day. Ethel and Alice would have good weather for their building project, and she would have good weather for her newest venture.

She had telephoned Viola last night and made arrangements to meet at her store. Viola would then drive Louise to the garage so Louise could pick up her car. Justine Gilmore was going to cover for Viola at Nine Lives.

She glanced at the brass-faced clock sitting on the mantel

of the fireplace. In twenty minutes Jane would be downstairs working in the kitchen. She still had time to practice some songs.

Louise closed the door, leaving it open only a crack, and took out the music for Sunday's service. As she sat at the piano, she felt again the moment of anticipation, just before her fingers touched the keys. Though she had played for orchestras and had accompanied many vocalists in public performances, she still felt a special thrill when she contemplated the music she would choose for a worship service. Knowing that the songs she played helped the members of the congregation to worship God created a combination of responsibility and humility.

She chose the first song, flexed her fingers and slowly, reverently began playing. As the notes filled the room, a smile crept over her lips. Music was for her a purer expression of her faith than that which could be conveyed through the medium of words.

She moved from hymn to hymn, discarding some, studying others. Finally a meowing interrupted her. She glanced over and saw Wendell nudge the door open.

"You don't approve of the music I'm choosing?" Louise asked as she slipped off the piano bench.

As she opened the door a figure detached itself from the shadow of the front entrance and moved up the stairs. Louise started at the same time her mind recognized Lynden's retreating figure.

She stepped out of the parlor, watching him, but he didn't turn around. An equally curious Wendell padded up the steps behind him.

She mused, *What was he doing outside the parlor, and why did he leave?*

Louise waited a moment longer, wondering if he would come back, but no one appeared at the top of the stairs. This was a puzzle indeed, she thought, returning to the piano and tidying up her music. Why had he been standing close by? The parlor was soundproof but, in the morning quiet, had he been disturbed by the faint sounds that made their way outside the room? If he had something to say to her, surely he would have knocked on the door.

Bemused, she walked down the hallway to the kitchen, the hum of the mixer telling her that Jane was already hard at work. Alice stood at the table, wrapping cutlery in napkins.

"Good morning. What can I do?" Louise asked, pulling an apron off a nearby hook.

"Morning, Louise. You could get out the warming trays and turn on the oven," Jane said, breaking a few eggs into the spinning bowl of the mixer. "I think breakfast for this crowd will be a long, drawn out affair, and I want to keep this French toast warm."

Louise went into the storage room off the kitchen and in a few moments had the warming trays set up.

"When are you leaving for the Habitat project?" Louise asked Alice.

"I told Ethel I couldn't leave until our guests ate breakfast, so I guess it depends on when the last ones are done."

Jane shut off the mixer and angled her sister a wry glance. "You might want to rethink that strategy. As I said to Louise, this crowd may use up the entire morning having breakfast."

"I thought those boys had to go early to Potterston for something."

"Maybe, but I'm fairly sure their alarm clock will ring, they'll look at the time and make a sudden change of plans."

"Are you sure?"

"Reasonably. They're students, and from my recollections of my days at college, morning was just a recuperation time from the night before. Especially summer vacation mornings."

"But Louise can't help you because she has a class—"

"And I'm perfectly capable of keeping food warm," Jane said.

"Are you sure?" Louise asked.

"Sure as a plumb line."

Louise frowned and Jane laughed.

"Little carpenter humor there, Louie," Jane said.

"Indeed."

At seven thirty on the dot, Jane had the French toast laid out, dusted with powdered sugar and garnished with orange peel. Another warming tray held sausage patties, seasoned with coriander. Fruit and plates of muffins and cinnamon buns sat ready on the sideboard as well.

At eight, Jane, Louise and Alice sat down to their own breakfast, listening for any signs of life stirring above.

At eight fifteen, Ethel knocked on the door, set her tool belt just inside the entry and joined the sisters for breakfast.

At nine, Alice reluctantly put her and Ethel's dishes in the dishwasher and bid her sisters farewell.

At nine fifteen, Louise put the last dishes into the dishwasher and turned to Jane. "I can cancel my class, if you'd like."

Jane flapped her hand at her in a shooing motion. "You go. I'll be fine."

"Are you sure?"

"Didn't we just do this?" Jane said with a cheeky wink. "Please, I don't have anything else planned. The garden is still too wet to work in after all that rain. All I had figured on doing today was going on an outing with Carita and planning the menu for the dinner yet again."

"Well then . . ." Louise washed her hands, dried them off, hesitated a moment, and left.

But as she walked to Viola's, she thought of the noise

and busyness of last night and felt as if she was abandoning her sister. Her mind slipped from the boys dropping by the kitchen to Lynden, and she remembered that he hadn't been there.

She wondered anew what he was doing at the bottom of the stairs this morning.

One thing was certain—Lynden was a puzzle.

∞

"Hard hats are mandatory. We don't want anyone going home with a concussion and then calling up a lawyer and suing us." The heavy-set, middle-aged man stood on a pile of dirt, arms folded over his massive chest, a tool belt, worn and cracked, hanging low on his hips. His grin showed them all that he was mostly kidding. "For those of you who are new, my name is Cal. Today we've got Jasmine, the owner of the house, and her sister Cordy helping us. The sun is out and we've got a good number of volunteers. That's great, so I'll be assigning you different jobs today." He clapped his hands together, rubbing them as if in anticipation of the work ahead. "Let's build a house."

Ethel grabbed Alice's hand. "Isn't this exciting? Let's go get our hard hats."

Ten minutes later Ethel, Alice and a young woman of about eighteen were getting instructions from Cal.

"What I want you ladies to do is nail down this particleboard on the studs. It's been tacked down already, so all you need to do is, essentially, fill in the blanks."

Alice looked at the wall section, puzzled. "But there are no windows in this section."

"That comes later," Cal said. "Once you're done tacking, we'll get a router and cut out the holes for the window. That way you don't waste time cutting and measuring, and the opening for the window is perfectly square." He tapped a stained forefinger to his forehead. "Always thinking, us carpenters."

He gave them a smile and then left.

The pounding of hammers and the whine of the skill saw filled the air as Alice pulled her hammer out of the pouch and turned to the young woman.

"I'm Alice, and this is my aunt Ethel." Alice had to raise her voice above the noise to make the introductions. "We've come from Acorn Hill to help."

"I'm Cordy."

"So I understand you're Jasmine's sister?"

Cordy simply nodded, her hand resting on the hammer still swinging from the canvas pouch many of the volunteers wore.

"Do you have a preference as to where you want to start?" Alice asked.

Cordy shook her head, the hard hat slipping over her eyes. She pushed it back over her thick red hair, her hazel eyes looking down at her feet encased in boots that looked two sizes too big for her.

"Don't care." She added a half-hearted shrug.

"Why don't you start on that side, Ethel. You can work your way along the top, and I'll start on this side with Cordy," Alice said, realizing someone needed to be in charge.

Cordy nodded, pulled out her hammer and knelt. But she made no move to start.

Ethel glanced from Cordy to Alice, her eyebrows lifted in question.

June Carter had explained that the future owners of the house they were building had to volunteer five hundred hours of their time to help construct the home. They could also bring in family members to contribute their labor. Cordy was one of those members, but no one said anything about making them work.

Alice and Ethel began.

"Now make sure you don't hit your thumb again," Alice warned her aunt as she took a handful of nails out of the pouch.

She carefully rearranged them, making sure she had all the points in the same direction.

"So, where do you live, Cordy?" Alice asked as she pounded the first nail into the particleboard. Though the worksite was noisy, holding a conversation wasn't impossible.

"Around here." Cordy narrowed her eyes as she watched Ethel carefully pounding in a nail.

"And where does your sister live?" Alice continued.

"Apartment. Just down the road."

"She must be excited about the house." Ethel gave the nail one last hit and sat back on her heels, surveying her handiwork.

"Yeah."

But Cordy didn't seem to be excited.

Alice set aside her campaign to get Cordy to talk for now and concentrated on putting the nails exactly the same distance apart along the chalk line laid out for them.

After putting in a few nails, she felt more comfortable wielding the hammer and got a certain satisfaction out of hitting the nail precisely on the head each time.

"You do this before?" Cordy asked after a few minutes of watching Alice and Ethel working. All around them crews were chattering and laughing above the noise. Cal walked around calling out instructions. Everyone else seemed to be having fun.

Alice shook her head. "First time for me."

"I've put a few nails in wood in my day," Ethel said with

all the authority of one who had been swinging a hammer since youth.

"That why you are using both hands on the hammer?" Cordy asked.

Ethel gave the young woman a smile. "It's my personal style."

"So, really, neither of you has done much carpentry work."

"Well, okay. Not a lot," Ethel admitted.

"I see." Cordy pulled a nail out of her pouch and set it in the wood. She gave it a few taps, then looked to see what Alice was doing. "So, is there any trick to this?"

Alice shook her head, realizing that Cordy was unsure of herself. "No. There's no trick and there's no wrong way to put in the nail . . . as long as you put it pointy-side down."

Cordy gave the nail a few more taps. "It's wobbling."

"You need to hold the nail steady," Alice said, walking over to show her how.

"Okay, but what if I hit my hand?"

Ethel held up her hand. "See that black mark on my nail? I was practicing my nailing and whacked my thumb good and proper. You don't want to do that. Hurts bad."

"So how do I make sure I don't?"

Ethel shrugged. "Just be careful, I guess."

Cordy sighed and gingerly tapped the nail, her fingers curled around it.

"You only have to hold it until the nail is steady, and just use your fingertips," Alice suggested. Then she took a nail out of her own pouch and demonstrated. "Once it's set, you can hit it without holding on. Then you won't hit your hand."

"Okay." Cordy tried again and this time got the nail in, and twenty taps later the head was flush with the wood. She shook her head when she was done. "There's no way I'm going to get good enough to be any help."

"Maybe if you hit the nail a bit harder," Alice suggested. "Like this."

She demonstrated and ended up bending the nail over. "Well, maybe not like that." Alice laughed and pried it out. "Guess I'll have to try again." She did, and this time the nail went in with five strokes of her hammer.

Cordy angled her head to one side, watching as Alice started another nail. "So you did that first one wrong."

"Yes, I did, but I got the second one right." Alice gave her an encouraging smile. "You're going to make some mistakes, but you shouldn't worry about that."

"But if we make too many mistakes the house won't turn out good."

"That's why Cal is here. To help us prevent the bad mistakes and to help us learn from the small ones. Why don't you try again?"

Cordy caught her lower lip between her teeth, set the nail in place and gave it a few careful taps.

"Good. Now just give it a good whack," Alice suggested.

Cordy wound up and pounded on the nail. Three hits and the nail head was flush with the wood.

"Hey! Look at that," she exclaimed. "I got it in."

"See. Nothing to it." Alice worked beside her for a few more minutes, guiding and giving a few words of encouragement.

"I might be okay at this," Cordy said.

"I think you'll do just fine, and I think helping out your sister is a wonderful thing to do," Alice said.

"Yeah, well, I hope she thinks so. I don't know nothing about building a house," Cordy said, setting another nail in place. "Jasmine told me I had to come..." Cordy stopped and narrowed her eyes as though concentrating on putting in the nail.

"Where is your sister?" Alice asked.

"Over there, talking to that man with the paper." Cordy pointed her hammer at a tall, young woman with the same flaming red hair as Cordy, who was consulting the blueprint held up by Cal.

"You two look a lot alike." Alice set another nail and pounded it in with a few solid hits.

"Mom says we act alike, though that's not true. I never had no kid while I was in high school like Jas did."

"That must have been difficult for her," Alice said. "I understand she is married now."

"Yeah. Though Grainger ain't doin' too well. Lost his arm in an accident. Jas has to work all the time while Grainger stays home with the kids."

"Your sister must be a strong person."

"Strong in lots of ways. Strong-headed, strong-minded. Stubborn, kind of. Pushy too." Cordy didn't look at Alice while she listed her sister's traits. The defensive note in her voice made Alice wonder if there was some conflict between the two women.

"Do you two get along?"

Cordy hit the nail she was pounding in a little too hard and it bent over. "Well, there's a question." Cordy sighed as she bent another nail. But she didn't answer.

"It's nice that you're here helping her," Ethel put in.

"Yeah, well, she told me I had to. Don't know why she wanted me here. She always tells me how I'm always doing things wrong. Like she's so perfect." Cordy hit the bent nail once more and it went deeper into the wood. She dropped the hammer and pushed her hard hat back on her head. "I can't do this. This is a waste of time."

Alice walked over and checked the nail with her fingers. "This isn't too hard to fix. You can get the claw part of your hammer underneath the head and pry upward, like this. Then you can use your hammer to get the nail out."

Alice demonstrated and sat back to let Cordy finish. She guided her through the steps and patted her on the shoulder when the nail was out. "See, that mistake wasn't so difficult to fix, was it?"

"Well. No. Except I made a mark on the wood now."

"That will be covered over, I imagine," Alice assured her.

"But it's not perfect," Cordy said, her voice holding a mocking tone. Alice wondered where that came from.

"Nothing in this world is perfect," Ethel pronounced, frowning as she gave her nail another hit. "But that shouldn't stop us from trying, should it? It didn't stop your sister from working and staying on course."

Cordy shook her head. "No. I just wish she didn't think the rest of us have to be better than she is. Have to be perfect." She pulled another nail out of the pouch, looked it over as if checking for defects, set it and tried again.

Alice watched Cordy, her mind processing the tone of the young woman's voice as much as her words. "I have two sisters myself and we don't always get along."

"Really? Even though you're, well, older than me?" Cordy sounded surprised.

"Unfortunately, wisdom doesn't automatically come with age." Alice set another nail, watching out of the corner of her eye as Cordy did the same. "But I've found when we disagree I try to see things from their points of view and that helps. I'm sure Jasmine is very happy you are here," Alice continued, trying to find her way through the moment of awkwardness.

Cordy's only response was to swing at the nail and miss.

Alice knew better than to push the matter. Ethel shot her a puzzled glance and Alice gave her aunt a slight shake of her head as if to discourage any questions that Ethel might fire Cordy's way.

For a few moments the only sound coming from their part of the worksite was the steady pounding of hammers. Finally Cordy sat back on her heels and sighed. "I didn't tell you the truth," she said to Alice, rolling a nail between her fingers. "Something is wrong."

Alice simply waited.

Cordy tapped her hammer lightly on the wooden wall. "Me and Jas had a big fight."

"Over what?" Ethel asked, frowning.

"She thinks I need to grow up."

"In what way?" Alice asked.

Cordy shrugged. "The usual. I'm not getting good marks in school, and she says it's because I don't go to classes. Says my mom spoils me."

"Does she?" Ethel asked in her usual no-holds-barred manner.

Cordy shrugged. "No."

"Does she make you go to school?"

"Sometimes, maybe, she lets me sleep in, and I miss some classes. But not many. I mean class can be so boring, and it doesn't always make any sense."

"The only way the classes will make sense is if you go regularly," Ethel said. "You can't learn if you don't go. And if you don't learn, you'll fail."

Cordy pressed her lips together, as if this was not the answer she was looking for.

"Hey, Cordy, I thought you came here to work."

A tall figure stopped beside them, and Alice squinted toward the sun to see Jasmine standing over her little sister, her arms folded over her chest. The sun backlit Jasmine's hair, giving her an almost ethereal glow.

Cordy didn't look up, but Alice sensed her anger from the set of her jaw.

"I was distracting her with questions," Alice said gently, trying to intercede for the young woman. "She's been working really hard up to now."

"Really?" Jasmine glanced at Alice as if she was surprised. "That's good. I guess." Jasmine frowned, then bent over, brushing her finger over a bent-over nail. "Aren't you supposed to take these out?"

"Probably." Cordy's answer came out sharp, and Alice saw Jasmine wasn't happy with her sister. She wanted to defend the young woman but sensed that neither Jasmine nor Cordy would appreciate a complete stranger getting involved.

"It was just a mistake."

"Well, then, maybe you should try to fix the mistake," was all Jasmine said. She looked as though she was about to say something more when Cal called her over to where he was working.

She left and Cordy picked up her hammer, twisted it around and started digging out the offending nail with jerky movements.

Alice took pity on her and came over to help. "Here, why don't I do that for you, and you can keep nailing."

"I can do this myself," Cordy snapped. Then she gave Alice a troubled look. "I'm sorry. It's just that Jas can get me angry when she gets going on me." She tapped her hammer on the wood.

"I think, in her own way, she's trying to help you."

"Help me have a fit." Cordy scowled. "I'm never good enough for her. She makes me so mad."

"But as Ethel said, you're here, helping her."

"Like I said, Jas told me I had to. Since she got religion,

she's been trying to get everyone else to be like her. As if it's done her any good. All her praying and churchgoing didn't stop Grainger from losing his arm. Didn't stop Jas from yelling at me about something that wasn't my fault."

"But now your sister and her husband are getting a home," Alice pointed out, preferring to emphasize the positive. "That could be seen as an answer to your sister's prayers."

"So you guys are church ladies too?" Cordy asked.

"We go to church to worship our God, if that's what you mean," Alice said gently. She had found when guests from the inn asked her about church, those who were not religious themselves often viewed their attendance as a cute quirk of some slightly eccentric older ladies. Now and again she tried to find a way to show whoever asked that attending church was an opportunity to worship God in community, not a habit like brushing one's teeth.

"Well, I guess that is kinda what I meant," Cordy said, looking a bit baffled by Alice's gentle response.

Alice felt a touch of remorse. "I'm sorry. I was just trying to explain that when we go to church, we go out of a conviction and a desire to worship our Savior with fellow believers. We go to hear God's Word and to be encouraged to carry God's name out into the world." Alice gave her a self-deprecating smile. "And now I sound like I'm preaching at you."

"No, you don't," Cordy said quietly. "It sounds nice. I never went to church, but I always liked the idea."

"Maybe you could come with us some time," Ethel piped up. "Rev. Thompson is always a good preacher, and Louise, my niece and Alice's sister, plays the organ. And she's quite talented."

"I might do that. Maybe if Jasmine thinks I got religion, she might lay off me for a change."

"Maybe you just need to show up here regularly. Let your actions speak for themselves," Alice encouraged.

Cordy nodded, as if processing the comment. "Maybe," was all she said.

"Alice, would you like a drink?"

Alice and Ethel both spun around at the sound of the voice behind them. Florence stood holding a thermos flask and some paper cups. "I've got some nice cold juice if you or your helper would like some refreshment."

"Sounds like a plan," Cordy said, putting her hammer down and jogging over to Florence.

Ethel looked over at her friend, as if hoping Florence would catch her eye, but she ignored Ethel.

With a gentle sigh, Alice asked Florence for another cup of juice for her aunt and then waited until Florence moved to the next crew.

Alice handed the cup to Ethel. "Some juice, Auntie?"

"Oh my, yes, I was so busy I didn't notice that Florence was here." Ethel put down her hammer, wiped her hands on the sides of her pants and took the cup. But Alice could see Ethel felt hurt by Florence's snub.

"That was real kind of her," Cordy said, finishing off her juice.

"She's just doing her job," Ethel said, handing Alice the empty cup when she was done. She opened and closed her fist, grimacing.

"Are you okay?" Alice asked, watching her aunt. She hoped Ethel's arthritis wasn't acting up.

"I'm fine," Ethel said quickly, lowering her hands.

"So who is going to cut out the hole for the window when we're done here?" Cordy asked, her hammer flashing in the sun as she pounded in another nail.

"I doubt any of us will be doing that," Alice said. "I've never handled a saw in my life."

"I'd like to try," Ethel put in, lifting her chin defiantly. "I think it could be fun." She gave Alice a significant look.

"I'm not sure about the fun part, but I am sure about the dangerous part," Alice warned.

Ethel wrinkled her nose in reply and went back to work.

An hour later the sheets of chipboard were all nailed down and the trio was ready for another job.

Alice was about to go looking for Cal when he came striding toward them, carrying a domed tool with a cord wrapped around it.

"Ladies, you ready for the router?" he asked.

"Um, shouldn't you be doing that?" Alice asked.

"It's not hard. One of you can handle this baby. I'll just get you started." He glanced at Cordy. "There's an extension cord lying on the ground behind you. Can you bring it here?"

A few seconds later, Cal had the machine plugged in. It was the oddest tool Alice had ever seen. A small bit poked out of the bottom of a flat, rounded plate. Above that plate was, she assumed, the motor that ran the bit.

"How does this saw work?" she asked.

"It's not a saw. This is a router and it works very simply," he said, crouching down. "What you do is find out where the hole for the window is. Luckily for you ladies, we marked it out with the blue chalk line."

Alice looked where he was pointing and saw the lines, just as he had said.

"So you get this started just a ways away from the edge, like this." He hit a switch and a whining sound filled the air. "Then you push the bit in, slowly."

As he did so, chips of particleboard flew out from the machine in an arc, releasing the pungent smell of cut wood.

"Then you move the router toward the line until it won't go any further, but don't force the tool too much. Like this." He demonstrated and sure enough, the router came to a stop, still whining away. "When you hit resistance, that means you've come to the frame of the window. Then you simply keep sideways pressure on the router and follow the line. The board framing the opening of the window keeps the bit from going the wrong way. Just follow the frame and you've got a nice rectangular hole for the window." He hit the switch, turning it off. "Who wants to try?"

Ethel jumped forward so fast, her hard hat slipped sideways. "I'd love to try."

Cal showed her how to turn on the router and what to watch for. Alice sent up a quick prayer as the machine started whining again, spitting out chips and sawdust.

Ethel pressed her lips together, her tongue poking out as she concentrated on slowly moving the router down. It wobbled a bit, but she straightened the cut and with Cal's guidance, she managed to work her way down and then across. "This is great," she called out, clearly enjoying her newfound skill.

"You're doing just fine, miss," Cal said.

"You and your friend might want to hold the section that's getting cut loose," Cal said, showing Alice and Cordy how to pry the board up with their hammers so they could get their fingers under it.

A few minutes later Ethel had come back to where Cal had started, with Cordy and Alice supporting the piece getting cut away.

"Done," Ethel said, pulling the router away just as the board dropped.

Alice and Cordy pulled it aside and stood back to admire what Ethel had done. Before them was a perfectly rectangular hole cut in the particleboard they had just nailed to the wall section.

"Well, isn't that just the cat's pajamas!" Ethel crowed.

"You can trim things up a bit," Cal said, pointing out a few places where the router had slipped to one side. "Just make sure you don't push the router too hard into the frame of the window."

When she was done, Ethel turned off the router, and she,

Alice and Cordy stood back again to appreciate their handiwork.

"I think that looks like a very nice wall," Alice said, giving Cordy a quick hug. "Simply perfect."

"Looks good to me too." Cordy beamed, then turned to Cal. "Now what?"

"Lunch time," he said, brushing the wood chips off his blue jeans.

"I think I'm going to be stiff tomorrow morning." Alice rolled her shoulder as they joined the rest of the group for lunch. "This is even harder work than I thought."

"Feels good though," Ethel said.

A cluster of chairs was set out on a vacant lot beside the house, and a group of women handed out bag lunches. One of them was Florence. Alice had to bite her tongue as she followed her aunt through the line. This time Ethel, as if acting on the slight Florence had given her a few moments before, didn't even look at her. She simply took the bag and walked on.

Alice cringed. Whatever was going on between those two seemed to be escalating. She hadn't imagined either Florence or Ethel being able to maintain her silence this long, but somehow they both had.

"Are you volunteering here every day?" Alice asked Florence as she accepted the lunch bag.

"I hope to. I can't work hard, but I am able to help with the food. I think I might even be helping Jasmine with some of her decorating decisions. Some people say I have quite good taste." Florence looked down demurely. "Not that I would say so, but other people have."

"I'm sure you can give her good advice," Alice said warmly, trying to offset her aunt's decidedly cool attitude.

"Not that I like to put myself forward, mind you," Florence continued, her gaze ticking to Ethel, then back again. "I know I can be opinionated, but so can other people.

And I find it puzzling when other people claim to be unable to help a friend, when they can clearly help someone they don't know."

The subtext in Florence's words was rapidly becoming full-blown text. Alice assumed the "other people" in Florence's little speech referred to Ethel. But she was not going to get involved. Not yet.

Chapter ⚒ Seven

Jane glanced at the clock, then went out to the dining room to check on the warming trays. The French toast was getting limp, the sausages were curling up and some of the fruit was changing color.

Should she wake up the young guests?

She stood in the doorway of the dining room, straining her ears for any sign of life coming from upstairs. Nothing.

Wendell rubbed up against her legs, and then strolled into the hallway and flopped down on the carpet with a muffled thud. He yawned, stretched and rested his head on his paws, as if bored by the lack of life at the inn.

Jane glanced over her shoulder at her rapidly deteriorating breakfast. She hated to leave food out so long, but what was she going to do? Start all over?

Wendell's head popped up, his ears perked and he got to his feet and padded over to the stairs, looking up.

A figure was coming down. *What a relief*, Jane thought.

Lynden came around the corner and smiled down at the cat. He bent over and picked him up, stroking Wendell's head with one hand and cradling him to his chest with the other.

Jane was surprised. Lynden didn't seem to be the animal lover type. He didn't seem to be any type except utterly reserved. Louise had told her sisters about his being outside the parlor while she went over her songs for the church service.

This was the first time Jane had actually seen him smile since he had arrived.

"Breakfast is ready," she said quietly, hoping she wouldn't startle him. She was fairly sure he hadn't noticed her in the doorway.

He jumped.

"Sorry," Jane said. "I didn't mean to startle you."

"That's okay. I was just . . . somewhere else . . ." He bent over and put Wendell on the ground. "Did any of the rest come down yet?"

"I'm pretty sure they're still sleeping. I doubt they would simply steal away without breakfast."

Lynden frowned. "I thought the other guys were going out early this morning."

"I thought so too. That's why I was cracking eggs at the crack of dawn." Jane gave him a self-deprecating smile. "Innkeeper humor."

Lynden only nodded his head.

Okay, Jane thought. *No wisecracks around this young man.*

"I'll get them up," he said, moving back toward the stairs.

Their phantom guest was on the run again.

"No, that's fine. They're on vacation, let them sleep."

A creak of the stairs made Lynden look back over his shoulder. And blush.

Carita came down, her hand trailing over the banister, a smile teasing out a dimple on her cheek. She wore loose fitting, linen pants topped with a bright yellow shirt. "Morning, Lynden. You sleep okay?"

He nodded, slipping his hands in the pockets of his blue jeans.

"Did you eat breakfast yet?"

He shook his head.

Carita saw Jane, and her smile grew self-conscious. "Morning, Ms. Howard. How are you?"

"I'm fine. Just wondering when your crew is going to be coming down for breakfast."

Carita shrugged, stifling a yawn. "I thought they were all done already."

"You and Lynden are the first."

"Well, that's great. We get dibs on all the best food then, don't we?" Carita said to Lynden with what Jane could only describe as a coy look.

He didn't catch it, however, and with a shrug, ambled into the dining room.

"There's fresh coffee and juice," Jane offered. "The French toast is aging, but it's still warm. If you want I can make a fresh batch."

Carita lifted the lid of the warming tray and grinned. "No need to do that. This looks just great, Ms. Howard. Thanks."

Jane fussed a bit with the cutlery, made sure the coffeepot was full and retreated to the kitchen. As soon as Louise and Alice had left, she had pulled out her cookbooks and had been leafing through them, alternately choosing and discarding recipes to go with the entrée. She had settled on chicken with roasted lemon, a recipe from an obscure cookbook she had bought a few years back. It sounded like it had the right combination of unique and comfortable that Stacy wanted. Chicken was the most versatile of meats and lent itself to a variety of spices and flavors.

She took out the recipe and went over the steps again.

". . . line baking sheets with parchment, arrange lemon slices, brush with olive oil . . ." *So far so good*, she thought. *Not too exotic or unusual.* She pulled out her grocery list and started jotting down what she would need.

"Capers, lemons, brine-cured olives . . . I could serve this with a side dish of steamed spinach, possibly a type of stuffed pepper, go with a Mediterranean flavor . . ." Jane muttered to herself, planning, visualizing. She could use that festive looking tablecloth Wilhelm had brought back for her from a trip to Italy. Possibly use some of those brightly colored canisters with the Greek pictures on them. But what else? Maybe her friend Sylvia Songer would have some ideas. Jane wanted to create warmth, an invitation to sit down and experience a slice of the Mediterranean. She had a decorating budget so she could provide atmosphere as she saw fit.

"We need more syrup, please."

Jane was yanked from visions of warm hillsides covered with olive groves and of sun sparkling on azure waters to the reality of Herbie standing squarely in front of her. He held out an empty syrup pitcher.

"Sorry to bug you, but we're all out."

"I'm sorry, I didn't know the rest of you were down here." Jane took the sticky pitcher, wiped down the sides with a warm, wet cloth, and refilled it from the jug in the pantry.

"Not the rest of us, just me, Carita, Lynden and Pete. Matthew and the others are still sleeping."

Jane couldn't help a quick glance at the clock. The time that she could devote to breakfast was running out. What should she do? They had set hours for breakfast and had never extended them like this before. But if she declared breakfast over before the other kids came down, she would have too much food to get rid of.

You have an inn to run, she reminded herself. *You need to maintain some semblance of order.*

However, Jane also knew what it was like to be a student, pushing yourself all year, then working all summer and only grabbing a few days of rest. Sleeping until noon on days off wasn't abnormal.

She gave Herbie the pitcher. "Do you have any more of that French toast and sausage patties?" he asked.

Jane stared, dumbfounded. She had made enough for seven adults. There were only four people in the dining room, one more than half of their guests. *And already they're almost finished with the warm food?*

But she pulled herself back and gave him a smile as if four people eating enough for seven was perfectly normal. "Sure. I'll get some together lickety split." Looked like leftovers weren't going to be an issue after all.

"That would be great. Good breakfast, Ms. J," he said, hoisting the syrup pitcher in a salute to her cooking.

As soon as the door swung closed behind him, Jane shoved the cookbook aside, jumping into innkeeper-panic mode. The unsliced bread was still frozen; thankfully she had enough eggs and milk, though she would have to make sure to pick up more when she and Carita went through town today.

She pulled a bowl out of the dishwasher, rinsed it and pushed it under the mixer. Then she cracked eggs, poured milk, defrosted bread and started slicing.

"Can I do anything?"

Jane started and turned around.

Carita stood right behind her.

Jane wagged a warning finger at her. "Honey, don't ever sneak up on a woman wielding a knife."

Carita held up her hands. "Sorry. I just wanted to know if I could help you."

Jane frowned. "You are our guest. You shouldn't even be in here."

"Well, I can still help. I told those lazybones if they didn't come down, there wouldn't be any breakfast left." Carita grabbed an apron off one of the hooks and wrapped herself in it. "I can take care of the French toast if you tell me what to do. You can do the sausage patties."

"What I want you to do is go back to the dining room and just relax. I'll be ready in a few minutes," Jane protested.

"In a few minutes the rest of the troop will be down and, trust me, you can't fry fast enough to feed them all." Carita removed the bowl from the mixer and reached for the bread.

Trying to take the bowl away from Carita would create an even more awkward situation. This wasn't right, but it looked like Carita was here to stay.

"It's not done yet. You need to put some vanilla extract in the milk and egg mixture," Jane said with a feeling of resignation.

"Okay. What else?" Carita said, pulling open cupboard doors in an effort to find the vanilla.

"Vanilla is over there," Jane said, pointing with the knife she still held. "And you need a dash of salt and a teaspoon of orange zest."

"Zest?"

"Grated orange peel. Oranges are in the . . ."

"Refrigerator. Got that."

A few minutes later Jane was frying up sausage patties, Carita stood at the stove earnestly cooking French toast and the noise level in the dining room was increasing.

It sounded as though the rest of the guests were downstairs. Jane couldn't help taking a quick glance at the clock.

The swinging door flew open and Matthew stood in the kitchen, scratching his head, his fingers running over his very short hair. "So, what can I do?"

"Nothing. It's all under control," Jane said with a forced smile.

Boundaries. We need to reset the boundaries, she thought.

Matthew sauntered over to the refrigerator. "Got anymore orange juice?"

"Yes." Jane wiped her hands on her apron. "I'll get it for you."

"No worries. I got 'er." Matthew snagged the juice container and carried it to the counter. He walked over to the cupboard that held the glasses, took one out and poured the juice while he was walking back to the dining room.

"I had set out glasses on the sideboard," Jane said, wiping her hands on a towel.

"Oh. Sorry. Didn't see them," he shot over his shoulder as he returned to his friends. "Got juice," he announced, holding the jug aloft.

Jane cringed. Usually she put the juice in a glass pitcher, but she didn't have time to correct the situation.

"I think these things need to be flipped," Carita said.

Jane returned to her cooking, trying to maintain her focus. A few minutes later, another batch of French toast and a plate of fresh sausage patties were ready to be delivered to an appreciative and hungry crowd.

Carita took one plate, Jane another, but they were both intercepted by Matthew and Pete.

"We'll just take those," Matthew said, relieving them both of the plates. Ignoring Jane's protests, he handed one to Pete and the two of them walked around the table, forking slices of toast and sausage patties onto the plates of the others.

Jane stood, dumbfounded, watching her job being taken, literally, right out of her hands.

"Please, boys, let me take care of that."

"You're too busy," Matthew called out, clearly enjoying his stint as a server.

"No thank you," Isabel said quietly as Matthew dropped another slice on her plate.

"I know you'll eat it if I give it to you," he said.

"But I didn't want more."

Matthew gave her another piece. "Keep talking and you'll be eating until lunch time."

Isabel glanced down but said nothing more.

"Good stuff, Ms. J," Rick mumbled, wiping his mouth with a napkin.

Ms. J? Once more Jane thought about boundaries.

"Very delicious," the usually silent Lynden put in.

And under Jane's fascinated gaze, the crowd sitting around the table devoured the French toast and the sausages. She cast a panicked glance at the muffins and fruit plate. Also empty. She picked up the plate to replenish it, and Carita followed her back into the kitchen.

"What else do we need to do?" she asked.

Jane bit back another protest and decided to embrace the chaos. "There's a white container in the fridge with more muffins and pastry inside. You can refill this plate with those. I'll take care of the fruit."

Carita saluted, took the plate and a few moments later was humming a little song as she arranged the food. "This is kind of fun. I remember when I was little, I always wanted to be a waitress."

"Waitressing has its moments," Jane said, setting the fruit out in a semiorderly fashion. She assumed artistic impression was less important than speed with this bunch. "It's sort of like the girl with the curl right in the middle of her forehead."

Carita cast her a puzzled glance.

"You know the nursery rhyme? When she was good, she was very, very good, but when she was bad, she was horrid?"

Carita shook her head.

For a moment Jane felt her age. She remembered so vividly having Louise read this and various other nursery rhymes to her as a child. She loved the pictures, the rhythm of the words and especially snuggling up next to her sister, Louise's arm around her.

"At any rate, that about sums up my waitressing experiences," she said, carrying the tray into the dining room.

She was spot on with her assumption about the need for

speed. No sooner had she brought the tray in than it was taken from her and plates were filled. Ditto with the plate Carita brought in.

"Honestly, you guys," Carita said, a note of reprimand edging her voice. "You act as if you haven't eaten for months."

"I haven't eaten *this good* for months." Matthew pointed his fork at the remnant of French toast swimming in syrup on his plate.

Carita sighed and glanced at Jane. "I'll go mix up another batch."

Half an hour later, appetites sated, the group sat around the table, full but still laughing and joking. Even Lynden, sitting quietly, had a smile on his face.

"So, now what, guys?" Rick said, his hands resting on his stomach.

"Now we head out to Potterston," Matthew said, pushing himself away from the table. He held his hand out to Carita. "Keys please, we depart in fifteen minutes."

"I'll be staying here," Carita said, clearing off the plates.

"What? Why?" Isabel sat up, looking startled.

"I've got plans," was all she said, giving Jane a wink.

Isabel glanced around the table, as if unsure of what to do.

"Just go, Isabel," Carita said. "You'll have fun."

Though Isabel didn't look convinced, she got up and followed the boys up the stairs to get ready.

"That girl," Carita said, shaking her head. "She can't seem to make up her mind until I tell her what to do."

"And now I'm going to tell you what to do, and that's relax," Jane said to Carita. "I don't want you to help me."

"I want to get things cleaned up so we can head into town," she said, waving off Jane's protests. "The sooner this place is clean, the sooner we can go."

Jane couldn't argue with her logic, so she reluctantly gave over yet another job to this young woman and guest.

While they were working Jane could hear the rumble of conversation and the thumping of feet above them.

"Sounds like the inn has been invaded by elephants." Carita shook her head as she scraped and rinsed plates.

"This is probably the most exuberant group we've ever had with us," Jane said.

"They're good guys. Lots of fun. But wait until they're getting ready for Friday night. Right now they're being downright civilized compared to when they're getting pumped to cheer their school on."

"That will be interesting," Jane said, trying to inject a note of enthusiasm into her voice. She couldn't imagine that this group could be busier or noisier. She didn't *want* to imagine this group any busier or noisier.

A few moments later Matthew and Pete poked their heads into the kitchen. "Sure you don't want to come, Carita?" they asked.

Carita looked up from the plates she was stacking in the dishwasher and nodded. "You guys go ahead. I've got a few irons in the fire."

"Isabel seems nervous about being alone with us," Pete said, settling his cap on his head.

"She'll be fine." Carita said, her voice taking on a bit of an edge.

And with a final burst of noise they closed the door behind them and peace fell like a soft blanket over the inn.

As Carita loaded the dishwasher, Jane wiped the counters, the stove and the dining room table. Next she pulled out the mop to clean the floor. *Memo to self*, she thought as she squeezed water out of the mop, *nothing with syrup for the next few breakfasts.*

Tomorrow was a brunch casserole. However, given how much food she had gone through at breakfast, she already knew she would have to double the recipe. As she had watched the boys wolf down their food she had put aside all thoughts of poached pear in crème brûlée sauce or meringue eggs with hollandaise sauce, both of which required smaller appetites than she was faced with.

"I'm all done," Carita said, wiping her hands on her apron. "Anything else?"

Jane leaned on her mop as she looked over the kitchen and dining room. "You know, I think we might actually be done here."

Ten minutes later they stepped outside, the bright sun pouring down like a blessing.

"Oh, it feels wonderful to see the sun again," Jane said, releasing a pent-up sigh and unbuttoning her cropped jean jacket. "I miss working outside."

"Is that your garden?" Carita asked, pointing to the tangled rows of plants edged by mounds of asters, pink lisianthus and orange mimulus.

"Yes. Usually it's much neater, but the rains really beat down my vegetable plants." Jane walked over the damp grass for a better look.

The beans needed one last picking, as did the peas. She could pick some squash too, she noticed. And the weeds had taken advantage of the wet weather to propagate like, well, weeds.

"I'm going to need to get at this as soon as it dries," Jane said, shaking her head at the work lying ahead of her. Then she gave Carita a smile. "But today I am at your disposal."

"Great. I brought along a notebook and some pens so I could write things down," Carita said, slipping a backpack over her shoulders.

"And I've got my grocery list. Let's go."

✑

"I thought we could start with the Coffee Shop," Jane said as they walked down the street toward town. "It's the first place on our way. Oh, there's Pastor Thompson."

He returned her wave before stepping into Grace Chapel.

Jane moved to one side to avoid a puddle just as a young boy zipped by them on his bicycle. "Hey, Ms. Howard," he called out.

"Where are you off to in such a hurry, Bobby?" she called back.

"Errand for Mrs. Humbert," he shouted back over his shoulder.

As they walked, they met a young couple strolling along the sidewalk.

"And a lovely morning to you both. What brings you to this part of town?" Jane asked.

"Just going for a walk," the young woman said.

"Have a nice day," Jane said.

"Who *don't* you know?" Carita asked as she and Jane carried on.

Jane frowned at her. "What do you mean?"

A rueful little smile played about Carita's mouth. "Before my family moved to Cobalt, I don't think I could step out my door there and even be able to say hi to a neighbor, let alone the first three people I'd meet."

"Acorn Hill is a lot different from living in San Francisco, where I was before. Sometimes I miss the city, but mostly I'm quite content to live here." Jane drew in a long breath of fresh, clean air and let it out in a sigh of contentment. "Not lots of excitement, but lots of people who know and care about you."

"Yeah. A person can get lost in the city. Either lost or caught up in the day-to-day business of making a living."

"That happens here too," Jane said. "Doesn't matter where

you live. Bills need to be paid, and money needs to be made, and there are obligations to the community that you are a part of."

"Like your sister working on that Habitat project?"

"Like that."

"Did she see that as an obligation?"

Jane shook her head. "No. She was excited to do it, and knowing my sister, she did it because she wants to help where she can. She wants to be a light, a representative of Christ in this world. As Saint Teresa of Avila said, 'Yours are the eyes through which He looks with compassion on the world. Christ has no body now on earth but yours.' Essentially she was saying Christ uses us to spread His compassion and love. And that's what Alice does and is doing with this project."

Carita didn't reply, and Jane thought she might have been too preachy. She didn't know where this girl stood spiritually. She and her sisters always strove to model Christ in their actions and words but at the same time be aware that not everyone shared their convictions.

"And here's our first stop of the day," Jane said as they rounded the corner onto Hill Street. She held open the door of the Coffee Shop for Carita.

The Coffee Shop was quiet this time of day. The breakfast rush was over, and the lunch crowd wouldn't come for a couple of hours.

"Hey, Jane," Hope called out from behind the counter as they stepped inside. "Be with you in a minute." Hope turned back to the coffee machine. "Things have been crazy here this morning," she said as she scooped coffee into a filter-lined basket. "I don't know if it's the weather or the fact that people have been cooped up so long, but I've never passed out so many breakfasts as I did this morning. It's like they hadn't seen food for days."

"I know what you mean," Jane murmured, giving Carita a conspiratorial wink.

Hope slid the basket into the machine and turned to Jane, grabbing a couple of menus as she slipped around the counter.

"Unfortunately we're not staying for coffee," Jane said holding up her hand to stop Hope. "Our guest Carita and I are planning a town scavenger hunt for the group at the inn. Carita, this is Hope Collins, a genuine, dyed-in-the-wool waitress." Jane saw Hope's faint frown and smiled. "Carita confessed to me this morning that at one time in her life she had aspirations to be a waitress."

"I always wanted to fill up the sugar containers and stack those little cream pitchers," Carita said.

Hope's laughter filled the Coffee Shop. "And I always wanted to be a movie star. Bloom where you're planted, huh?" She looked from Jane to Carita. "So tell me about this town scavenger hunt."

"We want to get the group from the inn to go through town and either pick up clues or some small items from various businesses."

Hope crossed her arms over her chest, her head bobbing as she thought. "Sounds like fun. How old are the little kiddies you're doing this for?"

"Nineteen and twenty."

Hope's eyebrows zoomed up into her bangs. "Now that's going to be an interesting challenge."

"Carita said they would enjoy it," Jane said.

"Trust me, they'll be stoked to try it," Carita put in.

"So, what could you do here?" Hope asked, looking around the Coffee Shop.

"Could you have June put something on the menu board?"

Hope wrinkled her nose. "She always puts that in the

window. I'm thinking you might want them to actually come into the place."

Jane imagined the group pouring into the Coffee Shop, taking it over. Second thoughts about this little venture bombarded her mind. "What do you think, Carita?"

"I had planned on splitting them into teams of two. That way there won't be a stampede. The point was for them to appreciate the town, so I'd really like it if they could do something here to make them take a second look at the place."

"Smaller teams would work." Jane was relieved at Carita's practical suggestion. While she felt a responsibility to her guests, she also was a resident of Acorn Hill and had no desire to jeopardize the inn's goodwill in the town.

Hope snapped her fingers. "I have just the thing. They could do a taste test and pick their favorite dessert."

Jane held up both hands and shook her head as she imagined either Matthew and Rick, or Herbie and Pete descending on the pie case. "I don't think that would work."

Hope glanced around the diner. "They could count the booths."

Jane waggled her hand as if considering this and finding it wanting. "That might be too simple."

"How about if we get them to ask Hope a question about the Coffee Shop?" Carita suggested. "When it started. Who owns it?"

"And what if they wouldn't know what question to ask me?" Hope's eyes widened as she clapped her hands together. "We could put hints on the menu board and they have to decipher the question from that."

Jane was pleased to see Hope buying into the silly scheme. If she was this excited about it, the group was sure to be as well.

Carita slipped off her backpack and pulled out her notebook. "Run that by me again," she said digging out her pen.

Hope and Carita slipped into an available booth and refined the plan, while Jane thought of the next destination. Acorn Hill Antiques was next door. A picture of those rambunctious boys lollygagging in the Holzmanns' store came to mind, and she shivered. Joseph and Rachel were fairly easygoing, but it would be best not to tempt fate.

The Good Apple Bakery would be a great hit. Clarissa, the owner, would be more than pleased to have those boys descend on her.

Sylvia's Buttons was just around the corner from the Bakery. Jane had to talk to Sylvia about decorating for Stacy's dinner anyway. Maybe her friend could give Jane some ideas.

"Okay. I think we got that figured out," Carita said, slapping shut her notebook. "That's great, Hope. Thanks a bunch."

"Any time. If you need more help, let me know."

As Carita and Jane exited the Coffee Shop, they almost ran into Fred Humbert. "Well, hey there, Jane," Fred said, pushing his cap back on his sandy-colored hair as he stepped aside. "Nice day to be out and about."

"I sure am glad to see the sunshine. Any idea if it's going to stick around?"

Fred Humbert dabbled in weather forecasting. He was impressively accurate. "Should stay for a couple days," he said, glancing up at the sky. "Barometer is holding steady and we've got no wind."

"Glad to know. I want to get at my garden in the next few days. If I don't, the weeds are going to stage a hostile takeover." Jane briefly introduced Carita and explained their mission to Fred. "We'll stop by your store on our way back. If you don't mind, we'd appreciate a few moments of your time to plan what we could do at your store."

Fred tapped his temple. "I'll think on that. I'll let you know when you come by."

"That'd be great." They said their good-byes. No sooner had Fred left them when Clara Horn came out of the antique store, pushing her baby buggy.

"That's her," Carita whispered, tugging on Jane's elbow. "The lady with the pig."

Clara waved, then hurried toward them, the baby buggy rattling over the cracks in the sidewalk. "Jane Howard. I need to talk to you."

Jane gave Carita a warning glance and had to stifle her own smile. Then she made brief introductions.

"Now, Clara, what can I do for you?"

"Have you heard what Florence is up to? She said she was going to be working on some house. Building things. Should she be doing that?"

"I can't see why not, Clara," Jane said. "I think it's quite safe. Alice and Ethel are also involved."

Clara looked shocked. "Ethel too?" She shook her head. "What were they thinking? Though it would have been nice to at least be told."

"It was rather spur of the moment," Jane assured her. "And how is Daisy?"

"Just fine." Clara angled the buggy so Carita and Jane could see for themselves.

Daisy sat curled up on a blanket, her eyes closed, the picture of porcine peace.

"Does she make a mess?" Carita asked, obviously curious about this pet.

"She's really very clean," Clara said, only too glad to be expounding on Daisy's many virtues. "And quiet."

Carita edged closer. "May I touch her?"

"Oh sure. Once she's down, she sleeps like a log. I just took her shopping, so she's plumb worn out."

Carita reached carefully into the buggy and touched the pig. Then she started to smile. "She's warm. Soft actually."

"I wash her every day. I use a lovely English soap."

Carita's eyes lit up and Jane could almost see the gears turning in her head. "What is it called?"

"I'll have to go home and check. Smells like vanilla."

"Thanks so much, Mrs. Horn."

"You're welcome." And Clara left, a contented smile on her face.

Love my pig, love me, Jane thought. "So I'm guessing you've got another idea for your little scavenger hunt."

"If Mrs. Horn doesn't mind people going to her house, I think I'm going to get the guys asking her the brand and the scent of what she uses on Daisy." Carita scribbled the idea in her notebook. "Now where?"

"Sylvia's Buttons," Jane said, unfastening her denim jacket. The sun gained strength with each passing minute. "My good friend works there. I need to talk to her about the dinner, and I'm hoping she can give us some ideas for the scavenger hunt."

They walked along Hill Street, past Acorn Hill Antiques. Carita paused to inspect the Holzmanns' window display of antique porcelain dolls and doll furniture. "I'm guessing you don't want the boys in here."

"And I'm guessing you're one smart lass," Jane said. "We could make up a riddle to do with the window display, but you're right. I'm sure Isabel would be fine, but best keep the boys out of this store."

Carita laughed. "Not all the boys are that active."

"Well, at least Lynden seems quiet."

Carita turned thoughtful. "Yeah. Like I said, he's a deep one. Though he's not the Lynden I used to know. I've tried to talk to him, but he's not saying much. He's changed a lot in the year we've been apart."

Jane thought of what Louise had said about Lynden's standing outside the door of the parlor. He seemed uncommunicative, and if Carita said he wasn't the same person she remembered . . .

What *was* he all about?

Chapter Eight

Regular washing will maintain the luster of the paint job, but waxing is important as well."

Louise stifled a yawn as Bart Tessier, the instructor for the course, showed them yet another slide of yet another car with yet another poorly maintained paint job.

She didn't want to glance over at Viola who, she sensed, was growing annoyed with the lack of what she regarded to be practical information offered in this hour-and-a-half lecture.

The course was held in a small room in Acorn Hill's library. Besides Louise and Viola, people in attendance included Martha Bevins, a tiny, birdlike, elderly woman; Delia Edwards; Derek Grollier, who sat scowling at the instructor over his glasses; and Harvey Racklin, who provided a mirror image of Derek with his grumpy demeanor.

Louise knew that neither Martha Bevins nor Harvey Racklin even owned a vehicle, but she suspected they were attending merely as a way to fill time. Martha loved nothing more than to find new and unusual things to talk about when she was getting her weekly "do" at the Clip 'n' Curl down the street from the library.

"So you realize you need to be diligent in which type of wax you're going to be using on your vehicle. Harvey, can you get the lights, please?"

Harvey, Bart's assistant, ambled over to the light switch, grumbling as he went. Louise didn't blame him. She felt like doing a bit of grumbling herself. This wasn't what she had in mind when she signed up.

"So, are there any questions about paint and wax jobs?" Bart glanced around the room, rubbing his hands as if anticipating a flood of questions.

Louise kept her eyes averted, Viola huffed, but thankfully no one was dying to know more about the qualities of paint.

"Okay then," Bart said, drawing the two words out as if he couldn't understand why anyone wouldn't want to continue the discussion. "Tomorrow Clyde is coming in to give us some pointers on batteries. I hope you enjoyed today's class." He beamed at the class, and Louise took a chance and put up her hand.

"I appreciate the information you gave us, but when I signed up for this course, I understood it was going to be more about driving than car maintenance?"

Bart frowned. "Well, in order to drive your car properly, you need to learn how to take care of it. That is the first emphasis of this course."

"So we won't be driving?"

"Not right away." He gave her a patronizing look, then glanced around the class. "Any other questions? No? Then be here tomorrow when Clyde will speak to you."

As soon as was polite, Louise got up, and she and Viola beat a hasty retreat.

"I don't know about you, but I think this might be a waste of time," Viola said as she and Louise walked out of the classroom. "I didn't think anyone could hold forth for so long on the properties of car wax."

Much as Louise hated to admit it, Viola was correct. "The course was rather drawn out for what we learned this morning."

"Or maybe we are too old."

"We are not that old," Louise protested. "I signed up and paid for the course so I feel obligated to go through with it to the end. Besides, this was just the first lecture. Perhaps the rest will be more practical."

Viola shook her head. "I didn't pay good money to learn that improperly applied paint can flake. As if I have any control over that when I buy a vehicle."

While they walked, Louise flipped through the course materials. "From the looks of the outline, we will be getting to the driving portion next week. Tomorrow Clyde will talk about battery and tire maintenance, so perhaps we'll get some valuable information. Maybe it will be more interesting."

"If you find tires interesting, I would say you need to get out more." Viola shook her head as they crossed over Berry Lane, then across Acorn Avenue. "I have to stop at Wilhelm's a moment."

"I'll go with you," Louise said. "I haven't seen Wilhelm for a few days."

The bell above the door tinkled a gentle greeting as they walked in. Strains of classical music soothed away any minor irritation Louise had accumulated listening to an instructor drone on for an hour and a half about paint jobs, glass maintenance and the amazing properties of leather conditioner.

"Good morning, Louise, Viola." Wilhelm greeted them from behind the counter, nattily dressed as usual. Today he wore a beige suit, yellow shirt and gold and brown striped tie.

"Very elegant tie," Viola said.

"Thank you. I purchased it in Sri Lanka," Wilhelm said, touching it briefly as if resurrecting memories of that trip. "Wonderful place. And the sheer variety of tea . . ." he sighed, lifting one hand upward as if mere words could not do the subject justice. "I shipped lots of it back."

"And I imagine we would be well-advised to taste some of the varieties when they arrive?" Louise asked.

"I brought a few sample packages back," Wilhelm said. "In fact, I am willing to give one to you as a prize, if you can—"

"Name that tune?" Louise finished the sentence, cocking an ear to listen to the music playing softly from the speakers located throughout the store. She listened a moment, concentrating. "Wassenaer," she said.

Wilhelm could hardly hide his smug smile. "I don't usually stump you, Louise, but this time I have. It is Giovanni Pergolesi's six concertos."

"They *were* attributed to Pergolesi," Louise said, almost hating to steal his thunder, "but a number of years ago Dutch musicologist Albert Dunning was successful in identifying the composer as a Dutch nobleman, Count Unico Wilhelm van Wassenaer. At one time it was thought that Bach had composed these pieces."

Wilhelm frowned. "I made a CD from an older record my mother had in her collection. When I copied the notes from the record sleeve I clearly remember reading that Pergolesi was the composer."

"Because the information comes from a record sleeve, that is not a surprise," Louise said, warming to the subject. "The record most likely predates the discovery. Dunning discovered this unknown manuscript copy of the score of the concertos. The concertos were made during the first half of the eighteenth century in the Wassenaer palace at Twickel in Overijssel, the Netherlands. The Count wrote the foreword to the score in his own hand."

Wilhelm stroked his thinning hair, a light frown creasing his eyebrows. Perhaps he regretted getting involved in this challenge. "But how is it the mistake was made? And why has the classical music world never heard of this man Wassenaer before these concertos, or afterward?"

"Apparently Count van Wassenaer was dissatisfied with the pieces. They were played initially at a musical gathering and one of the violinists playing with van Wassenaer wanted to make a copy. Van Wassenaer initially refused, but he was prevailed upon by another man, and when he finally gave in, it was on the condition that his name not appear anywhere on the copy. Granted, you are justified in assuming we have never heard of van Wassenaer as a composer before, but the evidence is apparently incontrovertible."

"Fascinating." Wilhelm shook his head, amazed at his friend's knowledge. "How did you know all this?"

"I'm always interested in what goes on in the musical world. I've always enjoyed these concertos, so when the information came out some time ago, I naturally remembered it and stored it away."

"And you were able to pull it out at the drop of a note," Wilhelm said, still full of admiration.

"I must say, Louise, you are far more interesting to listen to than the instructor we just had," Viola put in.

"What instructor?" Wilhelm asked.

"Louise decided she needs a refresher course in driving, so she enrolled." Viola gave Wilhelm a wry look, and turned to the bins of tea on display. "I thought I would join her, but for the past hour and a half we were inundated with terminology that I only hear on car commercials. So I'm ready for something more my style." She pointed to a blend of tea Wilhelm had displayed in a sealed glass jar with a note card describing the contents leaning against the jar. "Now that looks new. And interesting."

"It's a Rooibos blend with a hint of caramel and vanilla. I discovered it in South Africa. Very common there, but I thought the unique flavor would translate well to North America."

"I'll take a small package and a three-hundred gram bag of the Earl Grey mixture."

"That is also a new blend. I found a new source of Lapsang Souchong, which brings out a slightly smokier flavor. As well you might want to try . . ."

As Wilhelm expounded on the qualities of other blends, Louise wandered over to the tea sets. Wilhelm had a successful business on the side, selling china over the Internet. He often had several of the sets on display, and every time Louise was in the shop, it seemed he had yet another alluring pattern.

This time she was admiring a set whose hand-lettered sign stated that it came from Morocco. The silver teapot had a high, domed lid, and the small glasses were a lovely, clear sapphire blue, etched with a gold border on the rim.

The doorbell tinkled again and Louise turned. Jane entered the shop, looking over her shoulder as she spoke.

". . . but the real challenge is going to be to make sure we don't make the hunt too long or too easy."

Carita was behind her, scribbling something in a notebook she was carrying.

"Well, this is a pleasant surprise," Louise said. "What brings you here?" As far as she knew the inn was well stocked with tea.

"Looking for ideas," Jane explained, glancing around the shop.

Louise was about to ask for what when Carita scurried over to Louise's side. She gently picked up one of the glasses.

"Oh my, look at those lovely Moroccan tea glasses."

"How did you know what they are?" Louise asked.

"My parents took us on a Mediterranean trip, and we made a two-day stop in Morocco." Carita set down the glass. "They drink sweet mint tea in these glasses. It's great fun to watch them serve it. They lift the pot way up in the air, the higher the better, and the tea foams up in the cup. Everywhere you go, any shop you stop at, you get invited in for a cup. The ultimate expression of Moroccan hospitality, we were told. It's really good, but after a day of shopping and constantly being invited in for tea, you can feel really antsy, it's so laced with sugar."

"So you were in Morocco?" As if drawn by the mere mention of that ancient country, Wilhelm joined them, his eyes alight as if he were about to relive another one of his own adventures. After introductions he asked, "What parts did you see?"

"We stayed mostly on the coast. We went to a place called Essaouira, Casablanca, of course, and Marrakech. I even went on a camel ride." Carita's eyes sparkled with fun, as if she had been transported back to that particular experience.

"Morocco is on the top of my list of places to go," Wilhelm said. "I would love to find out more about it."

"I'm staying at the inn," Carita said. "Maybe I could stop by, and we can talk."

"That would be wonderful." Wilhelm rubbed his hands together, as if in anticipation. "And you'll have to explain precisely how to make Moroccan tea. I would love to be able to give out those instructions with the tea set."

"When you do, I'd like to know as well," Viola put in.

"I think these glasses would make lovely holders for votive candles. The light would glow quite nicely through these rich colors," Louise said. She glanced over at her sister, who was looking puzzled. "What seems to be the problem, Jane?"

"Carita and I are planning a town scavenger hunt," Jane said. "She wanted to keep our guests occupied one afternoon here in town. We have a number of things planned for the other businesses, but we need something for them to discover here."

"What could you do here?" Louise asked. She didn't want to dampen Jane's enthusiasm, but she was trying to imagine the rambunctious group of boys in this store. The phrase "bull in a china shop" seemed to fit the situation.

"Not sure." Jane glanced around the shop.

She walked over to the display case, glancing at some of the tea sets displayed under the glass.

"You're not too tired, are you?" Louise asked. From the sight of Jane's full grocery bag, it seemed that she had also been doing some shopping.

Jane waved away Louise's concern. "I'm fine."

But Louise saw a slight tension in Jane's face that hadn't been there this morning. She resolved to have a sisterly chat with her when they had a free moment.

"What about a quiz?" Wilhelm suggested. "You could give some obscure hints about tea, and they would have to guess or ask me."

Jane nodded, considering.

"How many different kinds of tea do you have here, Mr. Wood?" Carita asked.

Wilhelm slowly shook his head. "You know, I don't believe I've ever counted."

"They could try to find a dozen different kinds of tea," Carita suggested.

"And ingredients," Wilhelm added. "And where they come from."

"That would mean answering a lot of questions," Louise said. "Are you sure you want to?"

But when she saw Wilhelm's expectant expression, Louise had her answer already. Wilhelm loved expounding on the various kinds of tea and his own special blends. The only thing he liked more was discussing the many places he'd been.

"We could possibly get each group to come up with a name for a new type of tea," Wilhelm said.

"And we could vote on the answer," Carita put in.

Viola put down the glass and glanced at Louise. "We should go. My helper said she had to run a few errands yet."

Louise glanced over at Jane, but she, Wilhelm and Carita were already deep in discussion. So she simply said good-bye and left.

"Jane and Carita's plan sounds like a lot of fun," Viola said as they made their way down Berry Lane. "I wonder if they had decided on coming to the bookstore."

"I'm sure Jane will figure out something," Louise said. "Though I think she's taking on too much. I get tired just thinking of all the things she has to accomplish."

"I don't think you need to worry about Jane," Viola said. "She's smart enough to know when she needs to slow down."

Louise didn't say anything, but she wished she could share Viola's confidence.

"Are you going right back to the inn?" Viola asked.

Louise sensed that Viola was angling for a visit, but she had a few other things to do. "No. I have to stop at the church and go over the music for Sunday with Rev. Thompson."

"Then I'll see you tomorrow." Viola sighed. "Do you think it's worth going back to that driver's course?"

"I'll give it one more try," Louise said. "If I don't learn anything, I'll have to chalk it up to experience and lose the money I paid for the rest of the course."

"I'm of the same mind." Viola shrugged. "Let's hope for a more interesting topic tomorrow then. I hate to think I paid good money to be bored to tears."

Louise said good-bye, then made her way back up Chapel Road. As she walked, she tried to formulate a diplomatic way to tell Jane that she might be overextending herself.

∞

"I don't know if I can ever lift a hammer again," Alice said as she got out of the car.

Ethel was unusually quiet as they trudged toward the inn. All the way home, she hadn't said anything and simply stared out the window. Was the physical work too much for her?

"You're not too tired, are you?" Alice asked, trying to mask the concern in her voice.

Ethel merely shook her head, which only confirmed Alice's misgivings.

"I'm looking forward to a long, quiet soak in a hot bath and then bed. I just hope I'm not too stiff tomorrow."

When Alice opened the door to the kitchen, she was immediately inundated with the sound of voices, which grew louder as she and Ethel stepped inside.

What were all these people doing in the kitchen?

Herbie, Pete and Matthew were sitting at the table, large glasses of milk at their elbows. In front of them sat a plate holding only crumbs. Isabel stood by the counter mixing up something as Carita chatted with Jane, who was paging through her recipe books. Again.

"Hello everyone," Alice said, glancing from the boys to Jane.

Jane brightened. "And here come the resident carpenters," she said. "You must be starving. Do you want some tea? I've got a fresh batch of cookies in the oven."

Alice nodded. "That would be lovely." She gave Jane a questioning look, which was answered with a vague shrug of Jane's shoulders.

"Jane's making cookies," Herbie offered as if he caught Alice and Jane's wordless exchange. "And I couldn't resist the smell so I followed my nose and ended up here. Awesome, huh?"

Oh very, Alice thought, giving Herbie a warm smile. "And how was the day for all of you?"

"Tell you the truth, Ms. A, kind of a downer," Matthew volunteered, wiping his mouth with the back of his hand. "We were supposed to go to this car show, but it was only old, antique cars, which was kind of cool, but I wanted to see some souped-up cars. Something a bit more my style." He leaned back in his chair, his arms folded over his hooded sweatshirt. "Tomorrow's supposed to be pretty cool. Carita's got a treasure hunt thingy going on."

Alice accepted the "Ms. A" in stride. Jane had spoken earlier with her sisters, and all three had agreed to allow their young guests more latitude than was usual in addressing them—even if that meant that Louise might soon hear something other than "Mrs. Smith."

"I see," Alice said, though she really didn't.

"A scavenger hunt through Acorn Hill," Jane explained, setting the cookies on a wire rack to cool. "Carita and I made it up."

"In Acorn Hill?" Ethel asked, taking a chair at the table. "How will that work?"

"Well, I hope," Jane said with a rueful expression.

"Those cookies done yet?" Pete asked, looking up from the map he had spread out on the table.

"They're still hot," Isabel said, handing Jane a new tray of cookies to put in the oven.

"Where is Lynden? He might like some cookies," Ethel said, looking around the kitchen as if he might be hiding somewhere.

"On the porch reading."

"We probably shouldn't disturb him," Ethel said.

"Actually, I think we should," said Matthew with a mischievous glint in his eyes. "He's been on a downer since we came here, and this was supposed to be all about fun and fellowship and he's not really fellowshipping, now is he?"

Matthew pushed his chair back and grabbed Herbie by the front of his shirt. "C'mon, dude, let's go light a fire under that friend of ours."

Herbie, unable to stop Matthew's momentum stumbled

along behind his friend, throwing a beseeching look over his shoulder. "But . . . Matthew . . . cookies."

"Later. C'mon, Pete, let's get in the spirit of the game."

Pete folded up his map, tucked it in his back pocket, slipped his cap on and followed the two other boys.

As the front door closed behind them, silence fell on the kitchen.

"Thank goodness," Isabel said as she laid more cookies on the cookie sheet, "I'm getting tired of hearing about blue bottle kits—"

"That's lift kits," Carita corrected. "Lift kits and blue bottle mufflers. Those boys love to talk about cars and trucks and all the things they would do if they actually had one."

The curt nod of Isabel's head showed Alice that the young woman wasn't impressed with Carita's correction. However, Isabel didn't say anything and kept working.

"Sorry about these boys taking over, Jane," Carita said with an apologetic look. "I didn't think they would come right into the kitchen."

"That's okay," Jane said. She turned to Alice. "So how was the first day on the job?"

"I don't know about Aunt Ethel, but I'm tired. My hands are sore and my back is sore, and I think I got a bit too much sun," Alice said.

"But you're smiling."

"It was a lot of fun," Alice admitted as she eased her tired body into a chair. She bent over and unfastened her shoes, toeing them off. Her feet burned, her hands had blisters on them. But, as Jane had said, she was smiling. "It was not only a lot of fun, but satisfying to be a part of such a big project."

"How did you make out, Aunt Ethel?"

Ethel simply nodded. "Well. Real well. Looking forward to tomorrow." She pulled her tape measure out of her pouch and pulled out the tape, absently measuring the width of the table.

Alice frowned. "I don't know if you should go, Aunt Ethel. You seem very tired."

"I'm not," was all Ethel said. She let the tape slip back into the case but then pulled it out again.

Alice was certain her aunt was not as well as she claimed, but she also knew not to press her point. Tomorrow would be a determining factor. And, if need be, Alice could give Ethel a way out by claiming exhaustion herself. Yes, she was tired and yes, her feet ached, but it was a good tired. She would sleep well tonight.

"Why don't you girls join the boys," Jane said, taking the bowl of cookie dough away from Isabel. "You don't need to help me here."

"I don't mind helping," Isabel said.

"Besides, the boys just annihilated those cookies," Carita put in, glancing at the few cookies left. "You've hardly gotten anywhere."

"I'll just have to adjust my amounts next time I bake. Now, go." Jane waved her hand in a shooing motion. Carita got up, but Isabel lingered.

"Are you sure you don't need help?" Isabel asked.

"Absolutely. Now go have some fun." So Isabel did as she was told.

When the door closed, Jane brought the teapot to the table with a plate of gingersnaps she had kept hidden from the cookie monsters. "Those kids. What a pile of energy. I can hardly keep up with them."

"I can stay home tomorrow and help you," Alice said, seeing her chance to create an excuse for Ethel.

"But what about the house?" Ethel said, sitting up, a frown creasing her forehead.

"Well, I might be too tired . . ."

"Nonsense!" Ethel exclaimed, waving Alice's comment away like she was swatting a pesky fly. "You don't look the least bit tired to me."

Alice's tactic wasn't working, so she faced the situation head on. "But you do, Aunt Ethel. I don't want you to wear yourself out."

"I'm not tired." Ethel set aside her tape, poured the tea, then sat back, her arms folded over her bosom. "I'm just thinking."

"About . . ." Alice offered.

"Florence." Ethel tapped her fingers on her arm, then shook her head.

"I believe I did notice some strain at the building site today," Alice said, hoping Ethel would elaborate.

"She completely ignored me when she brought the juice around," Ethel said. "Didn't even offer me a glass. As if I wasn't there."

Alice didn't mention that Ethel had treated Florence in much the same way previously. "Maybe she didn't notice you."

Ethel wrinkled her nose, then shook her head. "She noticed me all right. I could tell the minute she looked my way."

"Why do you think she would do that?" Jane asked, dropping into a chair.

Ethel did not respond. Instead she stared into the steaming liquid of her cup as if trying to find an answer there.

Jane glanced at Alice, lifting her eyebrows in question. Alice gave a light shake of her head, indicating to Jane that she should hold off. For some reason Florence and Ethel's little pique had deeper roots that Ethel wasn't yet ready to discuss.

"And how is your menu coming along?" Alice asked, curious to see what her sister had planned for Stacy's dinner.

"I haven't had much time to work on it today."

"I can stay tomorrow . . ." Alice began.

Jane held up her hand. "Don't even suggest it. Things are going along just fine."

Alice wasn't sure about that part, but she also knew better than to buck her younger sister when she had a notion.

"I'm making a simple meal tonight. I have some ideas I'm going to try out tomorrow night for supper," Jane continued, stirring some sugar into her tea. "If my family doesn't mind being guinea pigs."

"We'll gladly test anything you come up with," Ethel offered. "You always have the most interesting ideas."

Jane smiled at her aunt. "Thanks for the vote of confidence. I'll do my best to maintain your faith in me."

The ringing of the phone broke into the moment, and Alice answered it.

"Is Jane there? Is Jane available?" The breathless voice on the other end of the line gave Alice a start.

"Yes she is. Just a moment, Stacy." Alice quickly handed the phone to Jane.

Jane's face drooped as soon as she heard Alice mention Stacy's name, but she held out her hand. "Hello, Stacy. No, I'm not terribly busy . . . I see . . . I'm not sure . . . I'll have to ask . . . I can't promise you anything. Sorry. . . . Yes, I'll talk to my sisters and get back to you." Jane nodded, made a few more abbreviated comments as she drummed her fingers on the table, making Alice more concerned the longer she spoke.

"Okay. I'll call you as soon as I know anything. Goodbye." Jane put the phone down and shook her head.

"What does Stacy want now?" Alice asked.

"Stacy can't find a place anywhere in Acorn Hill, in Potterston or any place within driving distance. She wants to use the inn."

"I take it you don't want the dinner here?"

"You take correctly." Jane smacked her hand on the table. "I knew it. I knew this would happen. From the minute she walked into the inn and saw the dining room, she looked as if she was going to have that dinner here no matter what other options were available to her."

"But wouldn't catering be simpler if she had her event at the inn? It would free you from a host of problems," Alice offered helpfully.

"And we could help you," Ethel offered, her eyes bright. Then she frowned as she looked at the calendar on the wall. "Oh, wait. That's Saturday, isn't it? Lloyd wants to take me to Potterston that night. But I'm sure Louise and Alice could help out," she said, glibly offering her nieces' services.

"I can help you," Alice said.

"You'll be too tired from working on the house," Jane said.

"I don't work at the hospital until next week, so I'll have lots of recuperation time."

"And the kids will be busy all day Saturday and Saturday night," Jane mused.

"And you wouldn't have to worry about whether the hall has the proper equipment. You could serve everything fresh and warm."

"I know all that. She's been—for lack of a better expression —a pain in the neck, and I couldn't imagine what she would be like if she got her hands on the inn. She quoted me a generous decorating allowance, but, knowing Stacy, she probably would want me to use some of that to repaint the inn."

"Now, Jane, that's where there's a difference. Here, in the inn, you are in charge. This is your territory, even if she is paying for decorations. Plus you have two partners who can be—and would be—as adamant as she is." Alice got up and patted Jane on the shoulder as she walked past her. "This could turn out just fine. Aunt Ethel, did you want some more tea?"

"I better get home and put my feet up for a while."

"Are you coming back for supper?" Alice asked as she rinsed out the teacups.

To Alice's surprise, Ethel shook her head. "No. I should stay home and cook for myself. Besides, I think I should get to bed early, and you seem to be quite busy with your guests."

Alice watched with concern as Ethel slowly got up from the chair and walked out of the kitchen with measured steps. Doing carpentry work all day was more than enough for Alice, let alone someone of Ethel's age.

Maybe she could talk her aunt into going to the project later in the morning to make a shorter day of work.

Chapter Nine

Jane yawned as she made her way down the stairs Thursday morning. As she hitched up the waistband of her khaki cotton capri pants and tucked in her bright yellow shirt, she paused on the landing of the second floor.

The silence on this floor was a direct contrast to the noise the young people made last night as they played a game Isabel had brought along. Though they were playing two floors down in the living room, their cries had filtered up to the third floor where Jane and her sisters slept.

Jane had been tempted to go downstairs and get them to quiet down, but at the same time she didn't feel right about chiding them as if they were unruly children. So she lay in bed, wakeful, fretting that Alice might not be getting enough sleep and hoping Louise wouldn't be upset.

Now, with morning, the inn was utterly quiet.

Nonetheless, she had a schedule to maintain, so she went down to the main floor, taking a moment to step outside.

The sun was warming off the early morning chill, drying the dew that sparkled on the grass. The faint growl of a car starting up drifted down the street followed by a mother's voice calling her child in for breakfast.

The neighborhood was slowly waking up.

Jane looked around, a smile on her lips.

"Thank You, Lord, for the promise of a new day," she prayed aloud. "For work and for health, for family and friends. For freedom and blessings we can't begin to count."

As she spoke she caught the muted sound of the tinkling of piano keys laying down a tranquil soundtrack to her spoken prayer.

Somehow Louise had slipped downstairs without Jane's knowing it and was already practicing the songs she would be playing in church on Sunday. The door was cracked open a bit, and the melody floated softly through the first floor. Jane should not have been surprised.

In spite of the noise from last night that surely had kept her awake, Louise was maintaining her disciplined schedule.

Jane crossed her arms, giving herself some time outside before diving into the busyness of her own day. She mentally ticked off her jobs, organizing her hours.

Finalize menu for the dinner Saturday night, keeping in mind that Stacy could call at any time with yet another food issue.

Help the kids get started on the scavenger hunt. Though she still had her misgivings about how well it would go over with the college crowd, Carita had assured her that they would have fun.

Get the laundry started and do some more baking to feed the insatiable appetites of these youths for homemade goodies.

Today she was going to make biscotti. Maybe the crunchy twice-baked cookies would slow their jaws down a bit. She had some lovely recipes she hadn't used in a while.

Feeling as if her day was now ordered, Jane opened the door behind her, whistling the same tune Louise had just played.

She stopped as she spied a figure hovering at the bottom of the stairs, outside the partially open parlor door.

Lynden. Today he wore a dark T-shirt and the baggy pants teenage boys often seemed to favor. A small book peeked out of his back pocket.

If she was startled, so was he. He pushed himself away from the wall, looking as if she had caught him with his hand in the cookie jar. *Not that he would have found anything there,* Jane thought. It was as empty as Mother Hubbard's cupboard.

She recovered in time to smile at him, pushing down a slight misgiving she felt at his lurking presence ... once again.

"Good morning, Lynden. How are you?"

He shoved his hands in his pockets and gave her a brief nod. "I'm good," was his terse reply.

"Lovely morning, isn't it?"

"Yeah."

In the background, Louise had stopped playing, and Jane wondered what her sister would think if she came out and found Lynden standing in the foyer as he had the other day.

"I'm glad the weather is cooperating for the scavenger hunt," she said, soldiering on. She was growing increasingly concerned over this young man and was determined to engage him one way or the other, inane conversation or not.

"I guess."

"I hear you're going to be hosting a tailgate party Friday night."

This time he simply nodded.

Way to get him to open up, Jane. "What are you going to serve?"

"The usual."

Four syllables. She was really getting somewhere. Jane was about to ask him another harmless question when Louise started playing again and Lynden's head snapped up, his eyes fixing on the parlor door.

Jane glanced in the same direction, wondering what he was looking at. Then she had a moment of inspiration. Something Carita had said came back to her. A throwaway comment she had made about a doting grandmother.

"She plays well, doesn't she?" Jane said, lowering her voice to a decidedly nonthreatening timbre.

Again Lynden only nodded, but this time Jane caught the faintest glint in his eyes.

"Does your grandmother play the piano?"

A look of sorrow crept across the young man's face. "Used to."

Jane sensed a whole world of pain and hurt wrapped up in those two words. Used to. Past tense. And suddenly everything became much clearer. This young man wasn't odd and he wasn't angry. He was still grieving the loss of someone he must have cared for deeply.

Taking a chance, Jane laid her hand on Lynden's arm. "I'm sorry to hear that. How long ago did she die?"

Lynden blinked and looked away. "Two months ago. She was sick for almost a year before."

She squeezed lightly, a gesture of silent sympathy.

"I lived with her." He spoke so quietly Jane had to strain to hear. "She took care of me since my parents died."

Jane remembered Carita's mentioning this. How her family had lived next door to Lynden and his grandmother. "How old were you when your parents died?"

"Ten."

A wave of sorrow washed over Jane. This poor young man had lost much in his life. No wonder he was taciturn. "Losing your grandmother must make you feel lonely."

He glanced at her, as if surprised she could empathize. "Yeah. Totally."

"I'm surprised you agreed to come along on this trip."

He shrugged. "I thought it would be fun. Didn't think I'd be such a loser." Lynden dragged his hand over his face and gave Jane an apologetic smile. "Sorry if you thought I was stalking your sister, but I like hearing her play."

"I'm glad. I was a little concerned, especially after your accident."

"That freaked me out," he exclaimed. "I thought for sure I'd hurt her or something."

Jane paused, letting his words settle in. "So you were concerned about Louise and not your truck?"

"My truck? Are you kidding? I mean, it's a great set of wheels and all, but hey, I didn't want to think I'd hurt her."

And one more mystery was solved.

"Louise was sure you were worried about it."

"Well, yeah. A bit. After I realized she was okay." He ran his fingers through his hair. "I mean, I got the truck from my granny. Before she died."

"So it reminds you of her then."

"I know it's just a truck. But she gave it to me. Said it was a small thanks for helping take care of her."

"Take care of her . . ." Jane let the sentence trail off, hoping he would finish it.

"When she was sick. I was supposed to go to college, but I canceled and stayed home when she got sick."

Jane felt a moment of shame for the negative thoughts she had harbored about this giving and unselfish young man. Amazing what the correct information could do to make a connection between people.

"You are a very remarkable young man," she said quietly.

"She was a great person. For a grandma, she was pretty cool. Taught me a lot. I miss her." He looked embarrassed. "Don't tell the other guys about this, okay? I don't know if they'd get it."

Jane thought of Matthew, Pete, Herbie and Rick. "I think underneath all that chatter, they're pretty decent guys. You might want to tell them, so they understand where you're coming from."

"I'll think about it." He pulled the book out of his back pocket and pointed it at the front door. "If anyone wants to know where I am, I'll be on the porch. Reading."

"You don't want breakfast now?"

"Nah. I'll wait until the rest come."

"Then enjoy the morning," Jane said. "The day is fresh and new."

He gave her an oblique smile. "Yeah. It sure is."

As Jane made her way back to the kitchen, she felt a shadow lift. In spite of Carita's assurances, she'd had her misgivings about Lynden and his reclusive behavior. Now that she knew what was happening in his life, she could regard him differently.

She whispered a quick prayer for him, creating another connection.

She pulled out her recipe book and turned to the marked page. If yesterday was any indication of when the kids would come down for breakfast, she had time to mix up a few batches of puff pastry. She would use part for the dessert for Stacy's dinner. The rest she could freeze for future use.

As she weighed the flour portions and measured out the water, she wondered if Stacy would call today. Since Jane had agreed to do the dinner for her, it seemed that Stacy called every couple of hours to give updates, ask questions and, in general, create an air of tension. Now that the inn was involved, Jane feared Stacy's calls and concern would only increase.

"Is there anything I can do for you?"

"Goodness, Louise, you startled me." Jane pressed a floury hand to her heart, leaving a white imprint on her yellow shirt.

"Jane, you seem rather jumpy."

Jane narrowed her eyes at her sister and caught a glint of humor in Louise's blue eyes. "I'm concentrating. I have a lot on my mind."

"Is that breakfast you're making? Shall I set the table and get the kettle boiling?"

"Please." Jane put the flour and a small amount of butter in the food processor, but before she pushed the button, she turned to her sister. "Lynden was hanging around the foyer again this morning, listening to you play."

"Again?"

"You don't need to be concerned, Louise. I found out why." Jane craned her neck to look through the door, into the hallway, to see if Lynden or any of the other guests were there, but the hall was empty. "Turns out his grandmother used to play the piano. He is just missing her, and he likes to hear you play."

"Indeed?"

"Yes. His grandmother passed away recently."

"Oh, that poor boy." The genuine sympathy in Louise's voice warmed Jane's heart. "Where is he now?"

"Outside. Reading a book on the porch."

"Do you think it would be a good idea if I joined him?"

Jane shook her head. "I talked to him already. He did say how much he liked your playing. Maybe more music might be the best thing for him."

"Very astute, Jane. I'll do that. And I'll be back to set the table," Louise promised. "So make sure you leave that chore for me."

"Wouldn't dream of taking that away from you," Jane said as her sister left the room. She hit the button on the food processor.

Making puff pastry was time consuming, and Jane could purchase it frozen, but she preferred making the food they served at the inn from scratch. That way she could proudly stand behind the word *homemade* appearing on their Web site and in their brochures.

She rubbed her marble cutting board with ice and wiped off the excess moisture. She rolled out the dough into a cross shape on the board, set the cold butter in the middle, folded the dough over and started rolling, being careful not to let the butter slip out of the cracks.

She folded again, getting lost in the soothing rhythms of the work.

A light knock at the doorway startled her again. It was Carita this time.

"Am I bothering you?" she asked.

"No, no," Jane waved the young woman's concern away with a floury hand. "Come in."

Carita looked pensive.

"Is something wrong?" Jane asked.

Carita merely shook her head, but she wouldn't meet Jane's eye.

Jane continued folding and rolling, occasionally glancing at the young woman. Carita shifted, her elbows resting on the counter, her dark eyes staring off into the middle distance. Jane sensed something was wrong, but she had already given Carita an opportunity; the only thing she could do was wait.

After a few quiet seconds Carita sighed, then turned to Jane. "You ever been in love?"

No light topics this morning, Jane thought.

"Yes. I was. I was married once." Jane thought of her ex-husband Justin. Though Jane had reconciled herself with their marriage break-up, there were times when her mind went back to those first few years, wondering if she could have done something differently.

Carita displayed a puzzled frown. "You make it sound like you didn't love him."

Jane brushed the flour off her rolling pin, then smiled. "I wouldn't have married him if I didn't."

"Have you been in love since?"

"No, but I'm quite content with my life."

"You don't want to get married again?"

Jane thought of some of the men that had slipped in and out of her life since Justin, then shook her head. "I've made a decision to focus my desire on my Lord first, to be content in my circumstances and to thank God every day for all the good things He has given me." She folded the dough over on itself and started rolling again. "I don't want to reject the idea that love might come my way, but for now, as I said, I'm content."

Carita folded and unfolded a napkin in front of her, and Jane could almost see the questions wandering through the young woman's mind.

"This is pretty heavy stuff so early in the morning," Jane said with a light teasing tone in her voice.

"Yeah, well, it's just I don't know what to do."

"About . . ."

Carita put down the napkin and sighed. "Lynden."

The morning had come full circle. "You like him." Jane stated the fact simply.

Carita nodded. "A lot. I've liked him all through high school. Before that even."

I'm on top of my game this morning, Jane thought. *I should hang up a shingle—Advice. Free.*

"You didn't stay in touch when you left for college?"

"I tried, but he stopped writing."

Jane had promised Lynden she wouldn't tell the boys about his grandmother, but would she be stretching her promise if she told Carita?

She weighed the thought, but discarded it. Lynden's loss was not hers to share. But she could possibly help things along a little.

"Do you know why he stopped?"

Carita shook her head.

"Have you asked him?"

"How could I when he wouldn't answer my letters?"

"He's out on the porch," Jane offered, rolling out the pastry one more time. "Everyone else is still in bed. This might be a good time to catch up."

Carita pressed her lips together. "What if he doesn't want me there? His mind isn't on me at all."

"Maybe you might want to find out what his mind *is* on," Jane hinted. "He could have a lot to think about."

"Do you think he'll tell me?"

"If you are old friends? I'm guessing he would."

Carita's expression brightened. "You might be right." She stood up, but just before she left the room she turned back to Jane.

"Just thought I'd let you know I'm getting everyone up in half an hour so that you don't have to make breakfast twice."

"Thanks for the heads-up," Jane said, glancing at the clock. Thirty minutes was not nearly enough time to finish up here, get a breakfast casserole together and bake it.

Scrap that menu item, she thought, thinking on the fly. She'd need something hearty enough yet tasty. Something she could make with ingredients on hand.

She wrapped the pastry dough, and as she set it in the refrigerator, did a quick inventory and came up with bacon, avocado and tomato salsa to make cheese omelets that would be tasty, fiery and full of zippy nutrition. *Just what the growing college students need. And just what the harried innkeeper can make in thirty minutes.*

She pulled out two cartons of eggs, bacon and the rest of the ingredients, and set them on the counter. How much would those kids eat? Better to err on the side of generosity.

Once breakfast was over, she might have time to put the final touches on the menu she and Stacy had decided on, and possibly make what she could in advance.

She also had to get hold of Sylvia Songer to help her develop a theme for the evening. Maybe Craig Tracy, at Wild Things, would be willing to rent some plants to fill some of the corners.

"*Yoo-hoo.*" Aunt Ethel stood behind her, dressed for work. "You're busy already."

"And you're up early," Jane said, surprised at how spry her aunt seemed compared to how tired she had been last night.

"I slept like a log," she exclaimed. "Haven't had such a good sleep in a long time. I think it was all that fresh air and exercise. Is Alice up yet?"

"Not yet," Jane said, taking out a bowl and cracking eggs into it. "But I'm getting breakfast ready for the guests, so I should ask Louise to wake her. What time do you have to be at the worksite?"

"Not for two hours," Ethel said, glancing around the kitchen. "I've got time to do a few chores for you. Do you need anything done?" Ethel fingered the hammer hanging from her pouch. "Any loose nails to be pounded in or something like that?"

Jane had nervous visions of her aunt working her way through the inn, flailing away with her hammer, causing more problems than she could fix. "No, Aunt Ethel. Trust me, everything is just fine."

Ethel's eyes flitted around the kitchen again, as if she didn't quite believe Jane's earnest protestations. "All right then. But keep it in mind, I don't mind pitching in where I can."

"I'll do that, Auntie." Jane prepared ingredients and scraped them into the bowl holding the eggs. She glanced at the clock. If she let the eggs settle, she'd have time to make a batch of biscuits to go with the omelet. And then . . .

"Good morning, Aunt Ethel," Louise said as she entered the kitchen.

Jane started at the sound of her sister's voice.

"You seem on edge," Louise said with a frown.

"I've got people hopping in and out of my kitchen like erratic rabbits," Jane said, a defensive tone creeping into her voice. She didn't want to admit that Louise was right.

"Well, this bunny has come to set the table," Louise said, picking up a tray and removing the place settings from the cupboard. "Which tablecloth do you want me to use?"

"The brown one is fine," Jane said, measuring out flour for the biscuits.

"I believe it's dirty."

"Then use the green one." She didn't mean to let the snappy tone enter her voice, but a questioning lift of Louise's eyebrows showed Jane that her sister was less than pleased with her younger sister's response.

While she added salt to the biscuit mixture she kept one cautious eye on Ethel. Her aunt wandered around the kitchen, testing the walls with her index finger, fiddling with the cupboard doors as if determined to find something loose to tighten or crooked to straighten.

"The table is set," Louise said, returning from the dining room with an empty tray. "When do you think our guests will be eating?"

"Carita said she was going to have everyone down here in thirty minutes. Actually, twenty, now." Jane rolled out the biscuits into a rectangle and instead of using the biscuit cutter, simply slashed the rectangle into squares and dropped them on the greased cookie sheet. She suspected the college group wouldn't notice if the biscuits were round or square or flower shaped.

"Where is Alice?" Louise asked, glancing around the kitchen. "I thought she would be up by now."

"I can go get her," Ethel offered, dropping her hammer back in its hook with a metallic click.

"You just sit down," Louise said. "I'll get you some coffee, and then I'll see what Alice is up to."

"And no weapons at the table," Jane said, pointing her whisk at Ethel's tool belt.

Ethel laughed and unhooked the leather apron, setting it down carefully beside the back door. "Funny how a person gets used to wearing it," she said with all the authority of a full-time carpenter.

Twenty-five minutes later, Alice had meandered downstairs,

the kids were settling in at the dining room table, and Louise and Jane were hustling food back and forth.

Sixty minutes later, the food was gone, the dirty dishes were piled up on the kitchen counter and Jane, Louise, Alice and Ethel were finishing up the last of their own breakfast.

They could hear Carita explaining the rules of the scavenger hunt as they ate.

Jane wondered what Carita and Lynden had talked about, if indeed they had talked at all, but she hadn't had a chance to ask the young woman about what happened. Carita sounded cheerful, though.

Ethel daintily wiped her mouth with a napkin. "That was delicious, as usual, Jane," she said. "I'm sure this breakfast will hold us for the rest of the morning."

"A carpenter's breakfast," Alice agreed.

Jane saw her sister stifling a yawn. Alice looked more tired than Ethel did.

"So, Alice, do you want to do dishes yet?" Ethel said, picking up her plate and bringing it to join the pile of dirty dishes the kids had created.

"I'll take care of the dishes," Jane said. "I'm not planning to go anywhere today."

"I thought you were helping with the scavenger hunt?" Louise asked.

"Carita has that well in hand. I've got enough to do," Jane said.

And as if to underline that comment, the phone rang again. Jane picked it up and the voice on the other end made her clench her teeth.

Stacy. Yet again.

She waved to her sister and aunt as they left. As Stacy expressed still more misgivings about Saturday night and what Jane was going to serve, Jane kept her smile fixed firmly in place while watching Louise clear and scrape and rinse and stack.

Fifteen minutes later she had a new list of marching orders and the beginnings of a headache.

"Everything okay?" Louise asked as Jane forced herself to end the call without shrieking.

Jane flashed her a bright smile. "Just peachy. Just peachy."

Louise's expression told Jane that her older sister was not convinced, but Jane didn't want to listen to another sisterly lecture on how she shouldn't have taken on this job. There was no backing out now.

Ten minutes later the kitchen shone, and Louise was getting ready to leave.

"Are you sure you'll be okay?" Louise asked one more time. "I can certainly skip my course. If the lecturer this morning is anything like the one yesterday, then I'm sure I won't miss much."

Jane answered her sister that all was well. "I just have to do some tidying in the rooms. The laundry is done. Go. Learn about cars." Jane knew her sister would have gladly stayed home to help, but she also knew that her budget-minded sister would want to get her money's worth for a course for which she had already paid.

Louise left and Jane sat at the counter, enjoying the first moment of silence the inn had experienced since she had come downstairs.

She let the quiet settle over her as Wendell padded softly across the kitchen floor and jumped onto an empty chair. He curled up, and the rumble of his purring was the only sound in the peaceful kitchen.

The ringing of the phone cut into the tranquility, and Jane let out a deep sigh.

The person on the other end of the line, however, was Sylvia, Jane's good friend.

"Hey, do you have time to stop by the shop today?" Sylvia asked. "I have some ideas for your dinner."

"I can come in two hours." She had to clean up the bed-rooms and vacuum with Ethel's wheezy vacuum cleaner, which would remind her what the money from Stacy's dinner would help pay for. "Is that soon enough?"

"Absolutely. I'll see you then."

Jane hung up the phone, pushed herself away from the counter and started in on the cleaning for the day.

Chapter Ten

If you look at the pictures of this battery, you can see the posts are full of corrosion," Clyde Gilroy, the instructor of the day, walked over to the screen and pointed to the white coating on the battery terminals. "You want to keep these clean so your battery is charging and discharging to its full capacity."

"Many of the things we are going to be talking about this morning, while basic, are important," Clyde was saying. "We're not going to have you doing engine overhauls, but I will be showing you a lot of preventive maintenance. I want you to feel comfortable around the various parts of the engine. I also believe the best way to learn is to do, and I have a few sets of batteries here for you to work on."

Louise glanced at Viola. This was a new twist and not entirely unwelcome.

"I think we actually might be learning something practical," Viola said, speaking Louise's thoughts aloud.

All the way here, Louise had felt bad about leaving Jane alone, and in spite of Jane's assurances that everything was fine, she saw her sister getting more tense every day.

The only thing Jane had requested of her was that she pick up groceries. Nevertheless, Louise had decided that if the course today was in any way a waste of her time, she would excuse herself and return to the inn.

"So if you don't mind breaking up into groups of two, I'll get each couple to stand at a table."

Louise and Viola paired up. On the table in front of them sat a battery, a few tools, rubber gloves and safety glasses.

"You need to remember that a battery is full of acid," Clyde was saying as he walked up and down in front of the tables. "Any time you work on one, you run the risk of exposing yourself to that acid. That's why you'll be putting on the glasses and gloves."

"This makes me feel right at home," Louise said, rolling her eyes.

Viola looked askance at the large, rectangular car battery squatting on the table in front of them. "At home? Perhaps you need to change the inn's décor."

Louise laughed at her friend's comment.

"The battery posts, as you can see, are encrusted with deposits. These deposits are a natural result of using your car," Clyde was saying, pointing out the green-and-white residue on the posts of a battery in front of Martha Bevins.

Louise stifled a smile at the puzzled look on the elderly woman's face. Louise was sure Mrs. Bevins would have been happier to listen to another lecture.

"When your vehicle and battery are operating, very small amounts of gas are released through the vent cap," Clyde continued. "When released, these fumes naturally combine with the heat, dirt and humidity in the air to form corrosion on your battery cables and terminals. One of the ways to get rid of this deposit is with a wire brush and a mixture of baking soda and water. You have to be careful not to get the mixture inside the battery. Baking soda can neutralize the acid in the battery."

"It's safe if you're careful," Clyde assured the class. "But

having said that, I do want to caution any of you when han-
dling batteries elsewhere to wear protective clothing. Older
batteries can leak and the acid inside can spill onto your
clothes."

"What about pennies for the corrosion," Harvey said, his
voice gruff. "Mechanic I knew used to use pennies."

"I've heard that pennies can actually draw all the corrosion away, using a chemical reaction between the copper of
the penny and the corrosion, but then you need to keep the
penny in place. I believe zinc works better than copper. But
for now we'll concentrate on simply cleaning the battery."

Clyde gave some further instructions, and Louise picked
up the brush and began scrubbing. In less than a minute, the
terminals were spotless.

"Well, now, that wasn't difficult," Louise said.

"And a simple cleaning like this, done regularly, will keep
your battery running well and, by extension, your car. Once
your battery is clean, you want to check how tight the cables
are on the posts. A loose cable can keep a car from starting,"
Clyde said. "You also want to make sure the battery is sitting
snug in its bracket. A loose battery can cause excessive vibra-
tion, which causes more wear and tear than on one that is
properly set." As he spoke, he walked to the side of the room,
heaved a tire up from the floor and rolled it toward the tables
where everyone stood.

"One of you was talking about pennies," he said. "Does
anyone have a penny on them?"

"I've got one." Harvey dug into his pocket and brought
it over to Clyde.

"If everyone could just come over here a minute, I want
to show you something," Clyde said.

When everyone had gathered around, he pointed to the
tire. "How worn is this tire?"

Louise was immediately all ears. Worn tires had been

cited as one of the factors in her accident with Lynden. But she hadn't been able to detect the wear from just looking at them.

"How much wear is left?" Clyde looked around the room. "Anyone?"

Louise was comforted to know that neither Harvey Racklin nor Derek Grollier could give Clyde a confident answer.

"If you don't want to put your trust in a tire store, which is, after all, in the business of trying to part you from your money, you might want to take note of this little trick. You first need a penny." He squatted down. "If you want to know if your tires are worn beyond what is considered safe, simply stick a penny into one of the tread grooves. Make sure you have President Lincoln's head pointing down. If the tread is lower than Lincoln's hair, the tire needs to be replaced. If his hair is covered, like this . . ." he indicated. Everyone moved closer to have a look, and sure enough, nothing could be seen of Lincoln's hair, "then your tires are fine." He pushed himself to his feet and handed the penny to Louise so she could try for herself.

Louise was impressed by this simple fact. Easy to remember and something she could do on her own.

"You have to check all of your tires though," Clyde was saying as Louise handed the penny to Viola, "Tires may wear at a different rate, even if they're on the same vehicle."

Louise made a mental note to write this down. As she straightened, she had to admit she was feeling much better about the course today.

"Correct inflation is also important. I've got my own car sitting outside, so I'd like us all to head out to the parking lot, where I can demonstrate how to use a pressure gauge."

As they followed him into the bright sunshine, he kept talking. "A decrease in tire pressure of only two pounds can affect your gas mileage by four percent. Now that may not seem a lot, but if you add it up, at today's gas prices, that does have a considerable effect."

They gathered obediently around Clyde's car, a midsize sedan, as he pulled out four pressure gauges.

"Mrs. L. Hey, there, Mrs. Louise!"

Louise stiffened, then glanced around to see who might be calling out her name.

Herbie and Isabel were waving at her from the sidewalk. She waved back and Herbie came charging over, Isabel trailing in his bulky wake. Louise excused herself from her group.

"We need your help," Herbie shouted. He was out of breath by the time he reached her. "We need to know who named Acorn Hill," he panted, bent over, resting his hands on his knees.

"We asked the lady who runs the paper, but she didn't know," Isabel offered quietly, standing a ways back from the group. Louise tried to catch her attention to give her an encouraging smile, but the girl kept her head down, looking at the papers she held. She seemed the most reserved of the guests, a complete opposite of her exuberant roommate Carita.

"Is this for the scavenger hunt?" Louise asked.

"Yeah. The one Carita made," Herbie said.

Louise frowned, trying to think. She glanced at Viola who shrugged. "Sorry, I don't remember," she said. "Though you might be able to find that information in the library."

"Yeah. Library." Herbie sucked in a few more deep breaths. "Where's that?"

"Right here." Louise indicated the building behind them.

"Okay. That's good. Who do we need to talk to at the library?"

"Nia Komonos," Martha Bevins put in, her bright smile taking in the two youngsters. "And what is this about a scavenger hunt? What are you hunting for?" Martha asked, obviously more interested in what the kids were doing than discovering correct tire pressure.

Herbie glanced at his list. "We need to talk to Wilhelm at Time for Tea and name a tea, we have to figure out a puzzle at the Coffee Shop . . ."

"Well now, I love puzzles," Martha said brightly. "Maybe I could help."

Louise caught Herbie's panicked glance.

"I think that would be an unfair advantage to the other teams," Louise said, rescuing the young man. "They divided up in pairs, and I'm sure they're not allowed to take anyone from the town along. You would simply have too much knowledge."

"Well now, that might be," Martha said, her smile smug. "I'm sorry I can't help you, though it sounds like fun."

"It is fun, but busy." Isabel rustled through the papers she held. "We should get going, Herbie."

"Yeah. I don't want Matthew to get ahead of us. Thanks, Mrs. L." Herbie waved good-bye, caught Isabel by the arm and hustled her off to the front of the library.

"What a fun bunch of kids," Martha said. "Where did they come from?"

"They are our guests," Louise said. "There are seven of them staying with us."

"Wouldn't that be fun, having all those young people around." Martha's voice held a touch of envy.

Louise thought of the other night. The noise, the busyness and the music that was finally turned off at 11:30 PM. Martha might be singing a different tune if she knew.

Clyde cleared his throat, getting the group's attention. "I'd like each of you to take a pressure gauge . . ."

"Mrs. L, Mrs. L . . ."

Louise sent Clyde an apologetic look and turned in time to see Matthew and Pete rushing toward her.

"More kids?" Martha asked.

"Sorry to bug you, Mrs. L," Matthew said. "We need to find out . . ."

"Who named Acorn Hill?" Louise asked.

He shook his head. "Nah. We're not that far yet, but if you know . . ."

"Sorry. We just sent Herbie and Isabel to the library to find that out," Louise said.

"Rats! But I'm really thirsty. Do you know where I can buy some water?"

"Go to Dairyland," Harvey said, his tone abrupt as if he was eager to get these young people out of their hair. "Down Berry Lane to Village Road. It's across from the Methodist Church."

"Thanks, Mister," Matthew said, giving him a quick salute. "See you at the inn, Mrs. L," he called out as he and Pete jogged off.

"Can we continue?" Clyde asked, tapping a gauge against his palm.

"I'm sorry for the interruptions," Louise said. "Please do. This is really interesting. I'm learning a lot."

She gave her fellow classmates an apologetic look.

"Okay. Tire pressure varies from vehicle to vehicle. You can find the correct pressure in the book that comes with your car, or often the number is printed on a door jamb or in the glove box." The group followed Clyde around his car while he showed them. "In the case of my vehicle, the correct pressure is thirty-two pounds per square inch." He demonstrated how to measure this and then gave each of them an opportunity to try it themselves. "I've got a piece of carpet on the ground, so you won't get your clothes dirty."

Louise glanced at the carpet and then at her narrow, gray skirt. With a shrug, she carefully knelt and pressed the gauge over the valve. Immediately the little white ruler popped up and stopped. "And there we have it," she said to Viola. "Thirty-two pounds."

"I keep hearing a hissing sound, but nothing is happening," Viola complained, fiddling with her gauge.

"You have to make sure you push down hard enough to cover the valve stem," Clyde instructed.

He walked around, making sure everyone understood the procedure, and then gathered up the tools.

"Hello there, Mrs. L," Another young male voice sang out across the parking lot.

Louise caught an annoyed glance from Clyde as Rick and Lynden walked past them. But Rick only waved and carried on. Louise thought of what Jane had told her about Lynden, and called out to them. "How is the hunt going, boys?"

To her surprise, Lynden stopped. "Goin' okay," he called back. Though he sounded less than enthusiastic about the entire expedition, Louise was pleased to see a faint smile on his face.

"Good luck," she called out.

And when she saw Lynden's careful smile, she knew it was worth risking Clyde's annoyance to make this small connection with the young man.

∽

"How are you feeling today?" Ethel asked Alice as they walked over to the building site. "You seem stiff."

Ethel sounded positively gleeful, Alice thought as she carefully adjusted the buckle on her pouch. Alice's arms were stiff. Her legs were stiff. Even her face was stiff. She had discovered muscles in places she had never studied in any anatomy class she had taken. Tiny muscles and big muscles, all of them stiff and sore and complaining with every move she made.

"I'm fine, Auntie," Alice said with a faint touch of pride. She wondered how her aunt managed. Ethel seemed as spry as she had yesterday, her hammer swinging as she strode up the wooden plank leading to the floor of the house. Two men in blue jeans and stained T-shirts were already at work, pounding nails into what looked like a wall section.

"Good morning, ladies," Cal said with a grin. "Glad you showed up today."

Ethel glanced around the quiet site. "Where is everyone else? Why are there so few people?"

"Oh, this happens once in a while," Cal said. "People offer to come, and then something else comes up and they can't make it. I've got Del and Jim setting out the wall section you'll be working on. You'll be doing the same thing you were doing yesterday."

As he spoke, another vehicle pulled up, and Alice was pleased to see June Carter emerge from the car.

Then she did a double take as Florence got out of the other side of the car wearing brand-new coveralls, a white visor, leather gloves and a new leather pouch.

"And it looks like Florence is going to be joining us on the worksite today." Alice gave her aunt a sidelong glance to see her reaction to this news, but Ethel was suddenly fussing with her pouch.

"I better stock up on nails. Don't want to run out." And off Ethel bustled toward the supply shed.

As Florence and June approached, Alice saw Florence frowning as she watched Ethel leave.

Alice had gently prodded Ethel this morning about her tiff with Florence, but couldn't get much out of her aunt. She wasn't quite sure how to deal with this situation. Usually Ethel or Florence would have discovered some vital and fascinating piece of gossip to pass on by now and would have been chatting away like magpies.

"Good morning, Alice," June said as she slipped on her hard hat.

"Good to see you, June. I imagine we'll get started pretty

soon." Alice stretched her arms over her head, trying to work the kinks out and as she did, she caught sight of Cordy walking gingerly up the gangplank to the foundation of the house.

She gave Alice a forlorn look as she came nearer. "I hurt all over," she said.

"So do I. I'm really glad you made it this morning."

"I didn't want to come and my mom told me I could just sleep . . ." She gave Alice a sheepish look. "Then I thought of you ladies coming here, and I figured I better get myself out of bed and get over here. Besides, I had fun yesterday."

"I'm glad to hear that."

As Ethel joined them, Cordy looked around. "Jasmine here yet?"

"Not yet."

Cordy's shoulders straightened. "Cool. I beat her here."

"Very cool," Ethel agreed, putting her arm around her young co-worker. "And once she comes she'll be proud to see you working again."

Cordy sighed. "I hope so. She's been on my case more and more lately. I don't like it that she's mad at me."

"I'm sure your showing up here every day will help," Ethel said, her voice growing soft. She looked down, fidgeting with the pocket of her carpenter's apron.

Alice was about to ask her what was wrong when Cal approached and started giving out instructions.

"So ladies. We're short of workers today," he said, glancing around the gathered group. "I thought today you could all work together. Alice, Ethel and Cordy, you can help these other women out. You'll be doing the same thing today as you did yesterday, only on a larger section, so there'll be enough room for all of you."

He pointed with his hammer to where the men were working. "We guys need to put up another wall, and there's too much bracing in the way for you to work on the floor of the house. Just ask Del what you need to do. He'll get you all started."

He gave them a quick nod and left.

"Aunt Ethel, can you and Cordy show Florence what to do?" Alice asked.

Alice didn't wait to see Ethel's reaction. She thought Cordy's presence could act as a buffer in case Ethel and Florence were still maintaining their campaigns of silence.

How long could they hold out?

"So, Cordy, are you ready to work through the pain?" Alice asked, turning her attention to the girl.

Cordy rolled her shoulder and grimaced. "This morning it hurt even to roll over in bed."

Alice laughed. "I know how you feel."

"Yeah, but you're old . . ." Cordy flashed her a contrite smile. "Sorry, I didn't mean like you were ancient or any-thing like that. Just, well . . ."

"I'm a lot older than you," Alice offered, flashing Cordy a smile to show her that she wasn't insulted at all.

Alice peeked over her shoulder and saw Ethel and Florence trailing behind, each making a point of looking in the opposite direction.

This tiff had to come to an end, Alice thought. Ethel couldn't explain the work in sign language.

Cordy moaned as she lifted a box of nails.

"When you use muscles you normally don't use, a per-son gets stiff. That's just the way the body works. As a nurse, though, I can assure you that once you get working, you'll work out the stiffness."

"I didn't know you were a nurse," Cordy said as she, June and Alice walked over to where Del was waiting.

"Alice works in the hospital in Potterston," June offered.

"Do you like the work?" Cordy asked. "I used to want to be a nurse, but Jasmine said I needed to be smart to do that."

"What are your grades like?"

"They're okay." Cordy said with a shrug.

"What grade are you going into?" June asked.

"Eleventh. But I have to redo some of my courses." Cordy flashed June an embarrassed grin. "The cutting thing is catching up with me."

"Then it sounds like you'll have time to make that up," Alice said.

"I'm trying to turn the corner. But it's hard to break bad habits."

Alice patted her on the shoulder. "It's even harder to get up in the morning and help your sister build her house, but here you are."

"Yeah. I should get my own alarm clock. My mother never wakes me up on time. Jas says I shouldn't lay the blame on Mom." Cordy sighed. "And my friends don't always show up at school. And when they do, they're always trying to talk me into leaving early with them."

"Maybe you need to find people who can be a good example for you."

"I know." Cordy shot her a discomfited look. "Not so easy."

Alice wanted to say more, but Del was waving at them to join the other people already gathered around him.

Del was a squat man and his stomach strained against his soiled T-shirt. "So, you ladies know what to do?" he asked, hitching up his pants.

"Cal told us we would be doing the same thing we did yesterday, so I think we'll be okay," Alice said.

"Good. Have at 'er." He dropped his hammer into his pouch and stalked away, as if he couldn't be bothered to spend much more time with them.

"What a rude man," Florence said while he was still within earshot.

Del glanced over his shoulder, his scowl easily visible.

"Okay. Let's get started," Alice said, preferring to let the exchange pass. "What we have here is, as Cal explained, a wall section—"

"An inside wall?" Florence asked.

"No. We are first putting up the outside walls."

"How odd. There are absolutely no windows on this wall," Florence proclaimed.

Alice waited for Ethel to explain the situation, but her aunt said nothing. "We first tack down the wood, then Aunt Ethel will cut out the windows with a router."

"What in the world is a router?" Florence directed her question to Alice.

Again Alice waited for Ethel to explain, but realized the longer her aunt kept quiet, the ruder she looked. "It's like a small saw with a bit that spins around to do the cutting. You'll see, once we get that far. For now we need to nail down the studs behind the particleboard. Space your nails about a hand's width apart."

"That would be Alice's hand width, not mine." Cordy held her hand up and grinned.

"I believe I can do this," Florence said with a tinge of haughtiness in her voice.

Alice knelt gingerly on the wall section, muscles in her thighs, calves and back protesting. In spite of her reassurances to Cordy, she wondered if she was going to be able to work all day.

Once she started pounding the nails in, however, the stiffness eased off.

"Is your sister coming today, Cordy?" Ethel asked as they started nailing.

"I don't know. The kids might be sick."

Alice watched Cordy working and was pleasantly surprised to see how much more accurate she was with her hammering today than she had been the day before.

"What is your sister's name?" Florence asked.

"Jasmine. Mom got the name off some television show," she said. "I'm named after a character she read in a book. My real name is Cordelia."

"That's a lovely name." Florence knelt down and glanced over at Alice as if to see what she was doing.

Alice pressed her lips together, suddenly frustrated with her aunt. Florence seemed to be trying in her own way, but Ethel wasn't responding at all.

"You don't know how to put the nails in?" Cordy asked Florence.

"Actually, I've never done much manual labor," Florence said. "When I signed up I saw myself as more of a consultant. My specialty is decorating. I like to change the décor of my house every year. I thought I could help your sister in that department. But today I thought maybe I would try the basic work."

"It's not rocket science," Cordy said with a light chuckle. "I can show you what to do."

Alice was pleased that Cordy took the initiative, but of course that wasn't her plan when she had put Ethel and Florence to work together.

Cordy walked over to Florence's side and showed her how to set the nails and how to avoid bending them.

"I did a bunch of that yesterday, but I soon got the hang of it."

Ethel was hammering away like an old pro. *Almost showing off,* Alice thought. *If she isn't careful she is going to hit her finger.*

Florence started working, but Alice saw her struggling. "Is there a trick to this?" she asked.

"Nails go pointy side down, you hit the flat top with the hammer," June offered with a laugh.

But Florence was looking at Ethel as she spoke.

Ethel kept working and didn't look up.

Alice stifled a sigh and started nailing. She was here to

help build a house, not build bridges between Ethel and Florence. They would have to figure out their problems by themselves.

For the next fifteen minutes the only sound was the ringing of hammers hitting nails. Alice was pleased to discover how much easier the work was today. She didn't take nearly as long to pound a nail in, and she hardly ever missed.

"You sure you know what you're doing?" Del stood above them, a dark shadow against the sky.

Alice glanced up, squinting into the sun, but Del was addressing Florence.

"You're supposed to follow the red chalk line, lady," he said, his tone disrespectful as he pointed with one stubby finger. "Don't you know that?"

"I wasn't told . . ."

Alice felt a flash of guilt. She should have explained things to Florence herself and not left it up to Ethel—or Cordy.

"It shouldn't be that hard," Del continued.

"I understand but . . ."

"Here. Let me show you." Del pulled the hammer out of Florence's hands and pounded the nail in with a few swift blows. "That's how we do it here."

"I know how to use the hammer," Florence protested.

Del pointed the toe of his grease-stained work boot at a bent nail. "Doesn't look like it. You maybe should try somethin' else."

At that Ethel looked up, frowning at him.

"Somethin' I can help you with, sister?" Del asked.

"I am not your sister, mister. And don't you talk to me or my friend like we're simpletons. You show some respect."

Del stood with his hands on his hips as if he was about to challenge Ethel.

"You might want to watch yourself," Florence put in. "My friend can take quite good care of herself."

Ethel's lips twitched a bit, and Alice took that as a good

sign. That and the fact the two women referred to each other as "friend."

"Just trying to help, is all," Del said, holding up his hands as if warding off the two women.

"You are not much help," Ethel said. "I think we can manage on our own. And if we can't, Cal can help us out."

"Suit yourself, you two." And Del stormed away, his hammer swinging at his side.

"I hope that nasty man stays away from us," Ethel said. "I can't believe how rude he was."

"I'm sure I could have taken him," Florence remarked.

"The two of us certainly could." Ethel gave Florence a cautious smile.

Florence held her gaze, then, finally, returned the smile.

Alice relaxed, pleased that these two were speaking again. She did find it interesting that it took someone else's berating Florence for Ethel to stick up for her friend.

Chapter Eleven

Jane glanced over her list as she walked down the street to Sylvia Songer's shop. Louise had been willing to take care of the groceries, leaving Jane free to plan for the dinner.

Decorations.

She needed Sylvia's advice on this.

Dishes.

Though Stacy, in one of her many calls, had talked about the possibility of renting dishes, Jane thought she could use her mother's lovely Wedgwood set.

She stopped in front of the Good Apple Bakery and glanced across Hill Street to Craig Tracy's flower shop, Wild Things. He might have some ideas about what to use for the dinner.

She crossed the street and stepped inside the shop, the scent of multitudes of flowers mixed with damp, fresh earth greeting her. A new shipment of houseplants must have arrived.

"Be right with you," she heard Craig call out from the back.

While she waited, Jane wandered around, checking out the new plants. She should get some for the inn, she thought. Some of their other plants were getting root-bound.

"Hello, Jane. Haven't seen you around for a while." Craig came through the door at the rear of the shop, wiping his hands on a small towel, his smile bright and welcoming. The apron he wore over his trim frame had a comical picture of a cartoon flower leaning over to look at itself in a puddle of water.

"I've been busy. Guests in every room of the inn, vacuum cleaners dying, a frantic catering customer and a dinner party to be put on by the hostess with the mostest."

"Ah, the ins and outs of inns."

Jane acknowledged his joke with a groan.

"Lame humor aside, what can I do for you, Jane?"

"For said dinner party, I would like to add a few plants or flowers to the décor. Not too pretty, not too plain, not too . . ." Jane caught herself. Goodness, she was starting to sound like Stacy herself.

"And the theme is . . . ?"

"Food."

Craig gave her a droll look. "Innovative." He put heavy emphasis on the first syllable.

"Please don't make me hurt you," she said, her grin belying the hidden threat in her words.

"So. Plants." Craig rubbed his hands together as if in anticipation of a new challenge. "Tall? Short? Foliage? Joking aside, a theme would help tremendously."

Jane wrinkled her nose. Stacy had provided her with a generous budget, but left the planning on her shoulders. "I'm going over to Sylvia's after this to see what she can help me come up with."

"What type of group are you going to be hosting?"

"The group is part of a Chamber of Commerce twinning program. These women come from towns paired with Potterston. They're coming from Japan, Canada, the Netherlands and New Zealand."

"That's an interesting mix of people," Craig mused, glancing around his shop. "When are they coming?"

"Saturday evening."

Craig whipped his head around. "As in *this* Saturday evening?"

"One and the same."

"That's cutting things very, very close," Craig said.

"Tell me about it. I keep having to change the menu because every time I plan something, my client lets me know about shellfish warnings and obscure allergies and her aversion to pasta."

"We could go with some tall plants in one corner, though if allergies are a consideration we could go with silk . . ."

"As far as I know, no plant allergies," Jane said. "I would prefer real plants."

"I agree. Besides, real plants cleanse the air," Craig said taking an exaggerated sniff. He dug into his apron pocket and pulled out a stub of a pencil and a piece of paper. "Let's make a potential plan," he said.

Twenty minutes later the plan was committed to paper, and Jane was happy with Craig's suggestions. Simple, elegant and not too tropical. They went with small topiaries on the sideboard and down the table with one large one repeating the theme in one corner of the room. They also considered a possible flower arrangement of lilies and ferns to provide some brightening.

"Thanks so much, Craig," Jane said, tucking her version of the plan into her pocket. "This is a good place to start . . ."

The electronic door chime sounded, and Jane turned in time to see Matthew and Pete scurry into the store, glancing behind them as they entered.

"Oh, hey, Ms. J," Matthew said, tossing off a quick salute as he ducked behind a plant, craning his neck to look down the street. "Has Herbie been here yet?"

"I haven't seen him, but ask Craig. He might know."

Matthew gave another quick glance out the window and moved closer to the counter. "He gave me and Pete totally wrong advice. Messed up our stellar record. I'm trying to get even with him but don't know how."

"How are you making out with the game?" Jane asked, not sure she should hear about any scheming he and Pete might be indulging in.

"Like I said, we got sidetracked. But we're getting close." Matthew tucked a pen behind his ear and pulled out a sheaf of papers he had rolled up and stuffed in the back pocket of his baggy jeans. "So according to this, we're supposed to talk to Mr. Tracy." Matthew glanced up from his notes, "I'm guessing that would be you," he said to Craig.

"Would be," Craig agreed.

Matthew sighed as he tapped his pen on the paper. "I gotta tell you, Carita has some weird idea going of a scavenger hunt. I thought we'd, like, be picking up stuff. You know?"

"Maybe she's trying to get you to expand your minds," Jane said.

Pete looked up, frowning. "Can't do that. My hats won't fit then."

Jane laughed. "I'm sure you'll do just fine, and I better get going," Jane said, slipping past the boys. "Thanks for your help, Craig."

"No problem, Jane. I'll be by with the plants and the arrangements on Saturday."

As Jane left, Matthew and Pete were peppering Craig with questions, and Jane had to smile. Carita had been absolutely correct. These boys did truly seem to be enjoying themselves doing something as innocent as a scavenger hunt. She was glad they had taken the time to put it together.

From the sound of Carita's plans, the group would be busy most of Friday. Then there would be the football game and come Saturday they would be gone all day. Then Jane would have the afternoon to prepare for the dinner, do the dinner and then collapse. But next would come Sunday morning, a time of rest. First thing, the kids would leave. And then a reprieve until Wednesday when the next guests arrived.

When Jane entered Sylvia's shop, her friend looked up from the bolts of cloth she had laid out on a large cutting table for the perusal of a couple of customers. Alongside the bolts was a vast array of squares for quilting, also in a rainbow of colors.

Today Sylvia wore a plain, white T-shirt with a cropped jacket in a unique material. Jane guessed Sylvia had done some fabric painting to achieve the watery effect on the surface of the jacket.

Very cute and very stylish, Jane mused.

"Be right with you, Jane," Sylvia said, glancing at her friend over her reading glasses, her reddish-blonde hair swinging away from her face.

"No worries," Jane said.

Jane recognized the women gazing at the material as members of the local quilters guild. They fingered the delicately patterned fabric, frowned over some choices, aahed over others and in general looked like they were thoroughly enjoying themselves.

While they debated fabric quality and color, listening intently to Sylvia's suggestions, Jane ambled through the store, checking out the newest quilt that Sylvia had completed. She had hung it up for display alongside a couple of Amish quilts she had picked up the last time she had gone to Lancaster.

Jane didn't sew quilts, but as an artist she could appreciate the way Sylvia had arranged the material to set off colors and patterns creating a harmonious grouping. As Jane let the symphony of colors wash over her, she had a momentary urge to take up quilting.

Too many projects, too little time, she thought with a wistful glance at the intricate work of the quilts. Life was too short to do all the things she would like to try.

Sylvia chatted with her customers as she cut and folded, discovering what they were working on and, in the process, finding out about their children and grandchildren.

She has that knack, Jane thought. Though in many social circumstances Sylvia could be somewhat shy and diffident, here in her shop she shone.

The women left, awash in smiles and good humor, their shopping bags rustling.

"And there go two completely satisfied customers," Jane said, as the door closed behind them.

"I love it when a customer knows what she is talking about, yet is willing to take some advice," Sylvia said, rolling up the rest of the fabric on the bolts. "These ladies are avid quilters, so that's great." While she chatted, she hustled from shelf to table, putting back material, sorting out the samples into neat piles and arranging them once again in the boxes they had come from.

When she was done, she picked up her tape measure and slung it back around her neck. "I feel like I haven't seen you in ages," she said,

"I stopped by the other day," Jane protested.

"I know. I'm just trying to tease you," Sylvia said, leaning on the fabric table. "So how is the scavenger hunt going? That's today, isn't it?"

"No one has been by here yet?"

Sylvia shook her head. "Not yet. What clue did you end up giving them?"

"They were supposed to figure out that they had to come here from reading the words of a song that Carita had scrambled up."

Sylvia frowned. "What song would that be?"

"'Needles and Pins.'" Jane said.

"Of course."

"Can you spare some time?" Jane inquired. "Remember I asked if you would be willing to help me do some decorating for this dinner?"

"I'm all yours."

"I was just at Craig's. We are going with small topiaries down the table, rather than more formal centerpieces, the same topiaries on the buffet and one large one as a corner display."

Sylvia thought for a moment, her eyes flitting around her shop, as if looking for inspiration in the myriad colors and textures surrounding her.

"I think you will want to keep things reasonably simple. You only want to create atmosphere for your dinner, not overwhelm it."

Jane and Sylvia discussed a few options, working in the flowers that Craig was supplying and the larger purpose of the dinner.

In the end they decided to go with an eclectic theme. The tablecloth would be a rich brown, set off with a gold linen runner. Sylvia had a variety of napkin rings she had collected over time, some in china, some bamboo, some in wood and some made from brushed metal as well as napkins made from different, patterned fabrics. Each place setting would be unique, but the dishes would tie everything together as would the place cards decorated with stamps from various countries.

As they talked and planned, Jane could visualize the setting and grew more excited about the evening.

"What are you going to serve?" Sylvia asked.

At that, Jane's excitement became edged with a hint of panic. "Every time I think I have a sure-fire, can't-miss menu Stacy calls and moves the target. So for now, I have three desserts picked out, a salad and possibly a soup or two. But for the main course, to tell you the truth, I'm stumped."

Sylvia frowned. "This isn't like you, Jane."

"I know, I know." Jane pressed the palms of her hands against the side of her head as if restraining her racing thoughts. "I am trying not to feel the pressure. I wish she wasn't paying me so much money. If this were just a simple catered dinner, I would feel far more comfortable. As it is, I feel like I'm not just serving a dinner. I'm putting on a production."

Sylvia patted Jane's arm. "Don't put too much stress on yourself. This woman obviously wanted you badly enough. You'll do a fine job. Just go with your instincts."

"I've been trying to, but she wants a dinner that isn't too 'out there' or too plain, or too simple. No fish, no potatoes, no hamburger—as if I would—and easy on the onions." Jane shook her head. "I can handle all of that, but she phones me constantly."

"I imagine having so many guests at the inn doesn't help."

Jane smiled. "They're not difficult to have around . . ."

"Finish that sentence, my friend," Sylvia said.

"Well, they do tend to take over the place," Jane conceded.

"I suppose they can be very boisterous."

"Emphasis on very," Jane agreed. "Oh well, tomorrow they have their pep rally, and they'll have lots to keep them busy on Saturday."

"Giving you time to concentrate on your dinner."

"Precisely. And I thank you for your help. At least the inn will look warm and welcoming."

"You'll do fine. I'll come by Saturday morning to help you get things ready."

"That would be lovely," Jane said. She glanced at her watch and gathered her lists. "I better run. Alice will be tired when she comes home, and Louise has a couple of extra piano students today, so I want to provide them with a meal that will replenish their strength."

"Their vigor will be completely restored, I'm sure."

With her friend's assurances ringing in her ears, Jane left. By the time she got back to the inn, she was ready to sit for a few moments before she had to work on supper.

She paused at the garden, mentally choosing which vegetables she could use for Stacy's dinner. String beans with fresh herbs? Too provincial. Carrots. Glazed and honeyed. She could make something with her own tomatoes, cucumbers and lettuce, but that sounded too plain too.

She knelt to pull a weed, found another and yanked it out, then tossed it aside. As she picked, she felt her fluttering nerves relax. A hymn came to mind, and as she entered the inn a short time later, the song was on her lips. She set her list on the kitchen table and became aware of the sound of voices coming down the hallway from the living room.

"I'm just saying this seems pointless." Lynden seemed agitated.

"It's just fun, Lynden. Nothing more," Carita was saying. "We're all going to be diving back into our studies in a couple of weeks. Surely some time off is appropriate."

"And that's the problem. Our whole lives are centered on fun and entertainment. We don't even take school seriously."

Jane felt sorry for Carita. She knew the girl cared for Lynden, and it sounded like they were having a fight.

Jane wondered if she shouldn't leave. But just as she was about to retreat, the voices came closer, toward the kitchen.

"You didn't used to take school seriously," Rick said. "And you didn't even go this year. What's the big deal now?"

"Maybe I've seen what a waste my life has been," Lynden was saying. "Maybe I want something different."

And suddenly they were in the kitchen with her.

Lynden was the first one in, and he stopped short when he saw Jane, Carita almost running into him.

"Sorry, Ms. Howard. I didn't know you were here,"

Lynden said, pushing his hands into the pockets of his leather jacket.

"Sorry, I . . . uh . . . was just going."

"This is your place," Carita said, brushing past Lynden, Rick in her wake. "We're the ones who should feel bad."

"Would you like something to drink? Some soda? Tea?" Jane felt a little awkward in the situation, but Rick seemed completely at ease as he dropped his lanky frame into a kitchen chair.

However, Jane was the hostess and they were her guests. She had to do what she could to make them feel comfortable.

"Thanks, Ms. J. I'll have a soda," Rick said.

"Rick, for goodness' sakes, Ms. Howard isn't here to serve us hand and foot," Lynden said, frowning at his friend.

Rick held his tattooed hand up in a gesture of surrender. "She offered."

"Yes, but . . ."

"I wouldn't offer if I didn't mean it," Jane assured him. "Now, please sit down while I get you something to eat and drink."

Carita held back a moment, then finally walked over to the table and sat down, her arms crossed tightly over her chest.

Jane thought of the conversation she and Carita had enjoyed, when Carita had said how much she liked Lynden. Well, it seemed the romance was not prospering. They sat as far away from each other as they could, not making eye contact.

Rick tapped out a rhythm on the table, bobbing his head in time to a tune only he seemed to hear, oblivious to the waves of animosity swirling around him.

"So, Rick and Lynden, you guys must have finished quickly?" Jane said, trying to make small talk as she pulled out the cinnamon buns she had planned on serving tomorrow for breakfast.

"Can I help you?" Carita asked.

"Could you put out the soda and glasses please?" Jane asked.

Carita set everything on the table and then sat down, folding her arms over her chest once again, looking put out.

Rick shrugged as he poured his soda. "Lynden quit. Said it was lame. I thought it was fun. But he's my partner so I go where he goes. He quits, I quit."

"Oh, that's too bad."

"I thought so too," Carita said, shooting Lynden an angry glance. "The hunt was supposed to be for fun."

"And like I said, I think we look for too much fun," Lynden returned quietly. "I'm sorry, Carita. I don't want to be a poor sport."

"I couldn't help overhearing what you were discussing earlier," Jane said, realizing she may as well be up front about what she had heard. "I'm just curious about what you mean, Lynden?"

He pulled in a deep breath, as if trying to decide what to say. "This whole trip was a good idea, that's true enough, and I really appreciate what Carita is doing . . ."

That should make Carita feel somewhat better, Jane thought.

"But the past few days I've been thinking—"

"Always a dangerous proposition," Rick said with a grin as he lifted his glass.

"—and it seems there's no point to what we're doing with our time. We spend money on ourselves, we buy all the newest toys—"

"Like that sweet unit parked outside?" Rick asked with a faint note of cynicism. "What did that set you back?"

"The truck was a gift from my grandmother. But don't kid yourself that it hasn't been on my mind. I feel like I've been wasting my life. Like all I've been doing is trying to find some meaning, some purpose to why I'm here." He shrugged and shot a pained look Jane's way. "I don't know anymore."

"So this is really about you, then," Carita said, relief edging her voice.

"Yeah. I guess."

"And your grandmother?" Carita continued.

Lynden took a can of soda and ran his finger down the side, making a line in the condensation. "She had such high hopes for me. Such big plans. Then when she died, she left me all that money, left me her house. And I guess I went overboard. I went out every night and blew money. When you phoned me about this trip, I thought it was a great idea." He gave a short laugh. "Except for the place you wanted to stay and all. I was all for going to a motel. I wanted to party."

"Instead you ended up here with a bunch of old women," Jane said with a light laugh to show him she was joking.

"Not proud of that comment, either," Lynden said, lifting his gaze to meet hers.

Jane's smile granted him absolution as she brought the plate of cinnamon buns, some extra plates and knives to the table, then decided while she was there, she could start working on the desserts for the dinner.

"So what made you change, dude?" Rick asked, absently scratching the back of his tattooed hand.

"The music Mrs. Smith played," Lynden said quietly. "My grandmother used to play the piano too. Same songs. As soon as I heard them, they came back. Words and everything. And it was like looking at myself through my granny's eyes. I didn't like what I saw." He fell quiet, his focus on the can of soda in front of him.

"And now?" Jane asked after a few moments of silence.

"I don't know what I want. I feel like I'm just marking time."

"That's why you thought this whole scavenger hunt was a waste of time?" Carita asked.

Lynden shot her a pained expression. "I'm sorry. It's just, I feel frustrated. That's why I couldn't finish."

"What was the prize?" Rick asked. "I mean, if there was a really cool prize attached, I could get seriously ticked off about missing out."

"Just some tickets to a movie," Carita said. "More entertainment."

"What were you thinking of going to college for, Lynden?" Jane asked, directing the conversation back to the young man's problem. While she asked, she measured out the ingredients for one of the desserts for Saturday, Nanaimo bars, trying to juggle making conversation and concentrating on her recipe.

"See, that's the problem. I've just registered for some general courses. Just filling time."

"Do you know what you would like to do?"

"Not a clue."

"Not knowing makes making a decision more difficult," Jane agreed. "I wish I could give you some solid advice, but I know I wasted a few classes myself in my time. Like you, I'm not proud of that either."

"But you do good work here," Lynden said. "You and your sisters. I read what you had put on that plaque in the front."

"'A place where one can be refreshed and encouraged, a place of hope and healing, a place where God is at home.'" Jane smiled as she repeated the motto. "My sisters and I strive to live up to that every time guests come here. When I was your age, however, running an inn was hardly in my long-term plan. There was a time when all I wanted was to make a big success out of my life. To be famous for my cooking."

"What happened?" Rick asked.

"Life. Disappointments. I returned here feeling a bit bitter and disillusioned. But God granted me healing through my sisters and through my community and my church, and I thank Him every day that He brought me back here to find my purpose."

Silence greeted this comment, and Jane wondered if maybe she had come across too strong. But the faint smile hovering at the corner of Lynden's mouth made her realize she might have said exactly the right thing.

"That's your church next door?" Lynden asked.

"Yes. My late father preached there. He taught me a lot."

"Your dad preached too?"

Jane nodded.

"I went to church all the time when my dad was preaching," Lynden said, a surprising note of wistfulness in his voice. "After he and Mom died, my granny used to take me till she was too ill. Then I quit going too."

"We could go to church here instead of leaving first thing Sunday morning," Carita suggested. "Isabel didn't want to leave so early anyway."

"Could." Lynden just looked thoughtful.

"And Saturday? We're still going to the reunion?"

"I don't know," Lynden said.

"I'd just as soon not do it," Rick said, brushing the crumbs off his hand.

"Are you guys kidding me?" Carita asked. "The reunion was the main reason we came out here."

Jane kept the smile on her face even as her heart plunged as plans were changed on the fly. But what could she say? These young people were their guests and if they wanted to change their plans, she couldn't really say much.

But she also had the dinner for Stacy on Saturday night. How could she juggle the two? She simply had to find a way to make sure they were out Saturday evening.

"Hey, ho, we're the winners!" Pete and Matthew's voices rang out as the front door slammed shut behind them. "We get the prize . . ."

But their voices faded away as they entered the kitchen and saw Lynden, Carita and Rick sitting at the table.

"Or not," Matthew said, scratching his head. "How did you guys get ahead of us?"

"They didn't finish," Carita said with a heavy sigh.

"Well, we are the winners then, cause we snuck past Herbie and Isabel still trying to figure out the menu at the Good Apple." Matthew exchanged high fives with Rick. "Number one, mister." He turned to Jane. "What are you working on?"

Jane glanced down at the chocolate mixture she was pressing into the pan. "Something called Nanaimo bars. They're for the dinner I'm having here tomorrow night," she added, just in case he might think they were going to be the recipients.

"Too bad," he said with a sigh. "But I'm sure we can find something else. There's always lots of food at Grace Chapel Inn," he said flashing a winning smile at Jane.

Chapter ⵀ Twelve

Louise checked over the list of groceries and other items that Jane had asked her to pick up after her course, double-checking to make sure she had purchased everything.

Some of the items seemed rather exotic, but Jane knew what she was doing. The rest of the list was straightforward, though Louise hoped that the containers of milk and the yogurt she had purchased were meant for their young guests. There was no way she and her sisters could gulp their way through that ocean of dairy produce.

She had originally planned on walking to the auto course and taking their pull-along grocery cart, but when Jane handed her the list, Louise did a double take and took her Cadillac instead.

She and Viola had been pleased with what they learned in the course, but Louise was less than optimistic about tomorrow. They were supposed to be learning about the care and feeding of windshield wipers. Viola had talked about not attending, but Louise was growing more dedicated. She was determined to learn something useful, one way or the other.

They were slated to do some actual driving on Monday with an instructor beside them to give them pointers and tell them what they might be doing wrong. Louise felt somewhat nervous about that, but at the same time, it was what she had signed up for.

Satisfied she had everything on the list, she got in her car and drove back to the inn. She would have time to help Jane before she had to go to the church to go over the songs she had chosen for Sunday's service.

As Louise gathered what bags she could and carried them to the house, she looked forward to a few moments of quiet with Jane. It seemed that since the college students had arrived, she and her sisters hadn't had much time to sit and go over the events of the day together.

When she set the grocery bags down on the floor of the porch to open the kitchen door, instead of silence she heard people talking. Lynden, Rick and Carita she figured, recognizing the various voices.

Louise stifled a sigh as she opened the door and carried rustling plastic bags into the kitchen. No sooner had she set the bags on the counter, than Lynden jumped up from the table where he sat with Carita and Rick.

"Would you like us to help, Mrs. Smith?" he asked.

Louise was about to say no when she caught Jane's pained look, and right behind her sister she spotted a pan of some dark substance on a cooling rack, probably the same something that was filling the air with a burnt smell.

Though it went against her concept of hospitality to have her guests do any chore, however small, she guessed Jane wanted a few moments alone with her.

"Thank you, Lynden," Louise said. "There are more bags in my car. Maybe the others could help too."

"Sure. Of course." Carita called out to Matthew to come and help, and Rick followed Lynden outside. As the door closed behind them, Louise hurried to her sister's side.

"What is the matter, Jane?"

Jane cast a quick look past Louise as if to make sure the

kids were out of earshot. "They're changing their plans constantly," she whispered, panic edging her voice. "Sounds like they might not be gone all day Saturday . . ." Jane's dejected expression clearly showed her turmoil.

"And you have a dinner to prepare, and they've been hanging around the kitchen all afternoon."

"I was going to make Nanaimo bars, especially for the Canadian women, but I burnt them."

"That's understandable," Louise said, consoling her sister. "Easy enough to do." Louise had burned enough things in her life to allow her to envision how that could happen.

"But they're a no-bake bar." Jane bit her lip, looking distraught. "I can't concentrate. I keep losing track of ingredients. I keep forgetting where I am in the recipe."

"You're under stress, Jane." Louise shook her head. "You never should have—"

Jane held up one finger. "No. You're not going to say it."

"All right, then I'll say this. We can all help on Saturday, Jane. Maybe find a way to keep the kids busy in case they change their plans."

But Jane's skeptical look showed Louise how much confidence she had in that course of action.

"Here you go," Matthew led the troupe, all of them carrying bags. "Do you want us to put this stuff away?"

"No. I can take care of the rest."

"Maybe it's time to try to find Isabel and Herbie?" Jane suggested with a hopeful note in her voice.

"Yeah. Sounds like a plan. Tell the losers they can quit now," Matthew said with a grin.

As they left, Jane settled back against the counter, rubbing her forehead. "I'm trying not to get flustered. Sometimes I wish I had been firmer in setting boundaries, but we always wanted the inn to be a place of refuge and peace. I've always hoped I could model the Lord to our guests."

"And you have," Louise assured her. "These kids love

being in the kitchen because they feel at home, and they feel welcome here. As for the dinner, it will all work out. I think you need to relax, trust your own instincts."

Jane gave her sister a smile. "Thanks for the pep talk, Louise. You're right. I've faced bigger problems when I was at the Blue Fish Grille in San Francisco. I can do this."

"Of course you can." Louise's gaze slipped past Jane to the clock on the wall. "I better go. I need to go over my songs for Sunday."

"And I need to try once again to make these Nanaimo bars," Jane said as she started unpacking the groceries. "At least Stacy and I have that part of the menu figured out."

"What are you having?" Louise couldn't help asking.

"It's quite innovative, really. Kumara soup from New Zealand and miso soup from Japan for starters, followed by a spinach and strawberry salad. Dessert will be Nanaimo bars invented in Nanaimo, British Columbia, something called stroop waffles or treacle cookies from Holland and apple galette, which is more French than anything, but I figured it didn't hurt to try to be as cosmopolitan as I can."

"And the entrée?"

Jane shrugged. "I haven't come up with anything that strikes any chord with Stacy. Though I'm leaning toward something Asian and, well, adjustable on the fly. Hence the special groceries on your list."

"I think you might be trying too hard to please this woman," Louise said.

"She's paying me such a large sum of money to do this, I feel like I have to give her as much say as possible."

"Still, if you are going to get this dinner under control, you'll just have to trust your own instincts and maybe even be a bit firmer with her."

While Louise spoke the telephone rang. Jane picked it up, said hello and when she winced, Louise knew who was calling.

Louise gathered her music from the parlor and exited out the front door. She wished she could help Jane. She was no cook, but she could pray. So as she walked to the chapel, she sent up a prayer for patience and forbearance for her sister.

And later, in the church, while her fingers drew songs of praise and thanksgiving from the keys of the pipe organ, she wove additional prayers for her sister through the songs.

∽

"Are you sure you're not too tired?" Ethel asked as she and Alice made their way back to Alice's car.

"Actually, I'm feeling pretty good." Alice glanced back at the worksite, pleased to see what they had accomplished. Three exterior walls were up and braced. One of those walls was one she, Ethel and Cordy had worked on yesterday.

Ethel yawned as she slipped into the car. "Too bad we had to quit early today," she said. "I would like to have seen those men put up another wall."

"And it sounds like they won't be back tomorrow," Alice said as she started the car. "I know Jasmine was disappointed to hear that."

Jasmine had come by the worksite later in the day. She had been inordinately pleased to see her little sister there, and Alice was glad Jasmine took the time to tell Cordy so.

Cordy beamed the rest of the day.

"I wonder if it's worth coming tomorrow if it's only going to be us women and Cal," Ethel said. "Florence may not be able to make it either."

"Speaking of Florence, I was glad to see the two of you make up."

Ethel nodded, looking rather discomfited.

"If I may play the part of a nosy niece, what was your disagreement about?" Alice turned onto the highway, settling into an easy speed. They had some distance until Acorn Hill and therefore had time to chat. She tuned the radio to a classical station for a comfortable ambiance, but kept the volume low.

"I feel foolish about our spat now," Ethel said, crossing her arms. "You know the saying, there's no fool like an old fool. Well, that sums me up just dandy. However, I wasn't the only one at fault. Florence didn't make things much easier. As I said before, she can be very opinionated. And very stubborn." Ethel stopped there and looked out her window.

The green hills slipped past them as Alice drove toward home. She waited, sensing that while Ethel wanted to talk about the problem, she also had her pride. The confession would have to come on her own time.

A mile later, Ethel sighed, took a breath and turned to Alice.

"Do you remember the day I brought you the vacuum cleaner? The day yours quit?"

Alice nodded.

"Florence had invited me to her place that morning. I thought we were going to have a cup of tea and chat about, well, things. I wanted to ask her opinion of a tie I was planning to buy Lloyd. And I had just found out that Nia had told Carlene that she had heard Patsy Ley saying that when she was in the Good Apple Bakery, Clarissa had told her that Betsy Long had gone on a date. With a man in Potterston. So naturally I thought Florence might have some more information because she had told me, when she got her hair done at the Clip 'n' Curl, that Rose Bellwood had said Ned Arnold had been in Potterston that same evening at the same place."

Alice tried to follow Ethel, but got lost in the Good Apple Bakery and was content to let her aunt meander along. Alice would catch up sooner or later.

"But when I got to Florence's ready to have a good chat, she told me she wanted me to help her carry some things up to her attic. Now Florence is a good friend and all, but I thought making someone my age tote stuff was taking advantage of our friendship, and I told her so. I understand that maybe she can't always get people to help her. She's hired women from time to time to help her clean her house, but I suspect that they just get tired of Florence's sharp tongue, and I don't blame them. Florence sometimes lets her mouth run off on her, and you can try to tell her and tell her, but she won't listen."

"I understand the feeling," Alice said.

"Oh, you don't know Florence like I do," Ethel said, wagging her finger for emphasis. "Anyhow, I told her that my arthritis was acting up and that I didn't think it was right to take advantage of our friendship."

"And that was what the fight was about?" Alice said, underlining the point.

"Not really a fight. More of a disagreement."

"But you carried it on for a while."

"When she found out I was going to work on this Habitat job, she phoned and asked why I was more than able to help with this house, but wasn't able to help her with her attic. And I said some things are more important." Ethel turned to Alice. "I didn't mean for it to come out the way it did, but you know me. Sometimes what's in my head doesn't always come out in my words. Well, she took offense in a big way. I tried to make things up to her, but she wouldn't let me, and that made me mad."

And around and around it went, Alice thought, *Florence ignoring Ethel, which got Ethel's back up, which made her ignore Florence.* But all Alice said was, "I was glad to see you stand up for her this afternoon."

"When I heard that man pushing Florence around, I got angry. That's all."

"Well, your defense seemed to be just what was needed to break the tension," Alice said. "She seemed very pleased that you were willing to intervene."

"I'm glad I did. Because when we started talking again, after I grilled her all about Betsy Long and her date, I found out why she wanted me to carry stuff to her attic. Seems she had a lot of items she wanted me to have but was afraid that if she out and out gave them to me, I'd be upset." Ethel sat back and blew out a breath. "And in spite of how angry Florence can make me, I realized I probably make her angry too. Not a good thing to see yourself like that. I like to think I'm easy to be with and easy to get along with."

"And you are, Auntie," Alice assured her, laying her hand on Ethel's arm for emphasis. "It's just that you and Florence, well, you have a complicated relationship. But I'm glad that you made up. I'm sure she missed your friendship too."

"I know I missed her. But we're working together now, and that's nice."

"As you said earlier, it might not be worth going tomorrow," Alice said as she made the turn off the highway toward Acorn Hill. "I guess I could phone Cal in the morning to see."

"That would be too bad. The house is really coming along. And Cordy's shown up two days in a row now. I'm sure Jasmine will be pleased to see that kind of progress in her little sister. Wouldn't be good for her to lose the momentum."

They pulled into the inn lot, and Alice parked the car beside Louise's Cadillac.

"How long are those students going to be around?" Ethel asked as she slowly got out of the car.

"They've got their rally tomorrow, some activities planned for Saturday during the day and evening, and then they're gone first thing Sunday morning."

"That will be nice for Jane if they are busy all day Saturday," Ethel said. "She'll have time to work on her dinner."

"She has been troubled about it. I wish she hadn't taken the job, but she wanted to make sure we could add to our funds and afford to buy a new vacuum cleaner."

"Well, that's just silly. I mean, you girls are more than welcome to use my vacuum cleaner as long as you need to."

Not exactly a long-term solution, Alice thought.

"My goodness, I didn't think seven kids could generate this much noise." Ethel raised her voice as she and Alice entered the kitchen. "I thought the worksite was loud, but this is way worse."

Alice had to agree.

"Well good afternoon, Ms. A, Aunt Ethel," Matthew said, looking up from the plate of cinnamon buns he was putting together. "You fine ladies are just in time to see what kind of culinary masterpiece I've concocted today."

"He didn't make them," Herbie protested, trying to filch one as Matthew walked past him. "Ms. Jane did."

"Would you like some tea, coffee, soda?" Carita asked, setting plates out on the table. "Isabel, we'll need two more plates," she called out.

Alice looked around at the bodies draped over kitchen chairs and was surprised Jane had allowed things to get this far.

"I'd love some tea," Alice said.

"Nothing for me, thank you." Ethel stretched.

"Here. Sit down." Lynden got up from his chair, and poked Pete who jumped up from his, offering it to Ethel, then perched himself on the kitchen counter.

"You're back early," Jane said, bringing the butter dish to the table.

"We ran out of workers." Alice accepted the plate from Matthew, on which rested a large cinnamon bun.

"Don't sit on the counter, Pete," Carita said, giving him a light hit on his shoulder.

"How do you run out of workers?" Pete asked Alice as he made a face at Carita, but slid off the counter and moved to a chair anyway.

"Not as many people came out as yesterday. The work is

strictly volunteer, so I guess that happens at times." The scent of warm cinnamon made Alice reach for her bun.

"Are you going tomorrow?" Lynden stood beside the table, leaning against the wall.

"I think Ethel and I will go. Cordy, the sister of the lady who will be getting the house, is going to show up, so we'll see what we can do with the three of us. And Cal, the supervisor. I'm pretty sure he'll be there. Maybe some more people will come, but Cal wasn't optimistic. He said Fridays are always a bad day."

"So can anyone just come?" Lynden asked. "Don't you need to have some experience?"

"It is helpful," Ethel said before Alice had a chance to reply. "I had quite a bit before I went to work on this project."

Alice didn't contradict her aunt, though Ethel's misadventure with the tool shed hardly counted as "quite a bit" of experience.

"I didn't have any, and I managed okay," Alice added just so they wouldn't get the wrong impression of what was required. "They are allowing some latitude on this project."

Lynden looked thoughtful, and Alice wondered what was going through his mind.

"So, Carita, what's up for tomorrow?" Pete asked, licking some icing off his fingers.

"I had planned a tour of Lancaster County."

Herbie pretended to snore loudly and Carita gave him a quelling look.

"Well, really, Carita. I bet it's all cultural and interesting, but kinda . . ." Matthew lifted his hands, as if he didn't know how to finish the sentence.

"Okay, okay, I get the message," Carita said, a sharp tone edging her voice. "Lynden was just talking about how so much of what we do is silly—"

"I didn't mean to offend anyone," he said.

"I thought we could do something more cultural. But I

guess that was a waste of my time. And I suppose now that we're at it, Saturday's plans will get canceled too. I honestly don't know why I bother." She got up, stuffed her papers into her bag, swung it over her shoulder and stalked out of the kitchen leaving behind a quietly stunned group.

Alice had to force herself to stay in her chair and not follow the obviously distraught young woman. Her sisters often teased her about being too involved with their guests.

But when she caught a glimpse of the pitying look on Jane's face, she realized she wasn't the only one concerned about Carita.

Matthew sighed. "Okay, guys, I guess we should go on this Amish thing."

Lynden pushed himself away from the wall and left the kitchen too.

"Bit of a downer," Rick said, scratching his tattoo. "So what do we do now?"

"Well, we got the tailgate party and a flag football game tomorrow night, so that's all good," Matthew said. "So we won't have to be on that tour all day."

"As long as we're back in time for the alumni barbecue, I'm good," Herbie said.

"And what about Saturday?" Isabel asked.

"We're going, aren't we?" Herbie asked.

"We better. That was the reason we came," Pete said, yanking his hat farther down his head as if emphasizing his point.

"Well I'm hungry, so I'm going to head to that Coffee Shop place and get some food." Matthew glanced around the kitchen. "Rest of you game?"

"Food is good," Herbie said. "Once we've got food in our stomachs, we can figure more stuff out."

As they left, Alice could feel the momentary tension ease.

"That was too bad." Ethel said. "I thought those kids all got along so well."

"They usually do, which is good to see," Jane said, leaning her elbows on the counter. "I think Lynden is frustrated about something, however, and doesn't know what to do about it."

Alice remembered what Jane had said about Lynden's grandmother. "Do you suppose he's still grieving?"

"I'm sure he is," Jane replied, "But he seems at a loss about his life in general. It sounds as if he has money, but no purpose."

"Which is interesting," Alice said. "We like to think money will solve problems, when, in fact, it creates its own problems."

"But money does buy vacuum cleaners."

Alice waved her sister's comment away. "I wasn't trying to make a point at your expense, Jane."

"I know. But I am. I just hope the kids don't figure on hanging around here tomorrow if they can't agree to go on that tour."

"Why don't we take them to the site tomorrow?" Ethel asked. "That Lynden boy seemed like he might enjoy it."

Alice glanced over at her aunt. "I suppose we could. I don't know if all of them would be interested."

"Interested in what?" Louise entered the kitchen, carrying a bundle of music books.

"The kids don't have anything definite planned for tomorrow, and Aunt Ethel suggested they come to help on the Habitat site," Alice said.

"Marvelous idea," Louise said heartily. "I am positive they would enjoy that, and it would keep them busy."

"Sounds to me like you want to get rid of our guests, Louie," Jane teased.

Louise fiddled with the chain of her reading glasses. "I have three music students coming tomorrow, and I don't want them to get scared off by all those college kids hanging around. One of the students is quite shy. So, yes, I wouldn't mind if the young folks were someplace else."

"Tell you the truth, I wouldn't mind either," Jane said. Then she hastened to add, "I really like them, and they're pleasant and fun, just rather . . . overwhelming."

"Then we'll try to convince them to go," Alice said. "I've been wanting to help you in some way, Jane, and if this is how I can accomplish that, I'll do my best."

"They'll need tools," Ethel warned.

"There are more than enough hammers on site, and I'm sure there are things they can do that don't require skilled labor. I know Cordy might appreciate having more people her age working."

"So our plan is to get them helping?"

"If they're interested, yes."

"Is the project going on Saturday as well?" Jane asked, a hopeful note in her voice.

"We'll see," Alice said, though she really didn't know if she could get herself to the worksite four days in a row.

Chapter Thirteen

As Louise opened the door into the darkened kitchen, she heard a hinge creak, but over the rest of the inn silence reigned.

She had gone out after supper to a book-club meeting at Viola's bookstore and the discussion went on for longer than usual. However, she had expected that even coming home this late, their guests would still be up and about as they usually were, laughing, joking and consuming vast amounts of food.

But the lights upstairs were out when she came home, and the only sounds permeating the silence were the low hum of the refrigerator and the muffled sound of Wendell's feet padding toward her.

A few moments later she heard soft voices outside the front of the inn, and she wondered who was on the porch.

With Wendell trailing behind, she walked to her father's study and took a few moments to straighten the desk. The past few days, when she had to do bookkeeping for the inn, she had taken refuge there to avoid any interruptions from the kids. She flipped through the accumulated envelopes and made a note to pay their bills and decide how much they could budget for a new vacuum cleaner. Though she still felt that the dinner was making Jane too busy, she had to admit she was thankful for the extra money.

Louise sorted the envelopes in order of importance, then set them on top of the checkbook as a reminder to pay the bills.

As she left the study, she heard the murmur of voices once more from the front porch. She listened.

Lynden and Carita. *What are they discussing at this hour?*

Just as she was about to slip up the stairs to give them some privacy, the front door opened and the two of them came inside.

"Oh, hello, Mrs. Smith. I didn't know you were still up." Carita glanced back over her shoulder at Lynden. "I had something I needed to talk to Lynden about," she said as Lynden followed her into the inn, closing the porch door behind him.

Ever the hostess Louise said, "Would you like something to eat?"

Lynden laughed. "It seems like all we've been doing since we got here is eat your food."

"You are our guests. We are here to make your stay as comfortable as possible."

"I'd kinda like some juice," Carita said, glancing sidelong at Lynden. "How about you?"

"Juice sounds good."

As Louise led them to the kitchen, she hoped Jane had done some baking.

She was pleased to find the refrigerator well stocked and the cookie jar filled to the brim. In spite of Jane's difficulties with organizing Stacy's dinner, she seemed to be on top of the day-to-day running of the inn.

Louise poured the juice, made up a plate of cookies and joined her guests.

As she sat at the table, she found herself at a loss for words. She didn't possess Jane's facility for making small talk with the younger set. Though she had regular piano students, they were usually much younger and, as a consequence, easier to talk to. In addition, they had the music she was teaching them as a conversation starter. That made Louise think of Lynden's appreciation of her music.

"I understand your grandmother played the piano," Louise said to Lynden.

He nodded, a wistful smile curving his lips. "I used to listen to her all the time." He glanced up at Louise. "I hope you didn't think I was some kind of stalker when I was hanging around outside the parlor while you played," he said.

"No, certainly not. I was sorry to hear that she had died. I'm sure you must miss her."

Lynden nodded. "I do."

Carita reached over and covered his hand with her own. "I keep forgetting she didn't die that long ago."

Lynden's smile seemed to absolve her. He turned his attention back to Louise. "Only trouble is, like we were talking about the other day with Jane, I mean, Ms. Howard, I feel like I've been wasting my time. Not sure what I want to do. This Amish trip is a good idea . . ."

"But you'd like to do something with some purpose?" Louise put in.

"Yeah."

"This is a vacation," Carita said with a smile. "Vacations are supposed to be about wasting time."

"I've done enough of that already," Lynden said.

Louise thought this was a perfect opportunity to bring up what she and her sisters had been discussing earlier in the day. "If you want to do something with meaning and purpose, and that could still be fun, why don't you consider helping out on the Habitat for Humanity project tomorrow?"

Lynden toyed with his cup, his expression thoughtful.

"You know, that sounds like a great idea." He glanced sidelong at Carita. "I mean, you could still do your tour thing with the rest, but I'd like to help out on the house."

Carita took a sip of juice, her forehead furrowed. She put down her glass, then gave Lynden a shy smile. "You know, in a way you're right about the summer break. It's not like we never have a chance to take it easy or relax." Carita looked down at her hands. "I think I'd like to help with the project too."

"So, what about the others? What do you think they'll want to do?"

"I'll bring it up tomorrow at breakfast," Carita said. "If they don't want to help, I'll take them on the tour. But the more I think about it, the more I like the idea."

"They might want to come." Lynden curled his hands around his cup. "Who knows? Maybe I'll find my calling by volunteering there," he said with a faint smile.

"Volunteering is an admirable place to start," Louise said, her heart warming at the thought of these kids taking time from their holiday to help someone else. She waited a beat, then got up and bid the two goodnight.

She could hear their voices as she made her way up the stairs to her bedroom.

Lying in bed, she sent up a quiet prayer of thanks to the Lord for His faithfulness through all generations.

❧

"Fantabulous breakfast, Ms. J," Matthew said, carrying a stack of plates into the kitchen Friday morning. "I don't know if we should stay all weekend. I'm gonna get superfat and in my line of work, that's suboptimal."

Jane looked up from the sandwiches she and Alice were assembling. "Don't you go to school?"

"That is my line of work, yes," Matthew said, dropping the plates on the counter with a clatter. "And if I get too fat, I won't be able to sit in the desks. 'Course I'll be working some of this off today." He swung his hand as if already wielding a hammer. "How many calories does carpentry work burn off?"

"I can't say."

This morning, Jane had been surprised to hear the youths' change of plans. When Lynden got up and suggested they all go to help Alice and Ethel on the worksite, the group, with the exception of Isabel, agreed that this would be a great thing to do.

Eventually, Carita managed to talk her friend into coming along.

And when Jane offered to pack a lunch for them, the entire group was convinced beyond a doubt.

Matthew glanced at the clock. "Not bad. I think we'll get to that site in time to do some serious damage."

"I thought the idea was to do some serious work," Jane teased, packing up the last of the sandwiches.

"Well, yeah. Same thing," Matthew said in a puzzled tone.

For a moment Jane felt every day of her fifty years. Sometimes these kids made her feel young, and then, in a matter of seconds, she keenly felt the gap between them.

Herbie followed Matthew into the kitchen, carrying a pitcher full of cutlery, and behind him came Pete and Rick, expressing their thanks and appreciation for breakfast as they brought in the empty warming trays and the fruit platters.

Jane stared at the clean trays and platters. Seconds ago they were heaped with breakfast burritos and fruit, and for a split second she wondered if the inn was going to realize any profit on this group the way they rocketed through food.

"You don't have to clean up, you know," she protested as Carita and Isabel came behind, bringing the rest of the mugs, cups and utensils.

"We want to. After all, you're making us lunch," Isabel said.

"You make sure to add lunch to the bill," Carita said.

"I will gladly feed workers heading out to do a good deed."

Lynden entered the kitchen. "The truck and van are full of gas. Oil checked. We're ready to roll."

Alice packed up the remaining snacks and put them in a cooler.

"I think we have everything."

"Did you and Ethel pack a lunch yesterday?" Lynden asked.

Alice shook her head. "Yesterday and the day before people came and brought lunch, but Cal warned us that the women who brought lunches for us the past few days wouldn't be able to come today."

"Sounds good to me," Matthew said, leaning over the cooler to inspect its contents. "I don't think anyone can beat the lunch you and Ms. J made for us."

The back door opened and Ethel stepped inside. "So, everyone ready to make some rafters? Put together some headers? Nail some drywall?"

Aunt Ethel must have found a carpentry manual at the library, Jane thought.

"I think we're ready," Alice said, closing the lid on the cooler. "Matthew, can you bring this out to the van? Pete, you and Herbie can take the other cooler, the one holding the juice and soda."

A few minutes later, Jane stood by the driveway, waving off the van, the truck and Alice's car, feeling like a mother sending her children off to school.

And then, like most mothers, she was sure, she returned to the quiet of her kitchen, enjoying the utter silence.

Until she saw the piles of dishes.

She suppressed a sigh, tied back her hair with an elastic band she found in her pocket and got to work.

This too will pass, she reminded herself as she started rinsing dishes.

∞

"Brought your own crew, did you?" Cal teased as Alice strapped on her leather pouch.

Alice glanced at the boys who were checking out the supply trailer, trying out some of the hammers, their laughter and joking streaming across the yard like banners of joy.

"I did. They're staying with us at our inn."

Cal frowned. "They a carpentry crew?"

"No. Our guests."

Cal gave her an odd look as if to say he would have second thoughts about staying at Grace Chapel Inn. Alice massaged her neck. Yesterday she'd been stiff; this morning weariness pulled at her limbs with a numbing force. How was she going to get through this day?

Ethel, however, looked as chipper as if she were ready to frame up the entire house on her own.

Matthew strode toward Alice and Cal and stopped, his hands on his hips as he glanced around the building site. "So, where do we start?"

"What do you know about carpentry work?" Cal asked.

"My friend Rick, he's worked construction before. I've helped my dad put up a shed. I can hit a nail without hitting my thumb." Matthew grinned.

"Okay. I need to get a few more outside walls framed up and braced and after that we can look at putting together the inside walls. I've been getting Alice and her crew to tack down the particleboard . . ." While he gave instructions, Alice looked around for Cordy.

She wasn't here yet, and Alice hoped the young woman hadn't changed her mind. Though yesterday Cordy talked about turning over a new leaf, Alice knew how difficult it could be to change when one didn't get much encouragement. Alice got the impression that while Cordy's mother meant well, she might not be the best person to create incentive in young Cordy.

An older car pulled up to the lot, bumping over the dried ruts, and Jasmine got out. Alice also saw her look around the worksite, then shake her head as she put on her hard hat.

As Jasmine came toward them, Alice saw her disappointment in not finding her younger sister, but she had a smile for Ethel and Alice.

"Thanks so much for coming again," Jasmine said. "Sorry I'm late. The kids were fussing as I was leaving, and I had to get them settled for Grainger before I came."

"I'm surprised you're here as early as you are. Can't be easy to get up on time with all you have to balance."

"And for some of us it seems impossible to get up, period." Jasmine's voice held a faint note of bitterness, and Alice guessed she was referring to Cordy.

"I'm sure your sister will be coming," Alice said. "She was here early yesterday."

"Cordy is a good girl," Ethel put in.

Jasmine only nodded, then noticed the rest of the crew. "Who are these people?"

"They're staying at our inn," Alice explained. "They heard about the project and decided to help out."

"They didn't have anything else to do?"

"They're on vacation before school starts."

"They came to work on my house on their vacation?" Jasmine's incredulous look made Alice proud of her young guests. And especially proud of Lynden, who was the motivator.

"They wanted to do something meaningful and helpful, and when we told them about this project, they thought they would come and help."

As Alice spoke, she saw a lone figure walking down the sidewalk toward the house.

And Alice's heart swelled with pride. She nudged Jasmine and pointed toward Cordy. "And look who else is here."

Jasmine's pleased expression said more than words could. "She's a wonderful girl," Alice continued. "She just needs some guidance and direction."

"Something she doesn't get much of from our mother, I'm afraid," Jasmine said with a light sigh.

"But she gets it from you."

"She doesn't want guidance or help or advice from me." Jasmine pulled her hand over her face in a gesture of frustration.

"I'm sure she resents what you tell her, but at the same time, I get a sense that she knows you're right." Alice touched Jasmine's shoulder. "What you think about her matters to her in spite of her reactions. She's still a teenager."

"I know." Jasmine gave Alice a grateful look. "I'm glad you ladies are spending time with her."

"Cordy simply needs a good example, and you've been able to give her one. But what she probably needs more than anything is encouragement when she does something good."

While she spoke, Alice glanced at Cordy. The girl seemed to be whistling as she walked, looking around. But as soon as she saw Jasmine, her steps slowed.

She kept coming, but more tentatively this time. Alice saw her gaze flick from Jasmine to Alice as if suspicious that she was their topic of conversation.

Perceptive little thing, Alice thought.

Cordy lifted her chin, a challenge in her eyes as she stopped in front of her sister. "I'm sorry I'm late."

Alice sensed Jasmine's hesitation. *Just hug her*, she thought, mentally urging Jasmine to do the right thing.

And, to her surprise and pleasure, Jasmine did exactly that. "I'm really glad you came, Cordy. I'm proud of you," Jasmine said.

Cordy's smile blossomed and Alice felt her joy.

"Don't tell me we have to do all that chick stuff." Matthew

stood beside them, his arms folded over his chest. "'Cause if we do, then I'm gonna find myself a different place to work."

Jasmine glanced over her shoulder, laughing at Matthew's comment. "Hello, there. My name is Jasmine and this . . ." Jasmine caught her sister by the shoulders and pulled her forward, "is Cordy. She's been helping me on the house."

"Cool." Matthew inclined his head toward Jasmine, then winked at Cordy. "So, what are we supposed to be doing here?"

"Cal didn't tell you?" Cordy glanced past him to where Cal stood by the other boys, waving his hand and pointing.

"Yeah, but he told me he only pretends to be the boss. Said you're the one I need to be talking to."

A flush crept up Cordy's neck, and Alice flashed a warning frown at Matthew, who gave her a cheeky wink back. She made a note to talk to him later. Matthew was an attractive young man and Cordy an impressionable high school student.

"I . . . uh . . . just work here," Cordy managed to squeak out.

"Well, that's great," Matthew said. He turned to Jasmine. "So, lovely lady, what's the plan?"

Alice resisted the urge to roll her eyes. Matthew was really pouring on the charm.

"Jasmine and her husband will be the future owners of the house," Alice said, putting extra emphasis on the word *husband*.

"Okay. That's cool." Matthew nodded, still grinning. "Is he here now?"

"He's home with the kids," Jasmine said, the beginnings of a smile teasing one corner of her mouth. "By the way, I'd like to thank you and your friends for helping out today. That's really neat."

"Well, it was either that or go check out the farms of some Amish people . . ."

He snapped his fingers.

"Matthew, get over here," Rick called. "We're ready to go."

"Talk to you ladies later," Matthew said, tipping his hard hat in their direction. Then he turned and jogged off.

"What a character," Jasmine said with a laugh. "I think he could be a lot of fun."

"Oh, that he is," Alice said dryly. "And now we better get some work done ourselves."

Alice saw Cordy look with a tinge of envy at Matthew, Rick and company and made a quick decision. "Cordy, I don't know if Aunt Ethel and I will be able to keep up with you. Might be better if you worked with the other group."

She laughed self-consciously. "No. That's okay."

Alice didn't want to press the matter, but as soon as she had an opportunity, she pulled Carita aside and asked her if she would invite Cordy to join them.

Carita had considerably more tact than Matthew, and a few minutes after Alice had asked her, she came over to where Alice, Ethel and Cordy were working.

"Hey, Ms. Howard," she asked, her shadow falling over the board they were nailing down. "I was wondering if you could spare Cordy? Isabel and I aren't quite sure what to do, and Cal is busy and the boys just laugh at us when we ask them."

Alice squinted up into the sun and grinned back at Carita. "I think that would be fine." She turned to Cordy, who was watching Carita with longing in her face. "Cordy, you wouldn't mind helping over there?"

"But then you and Mrs. Buckley will be working on your own."

A movement up the plank to the house caught Alice's eye. Florence was painstakingly making her way toward them.

"Here's Florence. I think we'll be okay."

Cordy gave another feeble protest, but when Florence came and Carita added her encouragement, she scrambled to her feet and followed Carita, grinning from ear to ear.

"That was nice of Carita to think of Cordy," Ethel said. "I'm sure she'll have more fun working with them than with us." As Florence joined them Ethel gave her a quick smile. "I thought you might not show up today."

Florence's only rejoinder was a pained look. "I hurt all over. I have muscles I was never aware of before this morning. But I'll meet the challenge."

"You've simply done some very minor straining of your muscles," Alice assured her. "If you slowly start working again, the stiffness will ease."

"I realize this is your area of expertise, but somehow that doesn't make sense. In fact, I thought of staying home and soaking in a warm tub of water."

"Trust me, Florence, the best thing you did was to come back and get moving again."

As Florence slowly eased herself down, Alice saw she remained skeptical.

Soon the whine of power saws and the smacks of hammers blended with voices and laughter and snatches of singing. Now and again a burst of laughter would come from the group of young people. Alice saw Cordy joining in and felt a surge of almost maternal pride.

That pride increased when they quit for lunch and Cal sauntered up to Ethel, Florence and Alice. "That is a great group of kids," he said, poking his thumb over his shoulder. "We're going to get lots done today."

"And even better, they seem to be enjoying themselves," Ethel said.

"Always makes for good production. Yesterday I was wondering how far we were going to get today, but now I'm real happy."

As he spoke, Herbie and Rick surged past. "Find a place to sit," Herbie called out. "We're getting the lunch."

"Come join us," Ethel said to Florence.

"I was thinking of finding a restaurant . . ." Florence said, obviously wavering.

"Nonsense," Ethel scoffed. "Jane packed us our lunch."

"Well, in that case I'll accept. I don't believe any meal I can buy in a restaurant could compare to a lunch put together by Jane."

A few minutes later Alice, Florence and Ethel were perched on a makeshift bench that Pete had hastily assembled —a plank of wood resting on concrete blocks. Carita, Isabel, Lynden and Matthew parceled out the food.

"I think I could get used to this," Alice said, accepting a paper plate full of food from Pete. "Thank you so much."

"Anything else I can do for you lovely ladies?" Rick asked, folding his hands in front of him as if eagerly awaiting their next request.

"You can tell me what you have on the back of your hand?" Florence asked, her expression clearly telegraphing what she thought of the tattoo.

Rick held up his dragon. Now that he wasn't wearing a long-sleeved shirt, Alice could see it snaking halfway up his arm.

"I got this done last year. You like it?"

Florence hesitated long enough for Rick to draw his own conclusion.

"Neither does my mom." He laughed. "Anything else?"

"If you don't mind, I would love something to drink," Ethel said.

Rick placed his hand on his chest. "I have a servant heart. Your wish is my command."

This elicited a guffaw from his friends.

"He's pulling your leg, Aunt Ethel," Matthew called out.

"Some respect, please," Rick said in an aggrieved tone as he went to get some cups.

"How are you making out over there?" Alice asked. "Cal is quite impressed with your work."

"It's going real well," Lynden said, looking up from his sandwich. "I'm enjoying it a lot. Cordy's been explaining how Habitat works. I think it's so cool that she can help out."

Cordy beamed. "When school starts, I won't be able to, though."

"What grade you in?" Herbie asked, wiping the back of his mouth with his hand.

"I'm going into eleventh, but..." she gave them a shamefaced look, "I'll probably have to redo some classes."

"Too tough?"

"No. Didn't show up."

"Oh no! A skipper!" Matthew called out in mock horror. "I don't know if we can be here guys. It might be catching."

Pete punched Matthew on the shoulder. "Says the king of school skedaddling." He glanced Cordy's way. "Don't let him get you down. He had a lousy attendance record last year."

"And I was a sorry, sorry student come finals." Matthew shook his head as if still regretting his impulses. "Let me be an abject lesson to you, missy. Don't skip. I spent way too much time trying to catch up. Totally wasted a year, a whole year of my life. Not worth it."

"Right on," Herbie agreed. "I was a nervous wreck come exam time. The whole hour I'm writing I'm wishing I could do the year over and not skip so much."

Alice watched as Cordy absorbed these nuggets of information. She hoped Cordy took them to heart.

"What do you want to do when you graduate?" Pete asked her.

"I dunno. I like animals, but I'm not sure what kind of job I could have working with animals."

"Be a vet," Pete called out.

"Dog walker," was Rick's contribution.

"Pet groomer."

The rest of them called out various suggestions, and Cordy laughed as they got sillier and sillier.

"I'm not smart enough to be a vet," Cordy said.

"Maybe you could be a vet's assistant," Lynden put in. "That way you can work with animals, and you won't have such a long studying period."

Cordy perked up. "I never thought of that before."

"I think it's an excellent idea," Ethel said. "You could probably do your studies at a local community college."

The conversation drifted from colleges to vocations and studying, and as the kids talked, Alice saw Cordy thinking through the various suggestions. She wondered if Cordy's friends ever talked about the future and the possibilities available to them.

Too soon lunch was over, and with exaggerated groans, everyone got up and went back to work.

Isabel rose and started clearing.

"I'll take care of that," Carita said, taking the plates from the girl's hands. "Why don't you help Cordy? Alice and I can finish this up."

"Things are going well, aren't they?" Carita asked.

"Looks like the boys are enjoying themselves," Alice remarked as Carita opened the back door of the van.

"They are, actually. In fact, Lynden's been asking a lot of questions about this organization. Seems like he's interested in doing some kind of long-term volunteer work."

"I sensed he's been searching for something in his life." Alice and Carita slipped the cooler inside and closed the door.

"We talked last night," Carita said quietly. "He spent a lot of time taking care of his grandmother, and now he feels a bit lost. She left him a lot of money, as did his parents, so he doesn't have to work. Trouble is, he doesn't want to hang around and do nothing."

"That's extremely admirable and mature on his part," Alice said. She glanced over at the boys. From here she saw Lynden's frown as he concentrated on what he was doing.

"I think so too . . ." but Carita's tone told Alice another story.

"But you were hoping he had other plans?" Alice asked, injecting a sympathetic tone into her voice.

"Yeah. I guess I hoped he would enroll in college, and we could spend more time together."

"Just because his plans might take him in a different direction than college doesn't mean you can't keep in touch."

"I suppose." Carita rubbed the side of her nose with her finger. "But I feel so shallow. All the things I did this week were, like Lynden said, just about having fun. About entertaining ourselves. And going to school for another year feels equally shallow."

"Not a chance. Education is a gift you give yourself and others. It broadens your horizons."

"Not when you're taking a general arts curriculum." Carita gave Alice a sad little smile. "And please don't bother telling me it will expand my mind. I'm only taking it because my parents wanted me to go to college, and I didn't know what else to take. I'm not even that committed to school." She folded her arms and leaned back against the van. "When Matthew was teasing Cordy about not going to classes, he could have been talking about me."

"Are you enrolled for this year?"

Carita nodded.

"What if you change your courses?"

"What if I just don't go?"

"And then what?" Alice asked.

Carita pushed back her dark hair, clutching her head with her hands. "Maybe do what Lynden is doing."

Alice felt lost at this point. She wasn't sure how to advise this young woman. In her day women didn't go chasing after men. At least not openly.

But things change, and it seemed Carita really cared about Lynden.

"Your silence tells me you're underwhelmed by the idea," Carita put in.

Alice had to dwell on the comment. Then she laughed. "It's not my business to be overwhelmed, underwhelmed or simply whelmed. But I do question the wisdom of planning your life around a young friend."

"I know. And I know exactly what my mother would say."

"And that would be?"

"Nice girls don't chase after boys. But I'm not sure Lynden even knows how I feel."

"Maybe you better tell him. Be upfront and then wait and see what he does with it," Alice suggested.

"Maybe. I don't know." Carita pushed her fingers through her hair. "This whole trip turned out completely different. Nothing turned out the way I planned."

"Welcome to life," Alice said with a light laugh. She put her arm around Carita and gave her a quick hug. "You obviously have things to think about, but in the meantime, let's have fun putting this house together."

"This work is fun, isn't it," Carita admitted as they walked back to the house. "I didn't think I'd enjoy building as much as I am. And it's great to know that we're helping out Cordy's sister. Cordy has been telling us a few things about what Jasmine has had to deal with. She's amazing, really."

"Jasmine has had to be a fighter," Alice admitted. "But so are you." Alice stopped, catching Carita by the arm. "I do want to tell you that I really admire what you've done for your friends. This vacation was not a waste of time at all. You showed them a good time, and you showed them a better way to have fun. I think that's worth more than you might realize."

Carita's smile widened. "Thanks for that, Alice."

Alice squeezed her arm. "You're welcome. You're a wonderful girl, Carita. And I don't think you're shallow at all."

Carita nodded, accepting the compliment, then returned to her friends.

"You and Carita seemed to have a lot to talk about," Ethel said, her tone suggesting that Alice had better spill the beans as soon as she could.

"Yes. We did." And that was all Alice was going to tell her dear aunt.

But while she worked, she surreptitiously glanced over to see what was going on elsewhere at the worksite.

Carita and Lynden were now working side by side, and when Alice caught Lynden watching Carita when the young woman wasn't looking, she suspected that it was possible that Carita's future might be in good hands.

Chapter ⊤ Fourteen

S h . . . you'll wake them up—"
"Your shushing is louder than my talking—"
"Could you all just hush up—"
"Sh . . ."

Jane stared at the ceiling listening to teenagers, one floor below, trying to be quiet and failing dismally.

They had come back from the Habitat for Humanity site exhausted and complaining how stiff and sore they were. They left for their Spirit Night, a listless and worn-out group. Jane wondered how much spirit they would be able show. In fact she thought for sure they would come home early from their evening and fall into bed.

But they must have caught their second wind at the rally. They stayed out until 1:00 AM, and now they were back at the inn.

She just hoped Louise and Alice weren't disturbed by the noise. Though as tired as Alice looked when she came home this afternoon, Jane suspected her sister was currently in a deep sleep.

Jane slipped out of her room and paused by Louise's door, listening. A faint sound of slow, steady breathing was the only sound coming out of her sister's room.

Well, that's good, Jane thought, creeping back to her bedroom. She crawled back into bed, fluffed her pillow, rolled to her side, pulled the blankets around her and waited for sleep to fuzz her thoughts and lift her off into dreams.

Fifteen minutes later she flopped onto her back, her arms crossed over her chest. A floor below, things grew more and more quiet.

She moved onto her other side, glaring at the alarm clock set to ring in five hours. She winced at the thought of all she had to do. Had she set the alarm properly? She grabbed the clock, checked and double-checked it. Though she doubted the kids would be up early for breakfast, she still had Louise and Alice to take care of.

And then there was the dinner.

Well, at least her challenge provided an opportunity to practice patience. Stacy had called almost every hour on the hour to double-check the arrangements, to fine-tune the menu and to tell Jane how stressed she was, how busy she was, how worried she was.

Jane had tried not to take on Stacy's fretting, but with each phone call Jane grew more anxious. She went over the menu again and again, rechecked her supplies, and finally satisfied that she had everything well in hand, she went to bed . . . and started tossing and turning. She was just drifting off when the kids came back a nd here she lay, wide awake again.

The soup is made and ready to be heated up tomorrow. The salad has to wait to be mixed up. The chicken breasts have been prepared. Tomorrow morning . . . no, this morning! . . . I will mix the stuffing for the chicken breasts, get the dry mixture ready for the biscuits and prepare the salad dressing. The more she could do in advance, the better prepared she would feel when the time came for the dinner.

The Nanaimo bars and the stroop waffles are done. Apple

galette can't be made until the last moment. The vegetables are cut up and ready to be cooked. The only thing left to do is . . .

Jane pressed her fingertips against her eyes to control her worries. She had gone over this dinner so many times, she was getting dizzy.

"Sufficient for the day . . ." she reminded herself.

But when she rolled onto her side, her worries intruded once more. *Have I prepared enough chicken breasts? Enough vegetables?*

Stifling a sigh of frustration at her spinning thoughts, she snapped on her bedside light, sat up and wrapped her arms around her knees. She needed to rest, to find comfort. And while she knew the stress from the dinner was nothing compared to some of the things going on in people's lives around the world, she did send up a prayer that the dinner would be a success.

Then she took her Bible off her bedside table and opened it to the passage she'd been reading just the other day, Galatians 5:22–23.

"But the fruit of the Spirit is love, joy, peace, patience, kindness, goodness, faithfulness, gentleness and self-control. Against such things there is no law."

As Jane read the words, she felt her focus shift from herself and the worries she carried to the Lord Who loved her. She had opportunities to show that love to those around her, and there were times, she had to confess, when she had fallen short.

"Forgive me, Lord," she prayed. "Give me the fruit of patience, gentleness and self-control." She read on and stopped at a passage that especially resonated with her.

"Since we live by the Spirit, let us keep in step with the Spirit" (Galatians 5:25).

Jane kept the Bible open, letting the words settle into her mind and recenter her thoughts.

I am put on this earth to serve the Lord and to serve others, she thought. *But I must make sure that in serving others, I don't lose track of serving the Lord.*

She took a deep breath and bowed her head to pray. And as she prayed, she felt peace settle upon her.

∞

"Where is Jane?" Louise asked Saturday morning, glancing at the clock in the kitchen. "I thought for sure she would be up by now."

Alice eased herself into a chair, nursing her cup of tea. "I didn't hear her get up this morning. Of course, I didn't hear much. I am still tired."

Louise gave her sister a look of sympathy. "You certainly should be. I am full of admiration for all the physical work you've been doing."

"I won't need to go for a walk with Vera for over a month," Alice groaned.

Louise finished her coffee and got up, pausing at the entrance to the hallway, listening. Upstairs, no one was stirring. Not Jane, not Carita, not Isabel and certainly none of the boys.

She rinsed her cup, put it in the sink and returned to the hallway entrance. "Do you think we should wake up Jane?" Louise asked, tapping her fingertips against her arm.

"I say if she can sleep, let her sleep." Alice yawned.

"My goodness, Alice, you look as if you should have stayed in bed yourself."

"I thought Jane was already whipping eggs and making whatever she had planned for breakfast this morning, so I dragged myself out of bed to help."

Louise glanced down the hallway. She didn't know what to do if the young people came downstairs before Jane.

While Louise could breeze through Chopin's *Prelude in F*

Sharp Major, any breakfast beyond boiled eggs and toast confounded her.

She walked back to the kitchen table and perched on the edge of her chair, fiddled with the cloth napkins already prepared for breakfast, straightened the plant sitting on the bright yellow cloth mat, pinched off a dead leaf, then got up and threw it in the trash can.

She wiped the counters, inspected the refrigerator in the faint hope that her usually organized sister had already prepared breakfast and that it only needed heating up. Surely Jane wouldn't be sleeping if she hadn't?

A plate of fruit, already cut up and covered, sat beside two casserole dishes covered in tin foil which, in turn, sat beside a plate of muffins and pastries. Aha! Breakfast.

"I would imagine these need to be heated up?" Louise asked, pulling out the tinfoil covered dishes.

"Probably," Alice said, stifling another yawn. "I know she said she was going to make a breakfast casserole for this morning."

"Should we put them in the oven for her? That would save her some time."

Alice didn't reply.

"I'm sure she wouldn't want the kids to come downstairs to no breakfast at all," Louise fretted.

Still no reply from Alice. Louise glanced over and saw her sister with her arms folded and her head down. She was sleeping.

Louise was about to put the pans back in the fridge when she heard footsteps above her. Then the sound of running water. Someone was up.

She looked from the pans to Alice to the hallway and made an executive decision. Jane had been busy enough the past few days. It wouldn't hurt for her to sleep a little longer, and if she already had breakfast here and all that needed doing was for it to be heated up, then Louise would do it.

She turned on the oven, put the pans inside and then went back to the refrigerator to get the rest of breakfast. She was about to wake Alice, then decided to let her sleep.

Feeling on top of things, Louise mixed up the orange juice, got the coffeepot going and set the table. A few more noises emanated from upstairs, but no one came down.

No matter. By the time anyone did, breakfast would be ready.

When the coffee was done burbling, Louise poured it into one of the carafes, set the carafe on the sideboard and immediately started another pot of coffee. A quick survey of the table satisfied her that all was in a perfect state of readiness. The only thing missing were the guests.

And Jane.

Louise allowed herself a smug smile while thinking of her sister. She would be surprised mightily when she came downstairs to find that breakfast was well in hand. Of course, Jane had done all the prep work, but Louise still felt quite proud of her own initiative.

She reached for the oven door to check on the casseroles.

"*Yoo-hoo*," Ethel sang out, entering the kitchen. She wore her cap, her overalls, a carpenter's apron and a huge smile. "How is everyone this lovely summer morning?"

Louise waved to Ethel and put her finger over her lips, and then indicated Alice who, miraculously, was still sleeping at the kitchen table.

"Oh, the poor dear," Ethel whispered, covering her mouth with her hand as if trying to recapture her words. "Has she been there all night?"

Louise shook her head and indicated that Ethel should follow her to the front room.

As they walked past the reception desk, Louise glanced

up the stairs, but in spite of the muffled noises above them, no one came down.

"What happened to Alice?" Ethel asked, settling herself into one of the chairs in the living room. She shifted, then moved her hammer so it wasn't banging against the leg of the chair.

"The poor dear is so tired. She got up because she felt she should help with breakfast, then promptly fell asleep at the kitchen table." Louise took a seat across from Ethel, but where she could still keep an eye out in case their guests came downstairs.

"Should we make her go back to bed?"

"We'd have to wake her to do that. I'll wake her up before the kids come down, though. I'm sure she wouldn't appreciate their finding her sleeping." Louise glanced at Ethel's attire. "I thought no one was working at the Habitat project today."

"Florence said she needed some work done on her fence today. So I offered to help."

"That's a wonderful idea," Louise said approvingly. Obviously the feud between the two women was over. Alice had said as much, but with Ethel and Florence one never knew. Sometimes hostilities would cease only to flare up at the slightest provocation. "Is her husband going to help?"

Ethel waved away that question. "Ronald may be a successful businessman, but he has no idea which end of a nail is up."

Louise somehow doubted that, but if fixing a fence would mend proverbial fences between Florence and Ethel, who was she to argue with her aunt?

They chatted for a bit about the Habitat project and Louise was pleased to know Ethel and Alice were going back again the following week.

"Alice has to work a couple of hospital shifts next week,

so I don't think she'll be going to the worksite as often. I'll have to get a ride from Florence—but now that we're getting along again I'm sure she won't mind coming here to get me, especially if I help her with her fence."

Louise nodded, half listening to Ethel, half listening to what was going on upstairs.

"Where's Jane?" Ethel asked. "I thought she would be up by now."

"I thought so too, but I have breakfast well in hand," Louise said.

"Do you now?" Ethel gave her a feeble smile. "I see."

"Are you going to join us?"

At the question, Ethel glanced at her watch, then jumped to her feet. "Oh my goodness! Look at the time. I promised Florence I would be there early. I should probably get going." She adjusted her tool belt, then sidled toward the back entrance. "I mean, we're just starting to get along again, and I don't want her to be angry with me if I come late. You know how she can be sometimes."

Her niece knew exactly what was going on in Ethel's mind. Her aunt was fully aware of Louise's culinary shortcomings.

"Jane prepared the breakfast in advance," Louise assured her. "I just put it in the oven."

"I see. Jane made it. So you're just heating it up."

"Which is happening as we speak."

"In that case, I'm sure Florence will understand if I don't come precisely at the time I said I would be there. What time will breakfast be ready?"

"In about twenty minutes. When the casseroles are done."

The sound of whistling came from the top of the stairs, followed by the thumping of a pair of feet taking the stairs two at a time.

"Morning Mrs. L," Matthew sang out as he landed on the floor of the hallway. His hair still glistened from a shower, and his shirt was partially unbuttoned. "Morning Aunt E." He stopped, pulled his head back as if realizing what he had said. "Hey. That's like a joke or something. Aunt E . . . Auntie. And it's not even ten o'clock yet."

"Actually you are up bright and early this morning."

"Yeah, well, I couldn't sleep. I'm still pumped from the game we had last night. Our boys won."

"Well, that's nice," Ethel said. "Did you have a good time?"

"We had a rocking time. Even the band was pretty good. And the bonfire. Whoa! Thought the fire department was going to have to come out."

"Sounds like fun."

"Way more than fun. It was awesome. We met up with some old friends, swapped some old stories. Even Lynden was laughing, and, hey, he doesn't laugh much. And how was your course? Learn how to fix a transmission?"

"That's for next week," Louise said. "Our focus yesterday was windshield wipers."

"Hey, you gotta crawl before you can run. You'll be lifting trannies yet." He headed down the hallway toward the kitchen as if this was the most normal thing in the world. "Do you need any help this morning?"

Too late Louise realized where he was going. What if he woke up Alice . . .

"Hey, Ms. A," Matthew called out. He stopped, looked from the still-sleeping Alice back to Louise who had followed him. "She okay?" he asked, scratching his head.

Alice slowly lifted her head, blinking as consciousness returned. The imprint of her hand blazed bright red on her cheek and her hair listed to one side.

"Good morning, Matthew," Alice said. "How did you sleep?"

"In my bed. How about you? Don't tell me you spent the night here?"

"I must have dozed off. Someone should have woken me before you came down." Again Alice gave Louise a reprimanding look.

"Someone didn't know you would fall asleep at the kitchen table," Louise said in her own defense.

Alice frowned, but then her usually sunny nature reasserted itself and she laughed. "I suppose it's not the best place to catch forty winks. I hope I wasn't snoring."

"I can't imagine that you snore," Matthew said.

Alice gave him a quick smile. "And how was your evening?

"Like I told Aunt E, great, fun and fantastic. I probably smell a bit like smoke." He then sniffed the air. "But that smells better. Smells like breakfast is cooking. I made sure we all got up so you don't have to feed us forever and ever. Besides, we got plans for the day."

"That's very considerate of you," Louise said. "I believe breakfast will be ready in about fifteen minutes."

"Great. I'll tell the gang." He paused a moment. "Isn't Ms. J up yet?"

"She's still sleeping," Louise said.

"Oops. If I'd known that, I would have told everyone to be quiet."

"I'm sure she'd like to be awake by now," Louise assured him. "In fact, I think I'll make certain of that immediately."

"Nah. Let her sleep," Matthew said. "She's been working real hard."

"So have you, I hear. Did you enjoy working on the house yesterday?"

Matthew scratched his head, as if contemplating the question. "Yeah. It was a lot of fun building the house. It's not a real big one, but looks like it'll be cozy. It was interesting talking to that Cordy girl. She's the sister of Jasmine, the lady who is getting the house. That Jasmine has had a real tough gig."

"Gig?"

"Yeah, you know, life I guess." He shrugged. "But now she's getting a house, and it's cool. She only has to pay back what she can afford. I think that's supercool."

"Good morning." Carita appeared in the doorway of the kitchen looking bright and chipper, followed by Herbie and Isabel. "Can I do anything?"

"No, you cannot," Louise said, giving her a gentle smile to offset a comment that might be construed as short. "You've done more than enough to help out."

"Smells like you've got breakfast cooking already." Herbie rubbed his hands in anticipation.

"Yes. I do. But I can't take any credit. Jane had it already prepared and ready to go. Now why don't you sit in the living room or enjoy the early morning on the front porch while breakfast is heating."

The group took her advice and left. Soon Louise could hear them boisterously reliving the events of the previous evening. She even caught a glimpse of Herbie backing into the hall, pretending to hold a football as he most probably reenacted a portion of the game.

"Those casseroles smell different," Alice said, sniffing the air.

Louise couldn't remember what the casseroles should smell like. "Maybe Jane used different ingredients this time." She opened the oven door, sniffed again, just because she felt she should. Seemed fine to her.

Fifteen minutes later the kids were gathered around the table and Louise brought out the casseroles. Too late she realized that Jane often used the warming trays for the heated portion of the guests' breakfast, so still holding the hot dishes, she hurried back to the kitchen.

"Where are you going with our breakfast?" Herbie cried out in dismay. "I worked pretty hard last night and need sustenance for today."

"Alice, I forgot the warming trays," she whispered as the doors flapped shut behind her.

"It's too late to get them going." Alice tugged open a drawer and pulled out a few hot pads. "We can use these. I'll put these on the table for you."

As Alice preceded her, the heat of the dishes was making itself known. "Hurry," Louise urged, her hands growing uncomfortably hot.

The pads went down, the dishes followed them with a "thunk" and Louise quickly shook off the overheated oven mitts. She gave the gathered group a weak smile. "There you go."

"I'm so hungry, I could eat a horse," Herbie announced.

Ethel scooted in behind Louise, carrying the fruit and pastry trays, which she set on the sideboard. Alice and Ethel went back to the kitchen and returned with bowls of yogurt, granola and cottage cheese. All was ready.

"Enjoy your breakfast," Louise said, feeling quite proud of herself as she peeled back the foil from the first of the casseroles.

And stopped. And frowned.

"What's wrong, Mrs. L?" Matthew asked.

Louise couldn't answer him. Her eyes were fixed on the strange looking casserole before her. She sniffed, bent closer.

"That doesn't look like breakfast casserole," Ethel said, peering past Louise.

Alice came to inspect as well and clapped her hand over her mouth, stifling her cry of dismay.

"What is it, Alice?" Louise asked.

"I think those are the chicken breasts Jane was going to serve for the dinner tonight," Alice said.

"They were right between the other breakfast foods. Why did she put them where she did if they weren't for breakfast?" Louise struggled to stifle a surge of misgiving.

She gingerly peeled back the foil from the second pan, hoping against hope that it was a breakfast casserole.

But all that faced her was a limp assortment of peppers, olives, celery decorated with blobs of melted feta cheese and the fast-growing smell of scorched vegetables.

"I suppose this was also for tonight?" Louise asked in a faint voice.

"I would think so." Alice said.

Silence fell over the table as realization hit the gathered group of guests.

"So this isn't really our breakfast," Pete asked.

"I'm so sorry," Louise said. "I don't think so."

"We can eat the yogurt . . ."

"If indeed it is yogurt," Louise said, no longer trusting her own instincts. She felt her shoulders slump as she stared at the casserole dishes. Jane was stressed enough over this meal. Now Louise had destroyed the entrée.

So much for feeling on top of things, she thought, wondering how Jane was going to react.

"This is yogurt, all right," Ethel announced from behind her.

Louise turned to see her aunt holding a small bowl and taking another sample.

"And I'm sure this other stuff is fruit," Ethel said gesturing toward the cut-up melon, mangoes and grapes with her spoon.

"I'm sure they are," Louise replied dryly.

"I could make toast for you," Alice said. "Won't take but a minute."

"I can fry eggs," Matthew offered.

"Nah. Scramble them," Pete said, getting to his feet as if he was going to do that very thing. "Goes way faster and you don't have to be as fussy."

"But . . . you . . ." Louise, still discombobulated from her breakfast faux pas, couldn't gather her thoughts fast enough to formulate a coherent objection.

"You must have eggs," Pete said, already walking toward the kitchen.

"If you put seasoning salt in them, that's really tasty," Rick offered, rushing to catch up to his friend.

"Don't put that in mine," Isabel protested, following them. "I like them just plain."

Alice stood by as the kids strode past her and then turned to Louise with a resigned expression.

So they gathered up the dishes holding what was supposed to be portions of Jane's dinner, brought them into the kitchen and found a place for them on a counter.

Pete was cracking eggs into a bowl, Carita was setting up the mixer and Rick had a pan on the stove by the time Louise and Alice got back into the kitchen. Herbie and Matthew were going through a cupboard, calling out the names of various spices.

"What can I do?" Isabel asked, tugging on Louise's sleeve.

"I don't mind helping either," Lynden offered.

"Toast?" Louise said, still trying to gather her thoughts. "Maybe you can take care of the toast?"

In a matter of minutes the pan on the stove was sizzling, toast was toasting and getting buttered, and Louise, Alice and Ethel were sitting at the kitchen table watching the spectacle.

"So how about that touchdown?" Herbie said, opening up another loaf of bread. "I don't think I played that well in high school."

"It was an awe-inspiring play," Matthew said. "Here, dragon man. Use this." He tossed Rick a container of spices.

"And the band did a great job," Carita said. "I really liked that last song they played."

The chatter continued, upbeat and positive and loud.

"Good thing Jane is still sleeping," Ethel commented, her

arms folded over her coveralls. "I don't know that she would appreciate having all these kids running amok in her kitchen."

"Well, at least *they* seem to know what they're doing," Louise said, forcing herself to relax. There was nothing she could do now except watch breakfast unfold.

A few minutes later they were instructed to follow the food into the dining room.

Ethel was already sitting at the table by the time they got there, so Alice and Louise gave in and sat down.

"So, dig in," Matthew urged, waving his fork at the huge platter of eggs and the mound of toast, and everyone did just that.

As their guests laughed and chatted, Louise, Ethel and Alice were treated to yet another account of strategic plays during the football game, a recap of the bonfire and the band and general college-age conversation.

The noise level grew and grew the longer they sat. Conversation was animated and punctuated by laughter and teasing.

Lynden joined in, and occasionally his glance would slip to Carita, and his expression would soften. Then, as if she sensed his gaze on her, Carita's eyes would turn to his, and she would return his look with a gentle smile.

Louise's heart melted at the sight. She wondered what lay ahead for them, but for now, it seemed they both truly cared for each other.

As quickly as the breakfast had been made, the food was consumed. The kids cleaned up, and as they did, the noise level in the kitchen rose dramatically.

"My goodness, what is going on here?"

Louise saw Jane standing in the doorway of the kitchen, blinking at the gathering. A few strands of hair had escaped her hastily tied ponytail.

"Hey, Ms. J, you missed breakfast, but we can make you more," Matthew sang out.

"Good morning, Jane," Louise said, forcing a cheery tone to her voice. "I hope you slept well."

"For some reason my alarm clock didn't go off." She blinked again and pushed the wayward strands of hair back over her ear. "Why didn't you wake me?"

"We thought you needed the sleep," Louise said, hoping that Alice would come to her assistance.

"Yes. You have been working very hard," Alice said. "So we took care of breakfast."

"Among other things," Ethel put in.

Louise saw Alice give her aunt a quick poke.

"What do you mean, other things?" Jane asked, stifling a yawn.

Louise sighed. She should have known Ethel was unable to keep anything she deemed interesting to herself.

"We can fix the problem, though," Louise assured her.

"It's not a huge problem," Alice put in helpfully.

"Whoa! What are you talking about?" Jane put up her hand as if to indicate she would tolerate no further delay.

Louise glanced at Alice who was trying to smile at Jane.

"I think they're talking about the chicken . . ." Ethel informed her.

Louise shot Ethel a frown.

"Chicken?" Jane's confused gaze flicked from Ethel, to Alice, to Louise.

"I'm sure you can do something with it," Louise said, walking to her sister's side. "You must have some kind of recipe you could use—"

"Recipe? Do something?" Jane tried to absorb what her sister was saying. "Could someone please tell me what happened?"

"Louise cooked your chicken."

"I thought it was a breakfast casserole—"

"—and the vegetables."

"Same excuse." Louise shot Ethel a warning look.

Jane scooted past Louise, glancing around the kitchen. Louise could tell the minute her sister laid eyes on the pan. Her expression became pained. "Oh no. Louise, what have you done?"

"I am *so* sorry, Jane. It was an accident."

Jane dropped into a nearby chair and blew her breath out in a sigh. "What am I going to do?"

"Change menus?" Carita said hopefully.

"I can't think of anything else to make," Jane said. "It took me about four days of wrangling to come up with this one, and I'm tired and worn out." Jane waved her fingers as if dismissing the entire menu out of hand. "I made suggestion after suggestion, and this was the only thing Stacy agreed to."

"That's rough." Matthew said, flinging a damp towel over his shoulder.

Jane nodded listlessly.

Louise felt even worse than Jane looked. "I'm so sorry, Jane. I should have been more attentive. I shouldn't have made such a quick presumption."

"Louise, you didn't mean any harm. I'll just have to think of something else."

"That's lousy. Can you do it?" Matthew put in.

Jane glanced across the kitchen counter and gave him a feeble smile. "I hope so. This was supposed to be a gourmet meal. Something unusual, yet not too—" Jane held up both hands and made air quotes with her fingers, "—out there."

"I hate to be the social planner yet again," Carita said with a smile. "But the clock is ticking and we need to get going."

Pete quickly wiped the counter and tossed the cloth into the sink. Matthew finished putting away the dishes, and the rest were leaving the kitchen when Isabel piped up.

"I'm going to stay."

Carita gave her a patient look. "I know you don't like this

stuff, but you bought a ticket for the barbecue and you should come."

Isabel looked from Jane to Carita and then shook her head. "No. I'm going to stay and see if I can help Jane."

Jane was surprised to hear Isabel speak up. The girl had been quiet and withdrawn most of the visit, preferring, it seemed, to let Carita do all the talking. "Don't worry, Isabel," Jane said. "I don't need any help."

"You do," Isabel protested, again surprising Jane with her vehemence. "You've been so great to us. You've let us invade your kitchen. And now I want to help you."

"I can help too," Matthew said suddenly. "I gabbed with all my buddies last night."

"I could stay," Pete said, adjusting the fit of his ball cap.

"No, don't do that," Jane said, raising her hands in a gesture of protest. She would get absolutely nothing done with the kids hanging around. Now more than ever she counted on their being away from the inn. "You have planned this for weeks. I don't want to ruin the day."

"You won't ruin my day," Isabel said quietly. "I don't need to go and be ignored by the same people who ignored me in high school."

Her voice held a plaintive note that called to Jane. She wavered and that was her undoing.

"That's it," Matthew said, returning to the kitchen and slapping his hands on the counter. "We're stayin' and we're helpin'." He turned to Isabel. "So, what should we do?"

Frowns met his question followed by some muttering as they talked among themselves.

"Where are your recipe books?" Pete finally spoke up. "I can look for some ideas."

"I can surf the Web," Herbie offered.

"We could come up with something," Isabel said. "I used to do a lot of cooking for my mom."

Jane was about to protest again, when the sight of seven earnest faces did her in. They weren't going to quit, and she didn't have the energy to buck them. So she simply pointed out the cupboard that held her recipe books, and while the kids bustled around the kitchen, she leaned her elbows on the counter, wishing she could think clearly.

"Should I go get some more groceries?" Louise offered.

Jane shook her head.

"Well, I'll be in the parlor going over my songs for tomorrow," Louise said. "Let me know if you need anything at all."

Jane nodded. Then she sighed.

Chapter Fifteen

She simply couldn't think. Jane glanced around the kitchen. Carita and Isabel were hunched over a set of cookbooks at the counter, while Herbie, Pete and Rick were surfing the Web at the front desk, printing out possibilities and running them back to Jane for approval.

The kids meant well and she appreciated their enthusiasm for the project and their sacrifice in staying with her, but if she was supposed to come up with something else for the dinner, she needed quiet.

So she looked over the recipes Herbie had printed out and tried to sort them into piles. Maybe, Definitely Not and Impossible to Do Before Five O'Clock Tonight. While she sorted, she struggled to keep her feelings under control, hoping the kids would eventually find something else to occupy themselves.

She had the dining room to decorate, the flowers to organize, the table to set. And a brand-new entrée to plan.

What happened to that moment of peace I had last night? She stopped herself, stopped her fussing as she remembered the words from Galatians. "The fruit of the Spirit is love, joy, peace, patience, kindness, goodness . . ." She took a long, slow breath, letting the passage once again still her soul, until the phone started ringing.

She darted a nervous glance at the clock. Seven hours and fourteen minutes till the dinner.

"Jane, it's for you," Alice said with an apologetic look. "It's Stacy."

"The fruit of the Spirit is love, joy, peace . . ." Jane repeated the words to herself as she took the phone from Alice, forced a smile, then said, "Hello, Stacy." She kept the smile intact while Stacy quizzed Jane again about the menu, about the place settings, the china.

"I might have to make a change," Jane said, knowing that she had to prepare Stacy in advance. "No, no shellfish or MSG . . . I'm fully aware of that . . . No potatoes. Of course. . . . Yes I realize you'll be here at five tonight . . . Yes, I'll be ready . . . I understand the pressure you're feeling. Everything will turn out just fine," Jane said with overly hearty emphasis. Then she made the mistake of looking over at Matthew who was shaking his head while spinning one finger in circles at his temple.

Jane almost burst out laughing at his irreverence. She shook her finger in reprimand, but he just grinned back and handed her another stack of recipes.

"But I should get back to the dinner, Stacy. You'll want everything just so, I'm sure. Bye." Jane hung up the phone.

"How many times does that lady call?" Matthew said. "Every time we're here, you're on the phone with her."

"She's just nervous about this meal," Jane said.

"It's just food," Matthew replied.

"You're right, Matthew, but she's also paying me quite a bit of money to serve that food and decorate the inn, so I am obligated to give my very best."

"As long as it's not too 'out there,'" Alice interjected.

"Precisely."

Jane scanned the recipes Matthew had given her and sorted them into her piles, then she flipped through the pile of Maybe's, setting aside the ones that might fit in with Stacy's criteria.

The pile was disappointingly small. And of those recipes, Jane could only realistically do one. She read through the recipes with a critical eye, mentally going over what she had in the house and what she might still need to purchase.

Would she have time?

"I've got it!" Isabel exclaimed. "I've got the perfect recipe."

"Where did you find it?" Jane asked.

"I didn't. This recipe here reminded me." Isabel held up an older recipe book Jane hadn't used for years. "My mom used to make this for us once in a while. She called it Fourteen Boy Rice Dish."

"The name sounds intriguing," Jane asked. "What's in the dish?"

"Everything you have in the house. And the best part, you start with cooked chicken and make a curry sauce, which goes over cooked rice. Then you set out bowls of diced pineapple, banana, mandarin oranges, mango, peanuts, cashews, coconut, raisins, dried cranberries, bird's eye peppers, green onion and diced lemongrass. People can then put any combination of these condiments on their rice that they want." She grew excited as she talked, showing more animation in the past half hour than she had during the whole visit. Jane wondered if Isabel had simply been over-shadowed by the more outspoken and exuberant Carita.

"Sounds a bit weird to me," Rick said with a note of skepticism.

"No way. Sounds awesome," Matthew cried. "All those different things, like a sweet and sour."

"And we could serve," Isabel continued. "Each of us could bring in a couple of bowls and set them on the table, which would add a little bit of drama to the meal."

While Isabel spoke, Jane imagined the combination of flavors, then envisioned the table filled with a dozen bowls of colorful and varied condiments. Hope flickered within her. This could work!

And having the kids serve? Genius.

"And the best part," Isabel continued, "is that the chicken curry is easy to make ahead because the longer it sits, the better the flavor. So if you're concerned, we can make the curry now and you can try it right away."

"We could have it for lunch," Matthew said, his eyes lighting up.

"No," Isabel and Carita said in unison. They looked at each other, then laughed, and it was as if an unseen barrier broke down between them.

"We could all help slice and dice the condiments before the meal," Carita said. But then she turned to Isabel. "Sorry. You figure out what we should do."

Isabel gave her a thankful smile. "I like the idea of us all serving the bowls for you. I mean, presentation is often a big part of a meal, right?"

"What do you think, Jane?" Alice asked with a worried look on her face. "It seems like a marvelous plan, plus it would use up the chicken breasts that Louise cooked this morning."

Jane nodded, still thinking. Making it ahead of time appealed to her, as did the idea of being able to taste it right away. If she didn't like it, she might, just maybe, have time to make the recipe she had set aside.

"Do you know how to make this recipe?" Jane asked.

"I can phone my mom. She would know." Isabel pushed herself away from the table, but just as she picked up the phone, it rang. She glanced at the call display. "It says Stacy Reddington," Isabel said.

"Didn't she just call?" Lynden asked.

"Let the phone ring," Alice said. "You just spoke to her. What on earth could she possibly have to say to you?"

Carita stood up just as Isabel was about to hand the phone to Jane. "I'll take care of this," she said. "Hello, Grace Chapel Inn, how may I direct your call? . . . I'm sorry, Ms. Howard is unavailable at this time. Can I take a message?"

Jane shook her head and held her hand out for the phone, when she felt Alice's hand on her arm. "Carita has the right idea," Alice said. "Stacy's constant phone calls are making you more nervous than the dinner itself is. You don't need to talk to her every time she calls."

Jane looked from Alice to Carita who was ending the phone call.

"You've been catering to this woman far too much," Alice said.

"I hope you're not making a pun, Alice."

Alice laughed. "No, but I am giving you some sisterly advice."

"You're probably right. Every time I talk to her I get more nervous." Jane gave Carita a grateful smile. "Thanks for running interference for me."

"Hey, if I'm going to be bossy, may as well be bossy for a good cause."

Half an hour later the chicken had been transferred to a larger casserole dish, and Jane was adding a rich blend of ingredients to prepare her new entrée. Isabel and Carita were going through the pantry, seeking out the other ingredients for the meal.

The boys were sent to Potterston to pick up whatever was missing and to stop at a thrift shop to see if they could find enough black pants and white shirts to add to those already on hand for the crew. Craig and Sylvia had shown up and were in the dining room with Alice, setting up.

Stacy had called two more times, and each time Carita answered the phone, shielding Jane. While this did make Jane feel like she was hiding behind Carita, the respite from Stacy's constant worrying and dithering was a relief.

"I think you can give the curry its first taste," Isabel said. She had a small bowl and spoon ready for Jane.

Jane couldn't help taking a quick glance at the clock as she walked toward the stove. *If this doesn't taste good* . . . she stopped herself right there. The curry will be fine. She'd made enough different meals that she knew which ingredients created which flavors, and this one sounded like a winner.

Nonetheless, she was apprehensive as she took the steaming bowl and spoon from Isabel. She blew some steam away, then took her first taste.

And smiled.

"This tastes wonderful," she said, relief washing over her.

She took another taste, enjoying the delightful flavors. "Though I would like to see a hint more cumin." She shook in some more, stirred the pot and sampled it again. "It will be a while yet before the flavor comes out more fully, but this should work quite well."

Isabel beamed. "I'm glad you like it. Adding all the other condiments makes the whole meal taste really good."

"Jane, come and see what you think," Sylvia said, standing by the swinging door between the kitchen and the dining room.

Jane walked over and stopped, her eyes wide. "This looks amazing."

Sylvia had draped gold silk cloth over the buffet, bunching it here and there to allow for placement of the small topiaries Craig had brought. The same gold cloth hung in one corner of the dining room from the ceiling to the floor, serving as a backdrop for a grouping of bamboo plants and a larger topiary. Sylvia had set the table with the bronze tablecloth and gold runner, complementing the dishes Alice was now setting out.

Four small topiaries, matching the ones on the buffet, marched down the long table, creating a formal, yet welcoming effect.

"All we need is the place cards and a menu card," Sylvia said. "I brought along some paper for the menu. You said you didn't have it settled the last time I spoke to you." She picked up a stack of dark brown paper and cream vellum. "I thought we could print the menu on the vellum and stick it to the brown paper using decorating brads."

"Brads?"

"Little buttonlike clips that hold paper together. Decorative and fun. I found some that look like postage stamps to match the place cards." Sylvia looked up as Isabel and Carita joined them. "Maybe these girls could help me put them together?"

"They've done more than enough already," Jane said.

"No way," Isabel protested. "I love working with paper. Carita and I can easily put these together."

"But you're here to have fun," Jane put in. She felt worse and worse at the amount of work her guests were doing for this dinner.

"And this is fun," Isabel said, smiling away Jane's protestations.

"While we're cutting," Sylvia said, "We can make up the place cards. I thought we could decorate them with these used stamps I found . . ." As they walked out of the dining room, Sylvia, Carita and Isabel talked about glue, placement and sizes.

"I didn't think this dinner party was going to take over

the way it has," Jane said to Alice who carefully laid out the last place setting. "I thought I could do the whole thing on my own, and here I not only have you helping, I have our guests pitching in too."

Alice adjusted a spoon, straightened a glass, then glanced at her sister. "They wouldn't help if they didn't want to. I haven't seen Lynden as happy and satisfied as he was yesterday. And today, I see that same satisfaction on the face of these kids. They appreciate what you've done for them, and they want to repay you."

"All I did was cook and bake . . ."

"And allow them into your life. And into your kitchen." And now, look how Isabel seems to have come out of her shell. And it's all because you let her help you."

Jane felt a flush of guilt at Alice's warm praise. There were many times she wished she hadn't been so open armed, yet, at the same time, she knew that these kids appreciated being in a kitchen where food was being prepared and where someone was around. She suspected, whether they wanted to admit it or not, some of them might be missing their families and missing the comforts of home.

"'A place where one can be refreshed and encouraged, a place of hope and healing, a place where God is at home,'" Jane said as the strains of the music Louise was playing filtered into the dining room.

"Exactly," Alice said, patting Jane on the shoulder. She glanced around the room. "And now, anything else we can do to make this place look welcoming and comfortable?"

"I have to say, the decorations look wonderfully elegant."

"I think even Stacy would approve."

"I hope so," Jane said, her fingers crossed.

⚭

"Avast, me maties. Vehicles approaching at ten o'clock," Matthew called out from the porch.

"Well, it's going on five now. What do we do till then?" Rick joked.

Jane gave a feeble laugh, wiped her hands on a tea towel and gave a quick glance at her reflection in the window.

She had opted for a more formal look for herself and had put on a soft, black-and-gray dress, spangled with tiny discs, which she had bought at one time for a formal dinner. The bias cut dress was shorter in the front, falling just below her knees, and longer in the back, creating a flowing look. She had topped it with a short black, collarless jacket. Alice had helped her with her hair, pulling it up into a sleek chignon. Carita and Isabel took care of makeup, something Jane seldom bothered much about.

But the effect was rather glamorous, she had to admit. She was about to lick her lips, when she felt the flick of a finger on her arm.

Carita frowned at her. "Don't. You'll smudge the lipstick."

"Sorry." She took a long, slow breath to steady her nerves as she glanced in the dining room one more time, allowing the soft glow of the tapers to soothe her. The room had been transformed into an elegant, but not too elegant, setting worthy of an international gathering.

She tried to distance herself from the whispering and giggling emanating from the kitchen. Even though the kids had exuded a laissez-faire attitude all day, now that the moment had come she knew they were nervous.

Louise was in the parlor, with the door open, playing some light classical pieces on the piano, the gentle music adding to the welcoming ambience.

∽

Finally the moment arrived. The doorbell chimed and Jane hurried to greet her guests. Pete stood by the entrance looking quite elegant in his second-hand pants and shirt. His hair, up until now covered by a baseball cap, shone and lay flat against his head.

Jane gave them a nod and with a wink, Pete opened the door. "Good evening," he said to the gathering, "and welcome to Grace Chapel Inn."

The group of women standing on the porch beamed back at him, then at Jane, who had come down to the entrance to greet them in person. Jane was relieved to see that they had all dressed up. Stacy stood to one side, clutching her purse, biting her lips as she glanced from Jane to their guests.

"Come in, please," Jane said, standing aside as the group filed in. They murmured among themselves as they entered and looked around. Jane recognized some Dutch, caught the twang of a New Zealand accent and the singsong cadence of the Japanese women. She knew the Canadian women by the English they spoke.

All of them looked around the foyer of the inn with interest, their faces lighting up when Lynden bowed and escorted them into the dining room.

Stacy introduced the group to Jane, who had found out in advance all the names and the proper spellings for the place cards, so she was able to greet most of the women personally.

As Lynden and Pete held out the chairs for the women, working their way around the table, she caught Stacy's worried gaze flicking around the room. Jane had to turn away for a moment. Everything looked wonderful. If Stacy could find fault with this, she could find fault with anything.

But Stacy's anxious expression slowly mellowed as the women oohed and aahed over the décor and the table. When they were all seated and had a chance to get settled, Jane glanced into the kitchen, tilting her chin up. Isabel caught her signal and made a motion to Herbie to stop stirring the soup.

Jane clasped her hands in front of her and looked around

the assembled group. Blonde women, dark-haired women, short and tall, plump and slender, women from all over the globe had gathered under her roof, and for a moment, she felt the weight of Stacy's responsibilities.

"If you would each care to look at the menu, I will try to make clear what we will be serving." Jane picked up a copy of the menu she had laid on the buffet and read it aloud, making explanations as she did so. When she was finished, she looked up to see the women smiling.

"You will also notice beside each plate we have placed a small gift bag that contains mementos of your visit here."

The gift bags had been Stacy's idea, and she had contributed most of the items, but Alice thought it was such a wonderful concept that she and Vera had put their heads together and come up with a few items from Acorn Hill to put in the bags as well. Wilhelm donated a few tea packets; the Holzmanns a pen with their store's logo on it; Lloyd Tynan, the mayor of Acorn Hill, gave them each a pin; Craig a package of seeds; and Sylvia had made up little sachets with soaps inside.

The women fell upon the bags, pulling items out and laughing as they compared the souvenirs. Jane was reminded of the young guests and their scavenger hunt. Games and presents seemed to transcend all age lines. Though these women had probably spent large sums of money to make this trip, they were tickled with items costing only a few dollars.

Once they settled down again, Jane announced, "Our first course, as you can see from the menu, is a choice of Miso soup or Kumara soup."

Pete and Matthew walked around the table politely asking the women their preferences. The boys were properly solemn, but Jane had to stifle a smile when Matthew winked at her once.

While the women were eating their soup and chattering away, Alice and Louise stayed out of traffic, relaxing in the parlor with a light repast. Jane hurried back to the kitchen to oversee the girls assembling the salads on individual plates.

The conversation in the dining room rose slowly with each course and Jane saw Stacy relax.

Jane herself, however, had a moment of misgiving when the girls put out the main course in bowls. She bit her lip as she looked over the meal. *Was it too plain?* But now was not the time to have second thoughts.

Go with it, she reminded herself. *Serve with confidence. As Isabel said, drama and presentation will carry this off.*

She returned to the dining room as Lynden and Rick cleared away the salad dishes. She gave them a moment to divest themselves of the plates and pick up the bowls they would be bringing in.

Jane cleared her throat and avoided looking at Stacy, preferring to zero in on a brightly smiling Japanese woman she vaguely remembered as Etsuko Yamada. Jane held her sparkling, dark eyes.

"This evening we are serving a unique dinner. We have researched this meal and found that it has two names. One is Fourteen Boy Rice Dish. The other is Snow on the Mountain." As she spoke, the youths filed in as they had been practicing all afternoon, and carefully placed the bowls of rice and the bowls of curry within reaching distance of the two ends of the table.

"The one bowl holds a chicken curry sauce, the other rice . . ."

She paused while the many small bowls with the condiments were set out.

"You may add whatever you wish to your sauce. The bowls hold mandarin oranges, pineapple chunks, banana slices, mango pieces, peanuts, cashews, slivered almonds, tomato, peppers, chopped celery, chives, raisins, dried cranberries and coconut."

She saw the women looking from her to the servers to the bowls gradually proliferating around them.

Jane nodded and the young people started serving the rice and curry. Then they showed the women what they might do next.

Slowly the noise level increased as women debated the various merits of each topping, trying to decide. One of the Dutch women was scooping merrily out of every bowl, spreading everything on her rice.

Another, from New Zealand, had taken a small portion of rice and curried chicken, and was cautiously adding minuscule amounts of the various fruits, nuts and vegetables, as if unsure of the finished product.

Jane allowed herself a quick glance Stacy's way, but Stacy was so busy watching the women's reaction to the unorthodox entrée that she didn't even notice Jane's look.

The sounds of cheerful conversation and, as the women started eating, the very positive comments about the food made it clear that they truly were enjoying the meal.

Stacy gave Jane a careful smile, then started putting together her own dish. Jane retreated, relief flowing through her.

In the kitchen, Isabel and Herbie helped Jane put out the desserts on plates. Then they put the plates on a cart to be wheeled in at the proper time. Jane sat down and let out a long sigh.

"I think we did it, people," she said quietly, with a satisfied smile as she glanced around the gathered group. "I think this meal went over remarkably well."

"I'll say," Matthew whispered, rinsing off the dinner plates. "That one Dutch lady would have licked the curry bowl clean if she could have."

"And how about the one Japanese woman?" Isabel said. "I don't think she stopped smiling the whole time."

Jane looked back, watching Herbie and Isabel bring out the cart, and let another sigh escape. Almost done, and the best part of all, Stacy looked relaxed and contented.

When all the desserts had been served and coffee and tea had been taken around, Jane wondered what was expected now. Should they retire to the living room with this group? Make small talk?

But then Stacy came into the kitchen, found Jane and hurried over to her side. She caught her by the hands, giving them a light shake. "Thank you so much for making this meal so memorable," she said, truly beaming. "And the kids helping you, they all did a standout job." Stacy glanced around the room, including each one of the youngsters in her praise. "The women will never forget this meal, I'm sure."

"I'm so glad you're pleased," Jane said.

"Pleased? My goodness, I'm thinking of asking you to do this meal again."

Jane's heart plummeted. Plan another meal with Stacy hovering over her? "I did say we don't do this on a regular basis—"

"You made that clear the first time, but this went so well—"

"And Jane's not going to have her hired help next time," Carita put in. "We're only on contract for this one time."

"Really?" Stacy's frown showed her complete puzzlement.

"Yes. We're college students and we, uh . . ." Carita glanced around, as if pleading for help.

"We prefer to pick and choose our jobs," Lynden put in.

"Yeah. Yesterday we volunteered at Habitat, but we never know where we're going to be from week to week," Matthew added.

"I...see." The way Stacy drew out the two words showed Jane that she clearly did not see. She turned back to Jane. "Would you be able to work without these kids?"

Jane shook her head decisively. "I couldn't do this without them. They are part of the package."

Stacy tapped one manicured fingernail against her chin. "I'm so sorry to hear that. The meal was a such a hit."

"I'm glad you have satisfied customers," Jane said, getting to her feet. "And I'm glad we could provide them with a memorable experience."

Stacy glanced back at Lynden and Carita, as if hoping they would change their minds. Then, with a long, drawn out breath, she pulled an envelope out of her purse and handed it to Jane. "Thanks again. And if you ever change your mind about the dinner..." she let the sentence hang as if giving Jane a chance to do just that.

"Thank you for your patronage," Jane said. "I had an enjoyable evening."

Stacy gave her a quick smile. "You've all been marvelous."

Jane thanked her as she handed the envelope to Alice, who had been supervising the kitchen clean up.

Alice signaled to Lynden and Pete. In a matter of minutes they were back at the entrance, chatting with the women, and in general just being their charming selves as they bid them all farewell.

Jane was thanked again and again for the lovely dinner and her charming staff.

Once they were gone, Jane leaned against the door and closed her eyes. *Done*, she thought.

"I think some tea is in order," Alice said, tucking her hand in her sister's arm and leading her to the living room, where Louise joined her sisters.

"But the kitchen needs to be cleaned up—" Jane protested.

"The 'servants' have that well in hand," Louise said.

Jane allowed herself to be guided as she settled into one of the chairs. She eased her high heels off her feet and sighed as she wiggled her toes. "Were you terribly inconvenienced?" she asked her sisters.

"Not at all." Louise's decisive reply showed Jane her sister wasn't just being polite.

Alice handed her the envelope. "Aren't you even a little bit curious what she paid you?"

"I know what she was going to pay me," Jane said, but took the envelope anyway. "We decided before I agreed to do this."

She slit it open, drew out the check and blinked. Read it again. Blinked again.

"She paid me far more than we had agreed on." Jane looked up at her sisters. "I can't accept this."

Alice got up and her eyes widened when she saw the amount.

"She put this with it." Jane pulled out a small note, cleared her throat and read, "'I know I was hard to deal with, so I let the check reflect that. Thank you again for being so gracious with me, when I have to confess, I was not always so gracious with you. You truly are an example of your inn's guiding principle.'"

Jane felt a moment of guilt. She knew she had not always felt gracious toward Stacy. "This could buy us four vacuum cleaners with lots of money left over. I don't deserve this," Jane said, letting the note fall into her lap.

"Nonsense," Louise said. "You put up with a lot for this occasion, and she made this dinner much harder than it needed to be."

Jane looked at the check again. "But still—"

"But nothing," Alice declared. "She gave it to you. Think of it as a gift."

"I suppose I could do that," Jane said, but she still felt uncomfortable with the final amount.

That night, as she lay in bed, Jane couldn't stop replaying the evening in her head, nor could she stop feeling a slight twinge of guilt at how much Stacy seemed to think Jane was worth.

She rolled over on her side, thinking, and as she thought, she knew exactly what she was going to do with the extra money.

Chapter ⊤ Sixteen

L ouise finished the last bars of the doxology Sunday morning, then glanced toward the front of the chapel, where Jane, Alice, Ethel and Lloyd sat along with Lynden, Carita, Matthew and Isabel. The others had elected to stay at the inn and sleep.

No matter, Louise thought. She was quite impressed that these young people changed their plans to leave early and instead came with them to church. Rev. Kenneth Thompson had a wonderful, thought-provoking sermon about servant-hood and how God uses us and our talents and calls us to build bridges across the chasms that can separate us from one another—chasms of age, abilities, resources.

Louise knew that she was challenged by the message, and when she saw the light of hope shining in Lynden's eyes, she knew he had received guidance and strength for the decisions lying ahead of him.

Louise started the prelude, watching as people came to greet the inn's guests and welcome them.

When the service ended and the majority of worshippers had left, Louise closed up the organ and went to join the others, who were already talking to the pastor. "You haven't had a chance to meet our guests," Alice was saying, introducing him to Lynden, Carita, Matthew and Isabel.

"Thanks for your message," Lynden said, shaking Rev. Thompson's hand and gazing earnestly into the minister's eyes. "I've been doing a lot of soul searching the past few weeks, and you really helped me clarify a lot of stuff."

Rev. Thompson looked pleased. "I'm thankful I could be a servant to you."

"Hey, I got that. Servant. Like you were preaching about." Matthew said, raising his hand as if he was going to give a high five to the pastor.

Louise's gaze flew to Rev. Thompson, but their pastor smiled and raised his hand to meet Matthew's.

Matthew slapped their pastor's hand, then rocked back on his heels, looking quite pleased with himself.

Louise gave him an indulgent smile. The boy was like a large Labrador puppy at times, but his heart was good and true. She was going to miss him and the others.

"How long are you staying at the inn?" the pastor asked, looking around the group.

"We're leaving right after this," Carita said with a note of regret.

"I'm glad you decided to come."

"I didn't realize how much I missed church and worship until I came here today."

Silence greeted her heartfelt statement.

Then the pastor put his hand on her shoulder, as if in benediction. "I pray you will be blessed by the service."

"I was. Thank you."

The pastor removed his hand and then looked beyond them. "I'm sorry, but I must excuse myself. Again, I'm so glad you came."

"And we should get going too," Isabel said. "Good-bye, Rev. Thompson. We have a long drive ahead of us."

The group walked together to the inn, the kids ahead, talking quietly among themselves, Louise, Alice and Jane following behind.

Louise smiled when she saw Lynden's hand slip sideways, capturing Carita's.

"So this has been an enlightening week," Jane said, simultaneously patting each of her sisters on the arm. "We certainly can't complain about a lack of challenges."

Alice massaged her right shoulder. "I know I've been challenged in more ways than one."

"I think we've managed to meet them all head on," Louise said.

"And how nice to know we don't do this alone," Jane said. She gave her sisters' arms a light shake. "Thanks again for all your help last night. The dinner went well and Stacy was so pleased that she called me again this morning to tell me, though I have to confess when I saw her name on the call display, I almost let it ring."

"Well, that challenge has come to an end for you," Louise said. "And I am pleased with how our guests conducted themselves."

"They were a huge help," Jane said. "I'd like to give them a discount on their stay. Stacy paid me enough money that I think we can easily do that."

"Excellent idea," Alice said. "Though you make sure that you keep some of that money for yourself."

"No. It's going into the vacuum cleaner fund."

"There is more than enough for that," Alice said. "You should buy something fun. Something just for you."

"What I think would be fun would be to make a contribution to the home you are building, Alice," Jane said as they walked up the steps to the inn.

"I'm sure that would be greatly appreciated," Alice said warmly.

Inside, Herbie, Rick and Pete were finishing up their breakfast. Carita, Lynden, Isabel and Matthew chatted with them a moment, then went upstairs to pack.

"And once again, great breakfast," Herbie said to Jane as

he carried a precarious stack of dishes into the kitchen. "I don't know if I can go back to dorm food after this." He set the plates on the counter and cast a curious glance around the kitchen, as if making sure he hadn't missed out on any culinary experience.

"Would you like me to pack a lunch for you and your friends?" Jane asked.

The joy on his face made Louise smile.

"That would be totally awesome, Ms. J."

"When you come downstairs, I'll have it ready."

Herbie disappeared around the corner, and Louise got up. "Do you want some help?"

"That would be great."

Fifteen minutes later Jane, Louise and Alice brought out the bag lunches. The kids were gathered outside. Matthew and Rick were tossing suitcases into the van and Lynden's truck.

Herbie was the first to say good-bye. He took his lunch, glanced inside, then clutched it to his chest, his eyes closed in anticipation.

"This is for *lunch*," Jane emphasized. "That comes later in the day."

"Of course." His wounded look made Louise chuckle.

Rick and Pete were next. "Thanks so much for everything," Rick said as he took his lunch. "You really made us feel welcome and made us feel at home."

"I was going to say the same thing," Isabel said with a wide smile. "I enjoyed helping out."

"And what a help you were. Your meal suggestion saved the day," Jane told her.

"That's kind of you to say. I'm glad the menu worked out."

"Perfectly," Jane said. "Thank you again."

Matthew gave them all a bearish hug. "I'm gonna miss

this place like crazy," he said, pretending to wipe away an imaginary tear. "But, hey, I'll send you a postcard from school. Just so you won't forget me."

"As if that would happen," Louise said with a wry tone.

Matthew grinned, then waved and jumped into the van. Carita and Lynden were the last.

"Thanks again," Carita said. "For everything. I had a wonderful visit with you. You ladies were awesome." She gave them all a quick hug, her eyes glistening.

"Again, thanks," Lynden said, shaking their hands. "I am really humbled by what I learned from you ladies." He held Louise's hand a moment longer. "Thank you so much for your music and for sharing it with us."

Louise felt a motherly rush of love for this young man. She gave in to an impulse and gave him a hug, which he returned with endearing enthusiasm.

When they pulled away, they were smiling at each other.

"So, a new year lies ahead of you," Louise said. "Do you know what you want to do?"

Lynden nodded. "I think I'm going to go see about enrolling in a program that lets me help people build a better life for themselves. I don't know what form or shape that will take. I'm counting on the college guidance counselors to point me in the right direction."

"That's admirable," Louise said. "I'm sure your grandmother would be very proud of you."

"I hope so." Lynden gave her a shy smile, then took a step backward, taking Carita with him. "We should get going. The crew is going to mutiny if we don't get moving."

Lynden and Carita walked to his truck and Rick ran toward the van. "Shotgun!" he called out, claiming the front passenger seat.

Doors slammed shut, windows rolled down and as the kids shouted out good-byes, Isabel got in the driver's seat.

She fiddled with something, then frowned. After a few moments, she lifted her hands.

"What's up, Isabel?" Louise asked.

"This van won't start," she said

A collection of groans greeted that remark. Matthew, Pete and Herbie all piled out, then Matthew held up his hand.

"You know, I think we need to give the resident car expert a chance to look at this."

He stood, waiting while Louise wondered who the "car expert" was. He crooked a finger at Louise, his grin lighting up his face.

"Hey, Mrs. L. Why don't you help us out here?"

Louise shook her head, raising her hand in a gesture of denial. "I'm afraid my expertise is limited to tire wear, paint jobs, windshield wipers and, well, batteries."

"See. There you go." Matthew lifted up the hood, stepped back, waving Louise on.

Louise looked from the boys to her sisters, who weren't helping her at all, then with a light sigh, walked over to the van. She hoped she could remember what she had learned, though she doubted she could offer any help at all.

She glanced at the engine. Oil dipstick. Transmission fluid dipstick. Windshield washer fluid container. And there was the battery. She frowned and jiggled the posts. Loose. In fact, the entire battery was loose in its casing.

"And the diagnosis is . . ." Matthew prompted.

"The battery housing needs to be tightened and the battery cables are loose. And, I might add, the posts are quite corroded." Louise gave him a wry look. "But then I'm guessing you knew that already."

Matthew shrugged, looking a little shamefaced. But not much. "I just wanted you to show off your knowledge," he said.

"And what if we hadn't gotten to the battery portion of the course yet?"

"Well, then, I would have given you a hint."

"Thank you for that." She stepped back and took a handkerchief that Lynden had been thoughtful enough to supply. "You might want to check your tire pressure too," she said, glancing at the one low tire on the front.

"See? A veritable fount of mechanical know-how," Matthew proclaimed.

Louise shook her head as the other boys went into action. They procured a small tool kit from the back of the van. While Pete tightened the battery cables and housing, Herbie checked the tire pressure, and Matthew offered advice and encouragement from the sidelines.

A few minutes later the battery was secure, the cables tightened, the van was running. Both vehicles left the yard trailing a chorus from within of thank-yous and good-byes.

Louise, Jane and Alice stood watching them as they drove down Chapel Road and then disappeared onto Berry Lane.

The silence they left in their wake was almost deafening. Louise let it settle around them, then sighed lightly.

"I do think I am going to miss them," she said.

"I agree." Alice nodded.

"Do you think they'll write?" Jane asked.

"Who knows? But it doesn't matter if they don't. Maybe they'll send some other guests our way," Louise said.

"Maybe." Jane agreed. "But if they do, I'm going to make sure I don't overschedule myself."

"Really?" Louise asked, raising one eyebrow.

"Really." Jane gave them both a smile. "Now, let's go have some tea and cookies."

"You have some left?" Louise asked.

Jane nodded. "Found four broken ones in the bottom of the cookie jar. The kids must have missed them in their final sweep of the kitchen."

"Sounds . . . tasty," Alice said.

"Bet your boots, Ms. A," Jane said.

They laughed and together walked back to the peace and quiet of the inn.

Jane's Butterscotch Cookies

MAKES THREE TO FOUR DOZEN

⌒⌒

1½ cups dark brown sugar

1½ cups butter

1½ cups flour

2 eggs

¼ teaspoon salt

1¼ teaspoons baking powder

12 ounces butterscotch chips

½ cup chopped walnuts or pecans

Combine brown sugar, butter, flour, eggs, salt and baking powder in a mixer. Remove bowl from mixer, and stir in chips and nuts, using a wooden spoon. Place a teaspoonful of batter for each cookie on baking sheet. Bake at 350 degrees for ten to fifteen minutes. Remove from oven and allow cookies to cool before transferring from sheet to serving plate.

About the Author

Carolyne Aarsen is the author of more than twenty books, including *The Only Best Place* and *All in One Place* and four books for Guideposts' Tales from Grace Chapel Inn series. She wrote a weekly humor column for ten years and lives on a farm in Neerlandia, Alberta, Canada.